MAIN STREET
MISTLETOE

MELA THOMAS

Names: Thomas, Mela, author.
Title: Main Street Mistletoe: A Contemporary Holiday Romance Novel/ Mela Thomas.
Identifiers: PB ISBN: 979-8-9930824-1-7 (trade paperback);
eBook ISBN: 979-8-9930824-0-0
Subjects: Romance fiction.

First edition: November 2025

For my partner, RT

MAIN STREET MISTLETOE

1

Kit

Coffee shops were one of my very favorite places to be, but especially on a bright snowy day. I hurried down the sidewalk toward my favorite coffee shop, The Bean. The windows had been decorated with snowflakes and snowmen. I pulled the door open and heard the gentle ring of their doorbell. The warm air was filled with the sweet smell of coffee and pastries. I inhaled deeply and couldn't help but smile. I loved all of it: the oversized furniture, the funky art, the festive Christmas music. For me, walking into The Bean was like walking into a warm hug.

It was the Monday after Thanksgiving, and the Bean was busy today. I joined the line of customers waiting to order. The pastry case was filled with holiday themed treats. I took another deep breath and smelled the seasonal, sweet smell of peppermint.

"Good morning," I said cheerily to the barista, Stef.

"Good morning, Kit." Stef smiled then asked, "Your usual?"

I tapped my finger against my chin thoughtfully and said, "You know, today I'm feeling the holiday spirit. Can I get the White Christmas Mocha and a chocolate croissant?"

"Of course!" Stef said, tapping the tablet. As she twirled the tablet to face me so that I could select a gratuity and sign, she picked up a platter of cookies and asked, "And would you like a complimentary snowflake cookie?"

"I would love one!" I exclaimed. I tapped the tablet with my card, signed my name, and selected a snowman cookie. "This is so nice. What's the special occasion for the free cookie?"

"Business hasn't been great," Stef admitted. We're trying to reward our regulars in whatever way we can so we don't lose their business over the holidays."

"Well, I think it's a brilliant touch, and it looks like it's working. You're busier than usual!" I said. Stef smiled at me as I put an additional tip into the tip jar. I know how hard it can be for small shops during the holiday season. We rely heavily on summer and fall tourism in our North Georgia town. The winter months are hard for everyone.

As I stepped to the side to wait for my order, I pulled out my cell phone to check my work email. Running a small-town library kept me pretty busy because we had such a small staff. I heard the customer behind me order, "Americano."

"Would you like a complimentary cookie?" Stef asked, offering the plate of snowflake cookies to the man.

"No, thanks," the man said and abruptly turned and joined me at the end of the counter to wait for his drink. I made eye contact with Stef, who raised both eyebrows. I blew a little air between my lips and said under my breath, "Bah humbug."

The man pulled his cell phone out of the pocket of his pea coat. His thick, dark eyebrows pushed together as he began scrolling with his thumb. I tried not to stare. He was well-dressed with a sleek overcoat and grey cashmere scarf. He had dark hair styled in a low maintenance way that accentuated his square jawline. Despite being well-dressed, he didn't have a pretty-boy vibe. Rather, he had the kind of rugged good looks that were striking. His broad shoulders filled the overcoat, which was tight around his biceps.

I averted my eyes before he noticed that I was looking at him. I reminded myself that being good-looking wasn't an excuse for being unfriendly.

Stef came over and set two white paper cups with lids on the counter. "Your drinks are ready."

"Thank you, Stef," I said.

The man and I both reached for the white paper cups and parted ways. I headed for a big comfy leather chair near the window. As I collapsed into it, I sighed. Ella Fitzgerald's "Sleigh Ride" started playing over the speakers. I bit the top hat off the perfectly decorated snowman cookie. Then I picked up my cup to take a swig, but was startled by a deep, gruff voice.

"I think you have my drink."

I fumbled my snowman cookie and coffee cup. I looked up into the dark, piercing eyes of the man from the coffee counter.

"Excuse me?" I tried to say, but my mouth was still full of cookie and a crumb escaped. Embarrassed, I covered my mouth. I could feel my cheeks turning pink.

"You picked up my drink at the counter," the man said without a smile. "This one is yours."

"Oh." I looked down at the cup as if I expected it to tell me if he was telling me the truth or not. "How did you know?"

"Did you order some kind of sugary thing?" He held the cup out as if he was holding something that totally disgusted him. "I didn't drink from this one, but it smells...Christmassy." He sneered, not trying to hide his dislike, as he pushed the cup out toward me.

We exchanged cups, and he opened the lid to examine the contents of his. With a crooked smile, he showed me. "See? black coffee."

"Okay," I said after finally choking down the dry cookie. As I awkwardly shifted in the overstuffed chair, I set my drink down with more force than I had intended. I practically grunted, "Crisis averted. Thanks."

"Yeah, no problem," the man said, shoving his free hand into his pocket. His smile had faded into a grimace. He turned on the heel of his brown oxfords and headed for the door. I watched until the door's bell stopped ringing.

Stef appeared next to me holding my warmed chocolate croissant and the plate of cookies. She gestured at the plate. "Would you like the city slicker's cookie?"

"The city slicker?" I asked, picking a snowflake cookie this time.

"Yeah." Stef put one hand on her hip. "That's what we've been calling him. He's been in here every morning for a week."

"How do you know he's from the city?" I asked, raising an eyebrow.

The corners of Stef's mouth pushed back into an assured smile. "Total hottie-city-guy vibes."

"Huh." I took a bite of the snowman's face, trying to be cool. "I didn't notice he was hot."

"Are you kidding me?" Stef said. "He's got a great ass. I bet those thighs could…"

"And you know he's from the city because of his ass?" I interrupted, skeptically.

"Yeah, and his license plate has a city tag on it," Stef said with a sly smile as she pointed at the window. I looked out to see the man as he was getting into his car parked on Main Street.

"Ah. Well, I'm happy to eat his share of complimentary cookies," I said to the snowflake cookie. "Who says no to a Christmas cookie?"

"I know, right?" Stef laughed as she walked back to the counter.

I saw my phone light up and tapped the text bubble.

Are you going to be able to make it to the meeting with the mayor? No pressure.

I laughed. Typical Aunt Rita—always trying to give me an out.

I texted back. *I'll be there, as promised!*

Before I could put my phone down, another message popped up, this time from my best friend, Veronica.

I know how much you love the holidays. Check out this cutie in the reindeer outfit.

I clicked on the text bubble and an adorable picture of Veronica's nine-month-old son, Preston, in a reindeer outfit popped up. I tapped the photo and sent a heart emoji.

I love the holiday spirit!

Three little dots appeared on the screen as I picked up my cup to take a sip of coffee. I couldn't help but sniff the cup before taking a sip. I guess the drink did smell a little "Christmassy," as the man had said earlier. But what was wrong with that? Didn't everyone love the holidays?

My phone vibrated in my hand. I looked down, surprised, to see that Veronica was calling me.

"Hey, chica. What's up?" I said.

"I thought it would be easier to just call," Veronica's cheerful voice announced.

"Preston is being a little fussy, so it's easier for me to hold him and talk rather than text."

"Oh, he doesn't like being dressed as a reindeer?" I asked, frowning because the thought of a fussy baby reindeer was so cute it pained me.

"Oh, he doesn't mind the reindeer outfit. It's the photo shoot that I put him through, trying to get that one cute photo I sent you. That's what he can't stand." Veronica laughed.

"So, what are you up to this weekend? Any hot dates?"

"No hot dates on the docket here," I snorted.

"Well, any potential hot dates?" Veronica asked hopefully.

"Please," I scoffed. "The only attractive man I've talked to in weeks was a rude out-of-towner at the coffee shop this morning."

Veronica didn't miss a beat and responded playfully, "Oh! That could be fun. Did you get his number?"

"No, we had a little back and forth about a confused coffee order. He was rude, though." I thought about the coffee cup guy's broad shoulders and deep voice and admitted out loud, "But he was really hot."

Veronica didn't need much more than that to jump onto her soap box. "Look, all I'm saying is: if a conversation with a random hot guy in a coffee shop is the most action you're getting, it's not enough action, amiga! You are young. You are good-looking. And you are incredibly single. You need to not only be talking to every cute, single man you see, but you need to be talking."

"Okay, okay. I'll put 'flirt shamelessly' on my to-do list."

"Please do! For both of us. I'm living vicariously through you. These days I'm just dealing with a crying baby boy all hours of the night, and he makes my nipples sore," Veronica lamented.

"Sounds like college all over again," I said with a chuckle.

"Right?" Veronica laughed and added under her breath, "I shouldn't have dated so many writers."

"Can we call what you were doing in college dating?" I joked.

Veronica laughed again and continued with a more tender tone. "But seriously, when we first met in college you were this smart, savvy, adventurous, black-haired, tawny-skinned goddess. And I get it; you wanted to move home to be with your mom when she got sick. But Kit, it's been over a year since she passed. You've got to get back out there. Your mom, of all people, would have wanted you to enjoy life, for fuck's sake."

I let a chuckle escape. Veronica was right. My mom loved life. No matter what her circumstances, she had a way of making everything seem brighter, especially the holidays. I felt that familiar lump in my throat. I took a swig of coffee, trying not to wince at how ridiculously syrupy sweet it was. "You're right," I said. She wanted me to be out here doing what I love." I added, "I do love my job at the library, though. So there's that."

"Turns out there are libraries all over the world," Veronica said sarcastically. She sighed. "Seriously, Kit. Your hometown of Creekstone, albeit very charming, really lucked out when you decided to move home. We'd love to have you closer to us here in Atlanta, and I know Matt misses you in Los Angeles. I mean...Creekstone is a tiny town in north Georgia. How many single people your age live in Creekstone?"

Before I could respond, Veronica's son, Preston, sounded the alarm that he was ready for his next meal. Veronica said hastily over Preston's cries, "Oh, let me call you back. Boobie-duty calls. Preston is hungry. Love ya!" Click.

I took a deep breath and watched a delivery truck drive through the puddles on the street. I leaned back in my chair and replayed what Veronica had said. Perhaps it was because she was so sleep-deprived, but Veronica wasn't letting up and was giving me a healthy helping of honesty about the state of my dating life. I guess that's what friends are for. Normally, I would have pushed back a little more, but I knew how hard these postpartum months were for Veronica. Before having Preston, Veronica worked as a real estate lawyer for a firm in Atlanta. She decided to take a year off to be with Preston, and I could tell she struggled to be at home instead of at work.

I didn't want to sink too far into this chair again. I shifted my weight in my seat. I thought about the feeling I got in the pit of my stomach when Veronica mentioned Matt, my ex-boyfriend. I knew that Veronica's husband, Gus, still spoke to Matt. After all, they had been college roommates like Veronica and me. That's how it all started. Veronica and I lived in the same dorm our freshman year of college. Once we met, we were inseparable. Veronica and Gus started dating, so Matt and I started spending more time together. We were always at the same parties, and Matt tagged along with Gus pretty much everywhere he went, so it seemed inevitable that Matt and I would end up together.

Dating Matt had been so easy and sensible. I wouldn't have said we had an immediate spark, but we worked so perfectly together. More than anything, I became aware of how happy our relationship made everyone else. I felt a pressure to be happy with what I had with Matt because everyone else felt like we were a perfect match. And Matt was the total package, right? Matt was attractive in that all-American way. He was not just conventionally good looking; he was also extremely smart and athletic.

After undergrad, I started a one-year fellowship in Washington, D.C., to work in archives. He moved with me to D.C. to study for his MCATs. While he was in D.C., Matt did volunteer work at a children's hospital and a clinic for the unhoused to help fill his time. He applied for med school and got into UCLA. I was elated for him. It's what he'd always wanted. Everyone immediately started asking me if I was going to move to Los Angeles with him. But a few weeks after we found out that Matt would be moving to Los Angeles, I got the call from my mom. She was sick again.

Breaking up with Matt had been hard, but probably not as hard for either of us as everyone thought it had been. We didn't break up right away. We decided to try and make the long-distance thing work. Matt was well into his first year of med school, and I had been lucky enough to get a position at the Creekstone Regional Library. In the same way that we had been good at going through all the motions of being college sweethearts, we were excellent at working out the logistics of being in a long-distance relationship. I would visit during short breaks, and he would come to see me during longer breaks. But then, less than a year after I moved back to Creekstone, something unexpected happened: the pandemic.

Like everyone else, our travel was limited, and the thought of someone working in a hospital being in close proximity to me or my mom was too dangerous. I told Matt that my mom's health would be my priority, that I didn't want to take any risks, and that this just didn't feel fair to him. He took it hard at first. He protested the appropriate amount. He insisted that he wanted to try, but like all other parts of our relationship, breaking up and moving on happened with relative ease for both of us.

That was five years ago.

I took a deep breath and exhaled slowly. Then I leaned back in the chair and took another bite of the snowman.

"Oh, sugar," a sweet woman's voice said from behind me. "What's eatin' you up?"

I turned around in the chair to see Ms. Pearl, a regular at the Creekstone Library. She was peering at me over the tops of her red glasses with a ball of yarn and two knitting needles resting in her lap.

"Oh, hi, Ms. Pearl." I turned in my seat and rested against the back of the chair. "I was just thinking about a meeting I have with Aunt Rita later," I lied. I did not need a second round of dating advice today. Ms. Pearl was a local who had lived most of her life in Creekstone. She had worked as a receptionist at a local law firm. Even though she had retired years earlier, she always wore her hair pulled back in a professional French twist, a matching cardigan sweater set, and a pair of tasteful pearl earrings.

"Is something wrong with our dear Rita?" Ms. Pearl gasped, clutching her knitting needles to her chest.

"No, no," I said quickly. I had slid down into the abyss that was the bottom of this chair again. I engaged my core and pulled myself forward. "Everything is totally fine." If other towns had rumor mills, Creekstone had a full-scale gossip factory. "We just have a meeting with the mayor later. Some development company is in town and interested in buying property out by the river."

Shocked, Ms. Pearl gasped, "You're going to sell the house and land by the river?"

"Oh, no," I said. "We are not selling the house. We're only considering a very remote possibility of selling the land by the river—not the land in town with the house. The whole meeting is probably a waste of time, but we just want to hear them out. I promised Aunt Rita I'd attend."

"Is that right?" Ms. Pearl nodded as if she was processing what I was saying, then she said with wide eyes, "Now that's interesting."

"Is it?" I squeaked out. That was the opposite of what I wanted.

I tried to pivot away from any piece of news that might be interesting to Ms. Pearl. I held up my decapitated snowman cookie. "Did you get a free cookie?"

"No one asked to buy my land," a gruff voice said from behind. I turned to see Ms. Patty.

"Well, who would want that lot?" Ms. Pearl chortled.

"Humph." Ms. Patty stood between Miss Pearl and me. She was a short, older lady, like Ms. Pearl. She had curly, grey hair that peeked out from under a homemade beanie. She wore a heavy canvas work jacket and her loose pants tucked into a pair of boots. Ms. Patty crossed her arms, dismayed. "It's a fine lot...It has character."

Ms. Pearl hooted in disbelief. "If by character you mean wetlands year-round, then that land has more character than a three-ring circus."

"That doesn't even make sense," Ms. Patty huffed. She turned to me and said, "Are you selling your land to out-of-towners?"

"We aren't set on selling the land," I said. "I think we're just going to listen to what the mayor and the development company have to say."

"I know that new, young mayor wants to help Creekstone, but I hate the idea of out-of-towners coming to town and building discount stores and bringing HOAs and all that nonsense to Creekstone," Ms. Patty said.

"And traffic." Ms. Pearl pursed her lips together in a frown. "Did you see how they did over near Dawsonville? I know it's closer to Atlanta, but who wants to sit in traffic to go from one side of the middle of nowhere to the other side of the middle of nowhere?"

"If there's traffic, it's not nowhere," Ms. Patty countered.

"Well still," Ms. Pearl said thoughtfully, "Maybe I'm glad they haven't asked about buying my land. Once we start selling our land, we really lose control and influence over the character of our community. Are you going to sell your house, too?"

I chuckled at the back and forth between the two, but I couldn't help but agree with Ms. Patty and Ms. Pearl. Creekstone was the perfect small town. My mom would say that of all the places she'd ever traveled, and she did quite a bit of traveling before she had me, Creekstone had the most heart, and that's why she decided to move back and raise me here. She marveled at the ordinary. She said that people spent entire lifetimes in pursuit of "the good life," but she believed that "the good life" was a state of mind, not a status.

Ms. Patty crossed her arms in front of her chest and took a deep breath. "Let me ask you something." She looked at me so seriously, as if what I said could really weigh on her.

"Sure. What's that?" I asked, my eyes wide in anticipation of what she might ask.

Ms. Patty lowered her voice. "Do you and Rita need money? Is that why you're trying to sell the land?"

"Oh, no," I said quickly. "We aren't trying to sell the land! They approached Aunt Rita about buying some lots. I think they want land near the river, so they're interested in the property we own on the edge of town. They want to meet to see if we're even interested in selling. But, please don't worry. We're doing great," I added a little too emphatically. This was partially true. Aunt Rita and I were approached by the mayor about selling our land, but the truth was Aunt Rita and I had started renting rooms in our house for extra income. My mom's medical bills had been more than any of us could ever have imagined, and we were still recovering financially.

"Well, sweetie. If you and Rita need anything, you just tell us," Ms. Pearl said softly. I know she was being sincere. Before my mom passed, Ms. Pearl had been one of the community members who kept a meal train going to help us get through those last weeks. She would appear every other day or so with a casserole or a basket of soup and sandwiches from the deli. She would linger in the kitchen to help load or unload the dishwasher. Sometimes Ms. Pearl would sit with my mom when Aunt Rita and I both had to be away.

"You two are sweet to ask." I forced a smile. "But we really are doing fine." I checked my watch. "And I should scoot because I don't want to be late for the meeting."

I stood up as Ms. Patty put a hand on her hip, turned to Ms. Pearl, and said, "And what do you mean, wetlands? I'll have you know that land is perfectly buildable."

"You're joking," Ms. Pearl exclaimed after she blew air through her lips. "You could sail a boat on that lake you call a buildable lot."

I smiled and gave a little wave as I exited the conversation and coffee shop. I hurried down the wet sidewalk toward the mayor's office. North Georgia wasn't a particularly snowy place in the winter, but we did get some freezing rain and ice storms that created a pretty glum atmosphere in the winter. I think this is one of the reasons Christmas lights helped brighten up everything on Main Street.

The mayor's office was in the middle of the town square. It was a historic brick building right next to the courthouse. The walkway was lined with hedges that were covered with lights. The doors and windows had all been decorated with wreaths and red bows. The black light post had been wrapped in green garland and had festive holiday bells at the tops. As I approached the building, a tall, thin man with wavy blonde hair walked through the front doors of the office building. Seeing me approach on the sidewalk, he started waving emphatically.

I waved back. The man beamed with a huge smile. He called out, "Kit! Hey, Kit!"

"Hi, Nick," I said as I climbed the stairs to the entrance to the building. Nick Martin, like me, was a native of Creekstone. But Nick was about ten years younger than me, a recent college graduate, and most notably, he was the youngest mayor in Creekstone history.

"Kit, I'm so glad you came." Nick sounded a little breathless. He extended his hand as I approached. Even though he was young, he was still a politician through and through. I shook his hand.

"I was worried you wouldn't come," he said.

"Aww, Nick. I told Aunt Rita I would come. Why would you worry?" I asked. I did want to show my support for Nick as our new mayor. Our former mayor, Brian Bigbsy, had been in office for nearly thirty years. The man loved his town. He knew his people, but you could only trust him as far as you could throw him. Nick's announcement to run for mayor was dismissed as foolishness...until he won.

Nick's campaign and victory was just what Creekstone needed. The town needed people who loved it and wanted the best for it, not just for themselves. Now Nick was being tasked with bringing about some of the changes he had promised, and this was proving more difficult than he could ever have imagined.

"Well," Nick nervously ran his hands through his hair. He still had a bit of a boyish charm to him. "I guess I assumed you wouldn't want to entertain the thought of selling that property by the river."

I nodded. "Yeah, I'm always happy to listen," I said, patting Nick on the shoulder. We walked into the building.

"Well, that's good. The folks from the company are here, and they're all set up in the conference room to give you and Aunt Rita a great presentation on the potential projects they could do here in town."

"I promise I'll listen with an open mind," I said, holding up three fingers, "Scout's honor."

Nick clapped his hands. "Kit, you're the best. You remind me so much of your mom. Did I ever tell you she was my art teacher in high school?"

"That's so nice," I smiled. One of the great things about living in a small town is that people always shared stories like this about my mom. "She loved teaching."

We headed into the office building. I spotted Aunt Rita in the lobby of the building, talking to a man as they both admired the Christmas tree. She waved at me, and I walked over. Aunt Rita was my mother's youngest sister. She was a few years younger than my mother, and they were best friends. My mom was seventeen years old when she moved out of the house to go to art school. When Mom was twenty-five, she returned to Creekstone seven months pregnant. My grandparents and Aunt Rita welcomed her back into the house, and Mom and I had been there ever since.

"Oh, hi! Kit, I'm so glad you came. I wasn't sure if you'd actually show up." Aunt Rita laughed.

"Why does everyone keep saying that?" I asked. "I said I was going to come."

"Well, honey, you aren't exactly pro-development in Creekstone," Aunt Rita said, a little under her breath. She turned to the man she was talking to and her smile returned. "Kit, I want to introduce you to Roger."

I shook Roger's hand. The man was holding his jacket in the other hand. He was neatly dressed with a flannel shirt tucked into his blue jeans. Roger looked to be quite a few years older than Aunt Rita, but I suspect she enjoyed being the younger, attractive person in the couple.

"Hi, Roger. I'm Kit Campbell—Rita's niece. Nice to meet you." I gave a little wave.

"Oh, yes, Kit. I've heard so much about you," Roger said politely.

"Is that right?" I said, raising my eyebrows. I looked over at Aunt Rita who was pretending to fuss over the Angel ornaments on the tree. I leaned forward with a wink and said, "Well, of course, likewise."

I had never heard of Roger in my entire life. This must be another one of Aunt Rita's conquests from a dating app.

"Okay, well. I think the mayor is expecting us, so we have to run," Aunt Rita said with a nervous laugh.

Roger spread his arms and gestured to suggest a hug. Aunt Rita forced a smile and giggle and allowed herself to be hugged. She looked at me over his shoulder and stuck her tongue out at me. I stifled a laugh.

I waved as Roger left the lobby. "Great to finally meet you, Roger!"

When I turned back to Aunt Rita, she was scowling at me. "You could have played that a little cooler."

"Ha! Do you remember my prom night? You and mom were the antithesis of cool," I said, crossing my arms. "I simply cannot be cool."

Aunt Rita's scowl broke in a grin. "He's cute, though, right?"

"I mean, I guess, he is—in that retired lumberjack kind of way," I said looking at the door he had exited out of. "I didn't realize you were dating him."

Aunt Rita waved her hands dismissively. "Oh, you know how it is. I'm just trying to find the right guy to spend Christmas, Kwanza, and New Year's with. And then I'll cut ties around Dr. Martin Luther King, Jr. weekend so I'm not tied down for Valentine's Day. I like to be single by spring."

"Wow. So, you're just securing someone to spend the holidays with?" I said, in disbelief. "And you want that to be Roger? How does Roger feel about being the Holiday Honey?"

"Oh, please! It's cuffing season. And don't you worry one bit about Roger. He's not exactly looking for his fourth wife. He just wants to have fun, sweetie." Aunt Rita said with a sly smile. Aunt Rita smoothed her sweater out while looking at her reflection in a nearby window. "Besides, you could learn a thing or two, little Miss Never-Dating."

"Hey!" I protested, but before I could say more, Nick walked up to us with an expectant look on his face.

"Ms. Rita. Kit. I think we're ready to start in the conference room," Nick said politely.

We followed behind Nick. Aunt Rita was slightly ahead of me. She was wearing a cute corduroy skirt, tights, and a sweater that I was pretty sure was mine. As we walked through the lobby, Aunt Rita raised her hand and gave her fingers a flirty waggle of a wave at two men walking out of the social security office. I rolled my eyes when she looked over her shoulder at me and gave me a wink.

Nick turned to me as we walked and asked, "How are things at the library, Kit?"

"Great. Things are busy as usual. Our circulation numbers are up. Trent is doing a great job with the programming," I said, shifting into work mode. I knew that Nick may be young and a little goofy, but at the end of the day, he was the mayor, and the library depended on funding from the city every year.

"That's great to hear," Nick exclaimed as we entered the conference room, which was as festive as the rest of the building. A small Christmas tree stood in the corner of the room and tinsel and garland adorned every corner. When we entered, I saw that one person sat at the conference table waiting, the man from the coffee shop.

"This is Kit and Rita Campbell," Nick introduced us. "They own the riverfront property at the end of the city limits."

"That's a wonderful property." The man extended his hand and gave Aunt Rita a firm handshake, "Great to meet you. My name is William Philips from Braithway & Randall."

"Oh, the pleasure is all mine," Aunt Rita said flirtatiously.

William turned to me. I could tell from his expression that he recognized me from the coffee shop that morning. "Nice to see you again," he said with a curt nod and extended his hand. His hand was warm and soft, but his handshake was firm.

"Are you from the area?" Aunt Rita asked coyly. I gave Aunt Rita a look to tone down the flirting.

"I work out of our New York office, primarily," William said. "But I do find myself in Atlanta quite a bit."

"How lovely. New York must be so wonderful this time of year," Aunt Rita marveled, then added, "We love living here in Creekstone, just two hours from Atlanta. Close enough to the big city, but far enough away to enjoy the mountains. The quiet life."

"That's great." William smiled warmly at Aunt Rita. I saw his eyes dart over toward me and then back to Aunt Rita. "The two of you live here in Creekstone?"

"Oh, yessss," Aunt Rita said with an extra thick Southern accent. "In addition to the property by the river, Kit and I own a house here in town, just over on Fifth Street."

"It's a beautiful historic home," Nick added as he gestured for us to take a seat at the table across from William. "They converted the bedrooms into studio apartments and rent them out."

"Oh, yes. With just the two of us now, the house is much too big. We had to find a way to use all that space." Aunt Rita smiled much too eagerly.

"Well, first I want to say thank you for joining us today," Nick started.

"Of course, Nick," Aunt Rita said, sitting back in her chair and crossing her legs. "We're always happy to find out how we can help Creekstone."

"Well, I think we're at an exciting point in Creekstone's history," Nick said. "For the first time in decades, we have a potential development project that could help keep our young people in Creekstone. You know as well as I do that to make a decent living, you have to leave Creekstone as soon as you graduate high school. You have to move away to go to college. You have to move away to get a decent paying job. This kind of out-migration is hurting not just Creekstone, but all the rural communities."

Aunt Rita and I exchanged glances. What Nick was saying resonated with both of us. We both had to leave Creekstone to go to college, and the only reason either of us returned was because my mom got sick. Since returning, we were barely getting by on Aunt Rita's nursing pay and my librarian salary. The rising cost of living and steadily rising property taxes were killing us. We decided the only way to make it work was to convert our upstairs rooms to rentals.

"The development firm Braithway & Randall approached me when I first took office about some redevelopment opportunities for Creekstone." Nick looked at William.

William started, "Creekstone is a lovely community. Braithway & Randall has worked in several communities like Creekstone." William picked up a remote for the projector and started moving through slides. He explained that there were opportunities to redevelop areas of town that were run down and opportunities to develop areas that had never been built on before, like our land. William had a deep, clear voice while he was presenting. I couldn't help but notice that he didn't smile much as he talked through the slides, but his face was still very handsome. Each time William clicked the remote a new slide with an impressive artistic rendering of our town glided across the screen.

"Wow." Aunt Rita said as she admired the proposed new buildings. "This is really impressive."

"Thank you," William said. He had a reserved, polished manner. I caught myself staring at him and made myself look back at the slides on the screen.

Nick picked up where William left off. "You can see that the proposed development includes quite a few infrastructure improvements for the town, stop lights to improve intersections, road widening, storm water drainage. All kinds of boring stuff, but if we don't have those things in place, we can't build new buildings because our infrastructure couldn't support more people."

"I get that from my experience at the library," I smiled encouragingly at Nick. I turned to William, "And your company would build these things as part of this development plan?"

"That's right," William nodded, measured and polite.

"And this plan requires us to sell our land to your company?" I asked.

"Well, not exactly," William started slowly. He remained composed. "We can still build on the land that we do purchase, but your land, with the riverfront, provides us an opportunity to build something the entire town can enjoy."

"Like a park?" Aunt Rita asked.

William used the remote to return to a slide he'd shown us previously. The drawing was not even recognizable as Creekstone, but in the distance, I could see the buildings that looked like the ones on Main Street. "We would work with our engineers and architects to build something like this."

"So, a shopping mall," I said flatly.

"Well, a mixed-use development," William said, turning to look more directly at me.

I tried not to squirm under his cool gaze. "It looks like a strip mall with houses on top."

"Ha." Nick let a nervous laugh out. We all turned and looked at him. "The truth is, we need affordable housing, and the apartments and condos that could be built would positively impact our whole community."

"I think apartments are great, Nicky," Aunt Rita said gently. Like me, Aunt Rita was trying to be supportive of the mayor.

"But you know, old timers around here won't go for apartments."

"Well, that's why we were hoping that you and Kit would show your support for the development by selling your property. I think it would show the town that you support the idea."

"We do support the idea of development," I said. Nick's eyes lit up with hope. "I'm just not sure about giving away control to a company that wants to profit from apartment and commercial rentals is the way to go. What would stop developers from going back on their promise to create affordable housing?"

"Are you trying to develop the land yourself?" William asked. I turned to him. I didn't like his tone. He seemed to be pushing back.

"Let me be honest. I am here as a courtesy to the mayor and my aunt. I like the way the land is now. Untouched. Natural beauty," I said.

"And what about the people in Creekstone? The development would offer tremendous opportunity economically and socially for them." Willam crossed an ankle over a knee and leaned back in his chair. My cheeks burned red with anger. I looked down at the floor and took a deep breath. I couldn't believe that someone who had never been to Creekstone before would be so bold as to tell me what was best for my family and for the town. William tried again, trying to restrain himself from seeming rude. "It's just that..."

I interrupted. "It's just that if we sell the land to your company, we give up our control over how the land is used. Not just Aunt Rita and me, but the entire town. We have to trust that your company will do what it says it's going to do with the land—and that it won't bring in dollar discount stores and storage units. Just look at what happened in Shelbyville."

I kept my gaze fixed on William. I wasn't going to back down. Willam pushed his lips together tightly. I saw his broad chest rise as he took a deep breath. He said slowly, "So what would it take for you to feel comfortable selling your land?"

"A Christmas miracle," Aunt Rita quipped, and raised her eyebrows. I could tell she was as interested as Nick and William in what I would say next.

"Well," I started, "I think I'd only feel comfortable selling to a company that had more of a stake in the community."

"Well, I'm local. And I'm very invested in the positive outcomes of this development," Nick chimed in. Then he nervously added, "I mean, otherwise, William would have to just move to Creekstone and become a local."

Nick and Aunt Rita laughed to break the tension. Aunt Rita slapped her knee and said, "And he'd have to rent one of our rooms in our boarding house because this town doesn't have any available affordable housing." This made Aunt Rita and Nick laugh a little louder.

"I'd do that," William said, almost expressionless.

"They aren't being serious," I said, rolling my eyes. "They're just trying to get under my skin."

Aunt Rita gave a little gasp. "I was being quite serious!" She winked at William. I scoffed.

"I believe in the potential of Creekstone. I think the development of your property is the cornerstone for this project. It elevates the entire development, and if moving to Creekstone is what it takes to show that our company has the best intentions with this project, then I'd be happy to do that. It's just that my job requires me to be in New York so frequently..."

I rolled my eyes. "Of course it does."

William placed his hands in his lap. He took a slow deep breath and then let a little sigh go. I tried not to shrink in my chair when I realized I had cut him off so rudely again. William's handsome mouth twitched a little and he said with composure, "Like I was saying, I think Creekstone is an amazing community. And Braithway & Randall would be lucky to partner with this community. If you're interested in working with us, we'd love to continue discussions."

"Definitely," Nick said with a smile. He looked nervously over at me.

"Well, this meeting has been really enlightening," I said, standing up abruptly. "We don't want to take up any more of your time. Good luck with everything."

Nick and I shook hands. Nick offered to walk us out, but I told him we could see ourselves out. I nodded curtly at William. Aunt Rita lingered behind me saying goodbye.

As soon as Aunt Rita joined me in the lobby, I hooked my arm into hers and walked with her side-by-side. I whispered under my breath, "Ugh. That was awful."

I forced a smile as we passed a few people and headed for the door. Aunt Rita replied in a louder whisper, "Oh, stop. I'm sure nothing will come of it, but renters aren't exactly falling out of the sky, so if that really good looking one happened to..."

"Aunt Rita!" I exclaimed as we pushed through the front doors of the lobby and back out onto the sidewalk. Aunt Rita squinted, looked down into her bag, and fished around for something. She pulled out a pair of stylish, oversized sunglasses and put them on.

"Oh, don't worry. I'm sure William knew I was just joking," Aunt Rita said dismissing my worry. She started digging through her bag again, pulled out a lip gloss, and began applying it.

I shifted my weight as I waited while Aunt Rita fussed around in her bag and then said, "So you're not mad at me for not wanting to sell the land right away?"

"Of course not," Aunt Rita said as she applied her lip gloss. "Why would you think that?"

"Well, my guess is they would have offered us a decent amount for the land, and well..." I sighed, hating to admit it aloud. "We really need the money, so I was just worried you'd be upset that I didn't jump at the chance to sell the land."

"Not in the slightest, my dear. We have to do what we think is right. Trust your gut. That's what your mom always said. Otherwise, we'll live with regret. And that is awful for the soul." Aunt Rita patted me on the shoulder. I felt a sense of relief wash over me hearing my aunt say she was okay with how the real estate meeting had gone.

Aunt Rita pressed and popped her lips together to evenly apply her lip gloss. "I won't be home for dinner tonight."

"Oh, yeah? Hot date with Roger?" I asked as I zipped up my jacket.

"Hot date with Hank." Aunt Rita tipped her chin down so that her glasses slid down her nose and she winked. Then she turned on her heel and gave me a little wave as she headed for her car.

As Aunt Rita bounced down the street, waving at strangers, I couldn't help but think how much she looked like my mom. I took a deep breath and let it go slowly. I felt the tension in my shoulders release. It was such a relief that Aunt Rita wasn't upset. It was true that I didn't trust an outside corporation to develop the land, but I also wasn't ready for Creekstone to change. I felt comfort knowing things were just as my mom had known and loved them. She loved the quaintness and quirkiness of Creekstone. I wasn't ready to let go of that yet.

2

William

As soon as I opened my laptop, I saw the email from Mr. Braithway. Come to my office when you get here.

The clock above the door in my Atlanta office read a quarter to 8 a.m. A dread began to build in the pit of my stomach.

I was the division director for the company. I managed teams that mostly worked on large scale urban development and redevelopment, literally millions of dollars in projects, but I knew what he wanted to talk to me about, and it wasn't one of my million-dollar development projects.

Two weeks ago, Mr. Braithway had sent me an email that simply said, Work this project. There were a few files attached. The project was a small-scale redevelopment in North Georgia. The project was so simple that I assumed Mr. Braithway had mistakenly sent me the email, but he wasn't the kind of person you could easily second-guess. Mr. Braithway was a giant in corporate real estate development. He understood his influence and how eager people were to please him. Mr. Braithway was intentional in keeping his inner circle impossibly small. And there was one person who commanded respect and dare I say even, deference from Mr. Braithway: his executive assistant, Marla. I knew she would help me get to the bottom of the Creekstone assignment.

I reached out to Marla and asked if he had intended to send the note to the division director of the rural redevelopment team. They usually work the smaller rural projects, but at huge volume. Marla assured me that Mr. Braithway intended for me to work on the project, and she gave me a stern warning not to delegate the project to a junior project manager on my team.

When I saw the email that morning, I knew he wanted to talk to me about the Creekstone project. I was not eager to report my progress, or lack thereof, to Mr. Braithway. I had spent the last few days in Creekstone, and while the mayor was extremely eager to start a project with us, the land owners were hesitant. I didn't understand the appeal of putting resources into working on a project like that.

I took a deep breath and forced myself up from my desk and down the hallway to Mr. Braithway's office. Our Atlanta office was in a high-rise downtown. The offices had glass walls with sleek contemporary furniture. This early in the morning, the lights were off in most of the offices. When I reached Mr. Braithway's office, I saw Marla sitting behind her computer.

She looked up at me and smiled as I approached. "Good morning, sweetheart. He's expecting you in there."

"Good morning, Marla. How's it going today?" I asked, pointing a thumb toward Braithway's door.

Marla laughed. "Good thing you're getting in there first thing. He's got board meetings later today, and you know the kind of mood that puts him in. But go on in. He's on the phone with his daughter, but he's expecting you."

I blew air through my lips and pushed the heavy mahogany door open. Mr. Braithway's office was a stark contrast to the rest of the office. He rejected any type of contemporary office interior design. In all six of our regional offices, Braithway had his own office, and every one of them looked like a Bass Pro Shop with a desk in the middle of it. Mr. Braithway stood at a table by the windows, his back to the door. He was organizing fishing flies in a clear container and looked up when he saw me.

Mr. Braithway poked his phone with his pointer finger and then held his phone up for me to see. He had put the phone on mute.

"I'm on the phone with Terra, my oldest. That coffee is for you and there's a chicken biscuit in the bag for you," Mr. Braithway said, using his chin to point toward the bag. Sensing that I might decline the biscuit, he added sternly, "You're in the South. Trust me. Do it."

Then he poked his phone again. I took a seat in one of the overstuffed chairs that sat in front of his desk. I heard Braithway impatiently sigh. I knew that sigh.

"What grade is Dash in?" Mr. Braithway asked his daughter, raising his eyebrows. I knew this look on Mr. Braithway's face. I knew this setup. He'd asked a question he knew the answer to.

I heard Terra's voice. "He's only in tenth grade, but Vanderbilt is really competitive. I think he needs some help."

"If it's too competitive, maybe he should go somewhere else." Mr. Braithway rolled his eyes.

"He wants to go to an SEC school so he can go to college football games, but I don't want him to go to a big party school. I think Vanderbilt is a good place for him. Can you call your foundation friend about him?"

"Honey, I would call someone at Vanderbilt, but your son is a turd," Mr. Braithway said, taking a bite of his biscuit.

"Dad! Please," Terra cried. I had worked with Mr. Braithway long enough to know how this would go. My guess was his oldest daughter also knew how this was going to go. I pulled the paper sack toward me and reached inside to find a warm foil-wrapped biscuit. I pulled it out, unwrapped the chicken biscuit, and took a bite. It was the best thing I had tasted in months. I held it up and nodded. Mr. Braithway looked satisfied.

"You can't call kids turds, Dad. Especially your own grandson," Terra scolded.

Mr. Braithway started laughing and said, "Well, he is a turd. Tell him to work on that and then I'll call any damn college he wants, but I'm not going to bat for a kid whose best and only quality is that he fell out of you, like a turd."

"Gross, Dad," Terra protested. "You have to say something besides he's a turd. What's the deal? You didn't hesitate to help the girls when they went to college. Is this just because you don't like his dad, Winston?"

I ate my biscuit and looked at the fly-fishing magazines on the table situated next to the overstuffed chair.

Mr. Braithway pivoted. "Terra, you're a dream. Your girls are amazing, intelligent women, just like you. Making a call on their behalf was merely a formality because they could have gotten there on their own. I did it as vote of confidence, an act of love and loyalty. I'm so proud of you and the girls that I can't even put it into words, but your son is a turd. Like your husband. Tell the kid to prove me wrong, and I'll help him. You said it yourself. He's only in tenth grade. That is plenty of time to grow some legs, stop floating around like a turd in a toilet bowl, and do something for himself."

"What is it that you think he should do?" Terra said with a sigh.

"Anything, Terra," Mr. Braithway said. "Hell, he can be one of these boys selling water on the corner of the streets in Atlanta for all I care, but he can't just do nothing."

"Dad, he has a 3.2 GPA at a prestigious private school. He's not doing nothing," Terra countered.

"Terra, a 3.2 GPA at a private school is like a 1.5 GPA anywhere else. Why do you think people send their kids to private schools?" Mr. Braithway said dryly. "It's because real competition against real talent would eat them alive. Rich people insulate their children from the real world and then make their kids believe they're really doing something, and that's a dangerous disservice to your progeny, my dear."

"Okay, Dad," Terra conceded with a heavy sigh.

"All right. I'll see you at dinner on Saturday night. Love you, honey," Mr. Braithway said.

"Love you, Dad." Terra said with another sigh. Mr. Braithway dramatically raised his pointer finger again and poked the phone.

I didn't know his four daughters that well, but I knew they were as tough as he was. They were an extremely close family. Mr. Braithway had lost his wife when his youngest daughter was still a baby. He'd never remarried, and he'd made his daughters his sole focus in his personal life. Everyone who worked closely with Mr. Braithway knew that every Saturday night he had dinner with his daughters. A few of my colleagues thought it was a bit of an inconvenience, always having to plan around his Saturday dinner. It made some coast-to-coast travel hard and planning international trips with Mr. Braithway was really tough. Once, when we had a project in Europe, I had told him that we were struggling to schedule a site visit around the Saturday dinners, and he told me, "Don't hold up a project for me. You handle it. I trust you." In the moment, I'd focused on the opportunity to climb a little farther up the ladder in the company, but later I realized Mr. Braithway had created boundaries that he was making everyone work around, and I admired him for that. I thought his daughters were lucky.

Mr. Braithway collapsed into his desk chair. He swiveled his chair to look at me and said very seriously, "The kid's a turd."

"I gathered that," I said, biting into my biscuit.

Mr. Braithway put his hand on his knee and tilted his head, as if he was taking a good look at me. "Good to see you, William!"

"Good to see you, sir," I said.

Mr. Braithway took a deep breath and exhaled through his nose. "You probably already guessed this, but I'm going to retire this year."

"Sir, congratulations," I said. "Is this a full retirement?"

"Sweet Jesus, I hope so," Mr. Braithway muttered. "I've been thinking about retiring for a while. I'm still young and healthy. I don't want to be one of those old farts who dies in the board-room. I want to go fishing and enjoy some of this shit my kids made me buy. So, I've been talking about it a bit with a few board members, just floating the idea. And I've mentioned you as my successor."

"I'm extremely flattered, sir." I tried to contain myself. I knew that my name had been in the running for a promotion, but I had no idea that Mr. Braithway intended for me to be his successor. "I...I...really, sir. Thank you."

"Your record is excellent. Everyone knows that." Mr. Braith-way said, scratching his chin. "I've kept you on our biggest urban accounts, and you've closed some pretty big deals. Every-one wants to keep that level of success going in those markets. No one is doubting you there. Because of your project leader-ship, our company has shaped the skyline in major cities. You have inspired imagination and hope in places others have aban-doned. Our company would do well with a leader like you. I'm proud of you."

I felt a heaviness in my chest. Like the breath had been knocked out of me. I don't think anyone had ever told me that they were proud of me before besides my mom. Sure, in the requisite places, I had been congratulated, but this was differ-ent. I took a deep breath and swallowed hard, trying to stay composed.

Mr. Braithway picked up a pair of pliers he'd been using to bend fly fishing hooks. "But to effectively lead this company, you have to be able to lead all the divisions. We work in other markets, not just urban development. Our investors will want to know the new CEO can handle the political landscape of rural development, and we have a substantial portfolio in rural areas. Those deals may not look as big on paper, but they matter to a lot of the regional relationships we have. And Rural deals cook a little differently."

Mr. Braithway pointed his pliers at me. "There have been some questions about whether you can manage rural deals. It takes a lot of tact and patience to make these projects happen."

"I assure you, sir," I said quickly. "I will do whatever it takes to gain your confidence."

"Always willing to go the extra mile. Proactive. That's what I like about you. Not a turd." Mr. Braithway smiled as he punctuated that last part.

I blinked. "Thank you, sir. I try."

"So then." Mr. Braithway sat up and leaned forward onto his desk. "What the fuck happened in Creekstone?"

I should have seen this coming. I inhaled sharply and steadied myself. I knew the best thing would be to level with Mr. Braithway, but he had just given me about a half a dozen reasons why I needed to prove to him I could handle this project on my own.

"I am just getting started in Creekstone, sir. I've met with the mayor, city council, and several landowners, and I think we have a lot of momentum."

"Then why didn't you get any landowners to agree to sell while you were up there this week?" Mr. Braithway asked, sitting back in his chair.

"I think there's an opportunity for me to earn trust in the community," I said. I tried to sound confident. "Like you said, these deals manifest a little differently."

Mr. Braithway snorted a laugh. "Sounds like you learned the first lesson."

"The first lesson?" I asked.

"Lesson one in rural development. Never underestimate the locals."

"Sir, I promise I didn't underestimate them," I said quickly.

"Well in that case, it looks like you got got." Mr. Braithway looked at me with his head tilted to one side, like he was sizing me up.

"Sir, I promise you that we will have a favorable outcome in this deal. I just need some time to work with the community." I tried not to let the panic show in my voice. I had been trained to pivot the focus. "We didn't get a no from any of the potential sellers. In fact, I think we got high engagement and interest from everyone involved."

"High engagement? We already have the mayor in our pocket," Mr. Braithway said with an exasperated sigh. He leaned back and looked at the ceiling as if collecting himself.

"Sir, I assure you. The development is still viable. I am going to make it happen."

"Look, this is a real sink or swim situation here, William," Mr. Braithway said. "Let me level with you. Ever since you were an intern, I saw the potential in you—even when other people told me not to take the risk on you. And now I want you to be the person who runs this company. I plan to retire next year, and I've started telling people that you are my top choice, but you have to show me and the rest of this company that you can win any kind of deal. You have to show the people you will lead that you understand their projects and work. They're the ones who need to believe in you. Think of Creekstone as the way you not only land this job, but also earn this company's respect."

"One year?" I asked. "I should be able to close the deal and break ground in a year."

"Oh, I know. And do you want to know how I know you're going to get this done?" He pressed his fingers together, making a pyramid.

"How, sir?"

"Because this is the only project you are going to work on until you close the deal," Mr. Braithway said.

"Sir," I started to object. But he held up his hand to silence me.

"You think you can do your job in New York and close this deal?" Mr. Braithway leaned back in his chair and pushed his lips together. "Tell me. What was the problem? Why didn't you get any of the land owners to start negotiations?"

"I think there is some concern about an outsider coming into the community and telling them what to do, but I could always host some focus groups and..."

Mr Braithway held up his hand again and I stopped talking. "Let me stop you right there. Focus groups and surveys and town hall meetings are all for show. If you want these people to trust you, you will need to spend time in this community. That's all there is to it."

"Yes, sir," I said. "Can I ask a question, sir?"

"I would hope so."

I hesitated. "What makes Creekstone a priority?"

"Priority," Mr. Braithway repeated as he leaned back in his chair and pressed the tips of his fingers together. He sighed and finally said, "Economic development."

I nodded, "Absolutely, sir. All boats rise when the tide rises." I repeated a commonly heard phrase in our industry.

"Yes, except that we want more than floating boats. I know you know this, but our business is more than just buying land and building on it." Mr. Braithway put his hands in his lap, "I'm on the board of the regional hospital; they're expanding. You want to know what one of their biggest issues is? Doctors and nurses don't want to live in the boonies. No matter how much you pay them."

Mr. Braithway continued. "I'm on the Board of Trustees for two colleges in the region; they want to expand. You know what one of their biggest issues is? College graduates don't have anywhere to work in the region."

I nodded, taking in his answer. He said, "I never want our teams to lose focus on the work they do, but the short answer is our work leads to economic development, then to community improvements, then to community resilience. And the world needs more of that. Especially rural communities like Creekstone." He slouched back in his chair. "So Creekstone isn't necessarily a priority or some magical diamond in the rough. It's like every other town in rural America, and if you can make it work in Creekstone...well then, William, I think you can make it work anywhere."

My head was reeling when I left Mr. Braithway's office. On the one hand, my hard work was being rewarded. I was being considered to take the top job at our development firm. This was my dream job. But on the other hand, I was being sent on a quest to prove myself. And this quest wasn't exactly an exciting high-profile project. It was a small scale, local deal. And as far as local developments go, it wasn't even a very interesting development.

I kept all these opinions and motivations to myself, though. The last thing I needed was for my coworkers, who were also my fiercest competitors, finding out that I needed to land a deal to become everyone's boss. They'd sabotage me for sure.

But regardless of my reservations or personal opinions, the ball had been set in motion. Mr. Braithway sent out one of his classically short emails letting the division know I had a special assignment and naming an acting director for my division in my absence. As soon as the email went out, my phone began blowing up with texts and calls asking to chat. I knew that everyone wanted the tea.

I decided to head back to Creekstone immediately. The sooner I could get this deal worked out and settled, the sooner Mr. Braithway would announce my promotion.

When I called the mayor, Nick Martin, and let him know I'd like to spend more time in Creekstone, he was ecstatic. Things had been left uncertain because the landowners were hesitant, and Nick worried that the project was dead. I reassured him that we were still moving forward and just needed to be patient. Nick told me he would help me find a place to stay for a few weeks so I wouldn't have to commute for meetings. I was determined to get up to Creekstone, close this deal, and get back to New York before the work vultures descended.

When I pulled into the parking lot at Nick's office, he was waiting near the front steps. He waved at me, with an enthusiasm that bordered on frantic. I sighed. In that moment, I realized how much I needed this skinny, twenty-something kid's help to close this deal. Nick seemed like a nice kid, but he was a recent college graduate who had upset an old-timer, incumbent mayor by running on a "change is needed platform." I had seen this play out dozens of times in my line of work. Small communities love the idea of having more but they don't want to give up small town life to allow it to happen, classic "not in my backyard" attitudes.

It's part of what has always drawn me to urban development. I like that folks in urban landscapes have already subscribed to the paradigm of city life, and convincing people to build something isn't the battle. Instead, our work focuses on the hope of improving or reinventing places and helping communities pick the "right" something. Unlike these small-town development projects. Towns like Creekstone are afraid to develop, so just getting started feels like a battle.

As soon as I opened my car door to step out, Nick was right next to me. "Hello! I'm so glad to see you today." Nick beamed. Before I could respond, Nick was walking around my car to the passenger side door. "Let's just take your car right to your rental, so you can get settled in."

"Okay," I said hesitantly, sliding back into the driver's seat. I started the car as Nick climbed into the passenger seat.

"Just pull out and take a left at the next light. It's two blocks away," Nick said. I listened as Nick chattered about how busy the holidays were in Creekstone, but that he thought this could be a great time to see everyone. "Right here. You can park on the street."

Nick was pointing at a large white house on the corner of a residential street. I pulled up in front. It had a charming picket fence. The front yard was small but had some tasteful landscaping. The house itself was a rather large colonial style farm house. It had a wraparound porch and gabled dormer windows that made it look quintessentially southern. Nick jumped out as soon as I put the car in park. I got out of the car and followed him through the white picket fence gate, up the walkway.

The house was tastefully decorated for the holidays. The red front door had a huge wreath on it. The porch banisters had garland and red ribbons. The white rocking chairs had boxes wrapped in cellophane paper to look like Christmas gifts.

As Nick reached out to ring the doorbell. I blurted out, "Are you sure this is a good idea?"

Nick turned to me. For a moment his smile faded, and it looked as if he were considering what to say next, then he shook his head a little, as if remembering. "Well, I do think this would be a great place to live, because you're right here in town."

"Yes, but Ms. Campbell, from our meeting last week. She didn't seem wild about me in the meeting and this might..." My voice trailed off.

"Ms. Campbell? Rita adored you," Nick said confused, then as if the realization had just hit him, he gasped. "Oh, Kit! Don't worry about her. She is the nicest, most agreeable person in town. Everyone loves Kit."

I blinked, trying to process the description Nick had just given me of Kit Campbell, the co-owner of not only the riverfront property I desperately needed to buy to make this deal work, but also the co-owner of this studio apartment I had agreed to lease. In my limited experience with Kit, she had been snarky and quick to judge.

"Plus," Nick said, leaning in a little and speaking out of the side of his mouth as if he were telling me a secret, "this is the only place in a thirty-mile radius that was vacant to rent on such short notice, so it's definitely the best option, because it's the only option."

Nick beamed a huge smile at me as he pressed the doorbell. I felt a familiar tightness in my body that I recognized anxiety. I took a deep breath, counting down from five, and then exhaled slowly counting back up.

I had moved around a lot when I was young and had rented my fair share of rooms since college and graduate school. Keeping to myself in this rental should be simple. My anxiety was high because all the pressure around the Creekstone deal had been magnified since I'd talked to Mr. Braithway.

I heard some shuffling around. Then, as the heavy front door opened, the bells on the wreath jingled so loudly they sounded like a laugh track from a sitcom.

"Hey." It was Kit Campbell. She smiled warmly at Nick but sighed when she looked at me. She pushed the door open wider, turned, waved a finger for us to follow her. "Come on in. Aunt Rita is working a double at the hospital, so she asked me to help you get into your apartment."

"Thank you. Your house is lovely," I said as I followed Kit into the house.

"Thanks. It's been in the family for four generations," she said flatly.

I heard Nick behind me clear his throat. "Hey, Kit. I would love to stay and get the tour again, but I have to run back to the office. I'll see you at the committee meeting later today, though." Nick waved with both hands and flashed his huge smile at us.

"Sounds good, Nick," Kit said, tilting her head and then added in an especially warm tone, "I just baked some Christmas cookies for the meeting."

Nick stood up straight, and his jaw dropped open, but somehow, he was still smiling. "Is that what that delicious smell is? I cannot wait! I'll make sure to have some coffee and tea ready." Nick waved again and pulled the door shut behind him.

I turned back to Kit, who had her arms crossed, looking at me skeptically. Despite her overall displeased demeanor, Kit was extremely beautiful. She was petite and curvy. She had her thick, wavy black hair pulled back into a loose braid that fell over her shoulder. She was wearing a hoodie and a pair of jeans that hugged her hips in just the right way. I tried to look as if I didn't notice.

"So, I guess Aunt Rita wasn't joking after all. You really are going to go through with this."

I let a puff of air out. I wasn't expecting Kit to roll out a red carpet for me, but this wasn't exactly the warm, agreeable person that Nick claimed Kit to be.

"What you said about needing to build trust makes perfect sense. But I'll be honest with you—I feel a connection with Creekstone, and I'm excited to be here," I said. I swallowed and smiled. The truth was I moved to Creekstone because my boss created this hoop I needed to jump through to get the most important promotion of my career. And I wasn't going to leave anything to chance. If I needed to temporarily move to this podunk town to get everyone on board, then so be it—and that included Kit. "I hear Christmas is the best time to be in Creekstone."

Kit rolled her eyes. "Well, I promised Aunt Rita I would show you around.' She limply held out her hand. "As you can see this is the foyer. We keep the front door locked at all times. Follow me, please."

The interior of the house had beautiful craftsman-style architectural accents. There was a large staircase directly facing the front door and two rooms, one on each side of the foyer. I followed Kit into one of the rooms. "Okay. This is one of our common areas. Feel free to use this as much as you want. The other renters come down here in the evenings, have drinks, and talk before dinner."

"This is great," I said. The room was warm and inviting space with two sofas and two arm chairs flanking a large wooden coffee table near a fire place. There was a large television above a credenza. In the corner stood a tall Christmas tree.

Kit said, "Okay, I'll show you where you can check your mail." Kit walked past without looking at me and back into the foyer. I followed her into the second room.

"This is the office. We put mail in your cubbies," she pointed. The wall had a nice shelf and a box that had been divided into mail cubbies. Kit walked over to the desk and shuffled some papers around like she was looking for something.

"I'll put your name on one of the boxes later so you know which one is yours."

"This room is also amazing," I said looking around in awe at the floor to ceiling built-in bookcases. "The craftsmanship on these bookcases is remarkable."

"Yes, my grandfather put them in. Renters sometimes borrow books. Feel free," Kit muttered as she continued to look for something on the desk. I tried not to let it bother me that she was so disinterested. I walked over and started looking at the books on one of the shelves.

"I guess it makes sense that a librarian would have so many books," I said, trying to make small talk.

"I found it," Kit said, ignoring my comment. She help up a white envelope.

Kit walked around the desk. She stood so close to me that I could smell the faint smell of jasmine perfume. I tried not to lean in. "Here are your keys," Kit said, handing me the envelope. I folded the envelope in half and put it in my back pocket.

Kit brushed past me, and I followed her. She walked past the stairs down a hallway. As we passed a closed door, she pointed and said, "That's a bathroom."

Then we kept walking. The short hallway opened up into a bright kitchen. The kitchen had a farmhouse vibe to it. "Every apartment has a small kitchenette with a little fridge, microwave, and hotplate, but most residents prefer to make large meals downstairs. They plan them together." Kit tapped a calendar on the refrigerator. "Feel free to put food in this fridge or in the cupboard next to the fridge. I'd just write your name on it if it's important to you."

"Got it," I said. Trying to be positive, I added, "The cookies do smell good."

Kit's mouth twisted. She looked like she was biting the side of her cheek. "I thought you didn't like cookies."

I didn't take the bait. "These smell too good." Before I could say anything else, Kit walked farther into the kitchen and into the next room. "This is the common dining room. Folks like to eat in here."

I walked to where Kit was standing in the doorway. I peeked over her head to see a sunroom that had been converted into a dining room.

"This room is incredible," I said. The room had floor to ceiling windows. Each corner of the room had beautiful ferns and Ficus trees. In the center of the room was a large dining room table. A huge antique chandelier hung low above the table. Every inch of wall space was covered in paintings and photographs. The chairs that surrounded the table were all Victorian-style chairs, but instead of traditional upholstery, they were covered in funky, eclectic, and colorful fabrics.

Kit turned around. I didn't realize I was standing so close to her. She crossed her arms and bit her lip again, but instead of looking annoyed, her expression softened. "This room, the art, the plants, the whole vibe—it was very much my mom."

I waited to see if Kit would say more. She looked down at the ground and shuffled her feet. "My mom passed away a little over a year ago. This was one of her favorite rooms in the house. It's nice that everyone gathers in here. She would have loved that."

"Is the artwork hers?" I asked. I couldn't take my eyes off her. She looked up at me and I felt completely lost in her perfect almond-shaped brown eyes. I said softly, "Beautiful...the paintings are beautiful."

Kit blushed and looked back at the floor. "Yeah, she was an amazing photographer, but an even better painter, as you can see." I could hear it in the softness and care in her voice. I could see it in her eyes. I understood her pain, her grief. I wanted to say more, but then Kit cleared her throat, and I realized I was blocking the door. I took a step back.

The corner of Kit's mouth pushed into a slight smile, and she brushed past me back into the kitchen. When I turned, Kit was crossing the room quickly and heading toward a doorway in the corner of the kitchen.

"I'll take you up to your room now. You saw the stairs in the front. They go up to the renters' rooms, too." Kit turned and looked to make sure I was following her. "But we can take the back stairs."

Kit disappeared through the doorway. I caught up to her and saw that she was climbing a steep, narrow staircase. I followed her up the stairs. As we climbed, I was eye level with Kit's thighs and butt. I shook my head and forced myself to look down. Kit had already made it clear that she didn't like me or my company. The last thing I needed was to get caught staring at her ass, even if it was practically perfect.

We reached the second-floor landing. Kit stopped there and said, "Okay, the second floor is for renters."

She saw me gaze toward the stairs that continued up to the third floor and said, "The third floor is where Aunt Rita and

I live. We converted the attic into an apartment when we re-modeled the house."

I followed Kit onto the second floor. The hallway was large, with bright light from the windows on either end.

Kit opened the first door. "Through this first door, there is a laundry room for everyone to use."

Kit kept walking. She stopped when we reached two doors, across the hall from each other. She pointed to the first door and said, "A professor at the local college rents this room, and a traveling nurse rents that room. Both work evenings and nights." I nodded.

Kit turned and kept going down the hallway until she reached two more doors. "This one is a newlywed couple. And this one is yours." Kit stopped in front of one of the doors and looked up at me. Her brown eyes examined my face. She bit her lip thoughtfully, as if waiting for me. "Uh, do you have your key?"

"Oh, right," I said. I felt a little embarrassed as I stood there staring at her and hoped it didn't show. I pulled the folded envelope out of my back pocket and poured the key into my hand. I held it out for Kit to take. I felt her fingers lightly brush mine when she picked up the key from my palm. I felt an undeniable spark. Her eyes met mine and lingered there for a moment. She cleared her throat and turned to unlock the door.

"This is it," Kit said as she pushed the door open. I followed her into the room. The room was bigger and brighter than I expected. There were large windows on both exterior walls and a fireplace. Kit walked over to the corner of the room and placed the key on the mantel. She crossed her arms and sighed. "Pretty straight forward. This is a real fireplace. Wood is on the back porch. These rooms get pretty drafty so you'll probably want to use it from January till about March, assuming you're still living here." She pointed at the far corner of the room. "You have your own bathroom and kitchenette over there."

"This is really great," I said. "Great light."

"I'm sure it's not as great as your apartment in New York," Kit said, her head tilted to the side. Her eyebrows raised as she waited for me to respond.

"Different but not better," I said with a smile. I wasn't going to take the bait. "Besides, I was living in a company apartment in New York. I'm happy to be out of that place and somewhere much cozier."

"And your boss just let you up and move to a town like Creekstone?" Kit raised her eyebrows.

I walked over to the window. I could see my car parked on a picturesque street lined with trees. Leaves were starting to turn from their golden yellow and brilliant orange to a crusty brown, but it still looked beautiful. I continued to look out the window as I said, "I was hardly in New York. I traveled constantly. But my job has changed, and I am going to be working more in this region, so moving here makes sense for me, and honestly, maybe I'll finally get some of that work life balance everyone is always talking about."

I conjured my best version of a sincere smile and turned back toward Kit. She was standing with her arms crossed, one eyebrow raised, almost suspiciously. Even when she was obviously doubting me, she looked sexy.

I kept cool. The truth was my relationship past was filled with hot, smart women just like Kit. I knew that somewhere in that defensive wall of skepticism was a crack where the light got in. And, I wasn't lying. I was moving to Georgia for a job, and right now, I was living in Creekstone. It's true that if all things went well, Atlanta was my final destination, but for now, Creekstone was the place I had to call home because it was my last mountain to climb before I was named CEO.

3

Kit

"Trust me, V," I said as I put my car in park. "His hotness is not enough."

"Are you sure?" Veronica's voice came from my phone. "I'm looking at his profile on the company's website. And he's super fucking hot."

"Yes," I nodded and sighed. She was right. "But being hot and charming isn't enough if your company wants to turn every small town from Atlanta to Charlotte into one big suburban sprawl. Women must resist the hotness to stop the sprawl!" I joked.

"Okaaaay." Veronica's voice sounded like she was conceding. "But I'm looking at his Instagram now, and it looks like he's single. Lots of pictures with work friends and lots of solo travel pics. Holy smokes, he doesn't have a shirt on in this one."

"It doesn't matter. He's one of my renters," I said. "I shouldn't be invading his privacy." As soon as I said that, my phone dinged. I pulled it off the dashboard clip and opened the text. It was a photo from Veronica. I swiped to open it and saw a photo of William Philips in a pool. My eyes nearly popped out of my head. Wow. His cut abs were glistening and his shoulders and arms looked much more muscular in this photo than they did in the business casual, three quarter polo zip-up he was wearing this morning when he moved into the house.

"Veronica," I pleaded, leaning my head against the steering wheel. "I live with this guy and we have to stay focused on keeping Creekstone safe from this predatory real estate development company. Not zoom in on his abs."

"Okay, okay. I'll stop, but just so you know, there are no photos of him with anyone who looks like they could be his boo thang. No hot girls or guys hanging onto him. So, I think he could be available. Not for you, of course, rather for some other eligible similarly-aged, hot Creekstone woman." I could imagine Veronica's mischievous smile as she said this.

"Ha, of course!" I chuckled and added regretfully, "I gotta run. We have our first Christmas tree competition meeting today."

"Oh, fun! You love the tree decorating competition," Veronica cheered into the phone.

I smiled. "I do love the tree decorating competition. Christmas is the best time of the year, and the tree competition is particularly awesome because the whole community comes together to celebrate."

"Bye, chica. Call me later."

It was true. My favorite time of the year was the holidays, but this year was going to be heavy. I was throwing myself right into the community activities so I wouldn't focus too much on missing my mom. I scooped up my plate of fresh baked cookies and headed into the library.

The Creekstone library was my favorite place in town. Ever since I was a little girl, I had spent endless hours there. As a high school student, I worked as a student volunteer. Then, in college, I worked during the summers at the library. So, when I moved home to be with my mom full-time, it was a no-brainer that I would go back. And, when the COVID-19 pandemic happened, the library manager called me in and told me he was going to retire, and he asked me to apply for the job.

The library was busier than usual. I immediately went to the circulation desk. As I approached, my assistant manager, Trent, was helping one of our senior patrons figure out how to put an e-book platform on her tablet.

"Good morning, Trent. Thanks for covering the desk this morning," I said as I peeled back the festive green plastic wrap on the plate and exposed an array of Christmas cookies.

Trent picked up a large gingerbread man and waved it at me. "You're lucky these little guys are so good! We've been swamped today. Must be the Christmas Tree Competition meeting."

"Oh, speaking of!" I said, covering the cookies. "I have to run to that meeting. I'll be back before lunch."

I hurried to the library meeting room. The room was packed with the usual community members. I waved at a couple of folks as I slipped into the room and put the cookies on the table. As I uncovered the platter, Nick appeared next to me.

"So excited to kick off the Christmas Tree Competition," he said with a huge smile that reminded me of a kid on Christmas morning.

"Me too!" I agreed. "I love the way the library feels with all the Christmas trees on display."

Nick nodded excitedly and then, noticing the cookies on the plate, he said, "Oh, yes. We brought coffee."

"We?" I said looking up to see William appearing behind Nick. William held up two containers of coffee from The Bean.

"Oh." I tried not to sound annoyed.

"Let me go get some cups out of the break room," Nick said, disappearing out of the room.

"William, I didn't know you were coming."

"Yeah, Nick invited me. He said it would be a great way to meet folks in the community. I'm excited," William said, setting the coffee carafes down next to the cookies. He stood close as he adjusted the spouts on the cardboard coffee containers. He was so close our elbows nearly touched. I tried to ignore the little flutter in my stomach, and I tried not to picture his cut abs under his button-down shirt. Nick reappeared with the cups, and William poured himself some coffee.

"Look, this is real smalltown stuff here. Are you sure this is where you want to meet people?" I said, trying not to sound rude.

"These are the exact folks I'd like to meet," William said with a shrug. William took a sip of his coffee. "This is why I moved here."

"Let's get started," Nick said from the podium at the front of the room. I turned and took a seat in one of the rows of chairs that had been set out for the meeting. Nick tapped his cell phone, and a slideshow of photos and Christmas music began to play on the screen behind him. William took a seat next to me. My look of surprise must have registered because he looked pleased and he loudly whispered, "This is exciting." I could smell his cologne, a musky but pleasant smell. I tried not to lean into it.

"Welcome to our annual opening meeting of the Christmas Tree Competition, one of Creekstone's favorite traditions," Nick said. A few old-timers in the front of the room started clapping. I smiled and began clapping as well. I looked at William, and he started clapping too.

Nick's presentation of the rules was pretty fast, but I felt myself squirming in the seat next to William. I could smell his aftershave, and my whole body was tense trying to make sure we didn't accidentally brush against each other. William's thighs made the conference room chairs seem small.

Nick concluded by saying, "So, in summary, each team will come to the library after hours today to decorate their trees. After tonight, no one can change the decorations on their tree. Simple touch-ups are allowed but no major decoration changes. The trees will be on display for public voting for two weeks until Christmas. The public can donate one dollar per vote. We'll tally the votes at the end of the two-week voting period. Then we'll announce the winners on December twentieth. Any questions?"

Ms. Patty was in the front row and her hand shot up. A frustrated sigh escaped my mouth with a puff of air. I checked out of the corner of my eye to make sure no one saw or heard me.

"I have a question," Ms. Patty announced once Nick pointed at her. "Are you all going to give preferential treatment to tree placement this year? Last year, our tree was off in a corner and no one could see it, so no one voted for it."

"Sounds like a complaint, not a question," Ms. Pearl said loudly. The crowd snickered.

Ms. Patty twisted around in her chair and narrowed her eyes at Ms. Pearl. "It's an honest question. Who decides where each tree is placed? If our tree is stuck in the section with all the reference books, no one will ever see it because no one even goes back there!"

Nick held up his hands. "Okay, great point, Ms. Patty. I'll work with the library staff to make sure everyone's trees are in high traffic areas of the library. Just remember, though, families visit the library, so if you're tree isn't family friendly, it will end up in the staff break room."

"What?" William whispered.

I leaned over and whispered back, "One year someone did a Santa Serial Killer themed tree inspired by the TV show Dexter."

"Wow." William turned to me with an amused wide-eyed look. I couldn't help but smile. Something about his smile was different at that moment. He looked more genuine, sincere, and incredibly handsome.

He leaned forward and whispered another question. "So, your workplace is just covered in Christmas trees for two weeks?"

"Well, it's longer than two weeks. We leave the trees up until January," I responded.

William's eyes grew wider.

"I love it!" I said, trying not to sound defensive. "Christmas is really the most magical time of the year."

"Sure, yeah," William said, nodding. I could tell he was trying to be agreeable. "I'm not a Grinch or anything, but that's a lot of Christmas spirit."

I felt a little self-conscious about how much I loved Christmas, so I further explained. "Well, it's for a good cause. The money raised from the entry and voting fees all benefit the Girl's House and the Boy's Lodge in Creekstone."

William's eyebrows raised as if surprised and his big smile faded back to his softer, more genuine one.

Nick's voice had raised to a polite shout as people started to talk amongst themselves. "If you're interested in registering for the competition, I'll be at the back table with Ms. Kit's famous cookies."

We both stood up. "I'd like to try one of your cookies." William stretched as he stood. I was eye-level with his chest, and I couldn't help but notice how his shirt was snug around his pecs as he stretched.

"Excuse me?" I asked.

"Your famous cookies," William said, pointing at the table. "I hope they don't run out. There are a ton of people here."

"Well, you can taste my cookies back at the house," I said and then immediately stammered and tried to hide my blush. "I—uh...meant that I made extra and put them in a Christmas cookie tin on the counter by the fridge. You can have some. That's what I meant."

William raised one eyebrow and one side of his lip curled into a slight smile. He shoved one hand into his pocket.

"I have to go and give my assistant manager a break from the circulation desk." I practically squeaked as I turned and scurried out of the room.

As soon as I arrived at the circulation desk, Trent looked relieved. "Boss Lady, I am so glad to see you. I have got to eat something. I'm getting hangry." He made prayer hands and bowed as he backed away from the circulation desk and disappeared behind a door that read "Staff Only."

I let out a puff of air as I collapsed into the chair. I felt a sense of relief, but I couldn't quite explain why. Maybe I was just anxious about the Christmas Tree Competition kicking off. Before I could give it too much more thought, a library patron appeared in front of me with a stack of books, and I got to work. There was a steady stream of library visitors until finally Trent returned.

"You look refreshed," I said as Trent took a seat next to me.

"That I am," Trent said as he logged into his computer next to mine.

"Are you participating in the Christmas Tree Contest this year?" I asked, spinning around in my chair to face him.

"That I am," Trent said again. I chuckled. Trent and I were the only full-time employees at the library. We had a handful of part-time employees and volunteers. Trent was a few years younger than me, in his mid-twenties. When we went to library conferences, we were the youngest library team in the state by far. Trent had also been a Creekstone Library teen volunteer. Trent stayed in Creekstone, though, and worked at the library while he commuted to a nearby community college. I think his degree was in literature or history, but Trent's real love was his alternative bluegrass and folk-rock band.

"That's exciting," I said, leaning back in my chair. "What team are you working with?"

"I'm going to work with the afterschool music program. I think we're going to do a 'Rockin' Christmas' theme," Trent said and immediately went shredding on an air guitar.

"I like it," I said. "Good theme!"

"Yeah, we had the kids make ornaments after school last week. They each made one that represented their favorite Christmas or holiday song."

"How sweet!" I crooned. I couldn't wait to see all the trees. "So, I'll stay tonight and keep the library open so that the teams can come in after hours and decorate their trees."

"Are you sure?" Trent asked. "I'll already be here. I can handle it."

"As your boss, I see you as a capable leader and manager here at the library," I said in a soft matter-of-fact way, "but as your friend, do you really think you can referee Ms. Patty and Ms. Pearl when they start going at it about extension cords and tinsel rules?"

"You're right. That would be an awful way to die," Trent said, wide-eyed. "But if you're going to stay, at least come out with us and get a beer afterwards?"

I stood up and said, "Okay, that sounds nice. I'll be in the back doing payroll. Then I'll go to get some supplies for the trees out of the storage room."

Trent clapped his hands and held them up. "Yes! You're going to come out with us. Finally!"

"Oh, come on," I protested. I crossed my arms. "I go out with you guys—sometimes."

"Boss Lady, community events don't count." Trent pointed a finger at me. "You're becoming a bit of a hermit."

"Okay, okay!" I said, feeling a smile creep across my face. Trent had a point, a very similar point to the one Veronica had made on the phone earlier today. I needed to get out there and be more social.

I headed back to my office. Even though I worked for several hours on the end-of-year reports, I kept zoning out while looking at the spreadsheets. Instead of focusing on the budget, I was thinking about how incredibly good William looked this morning in the kitchen. When we first met in the coffee shop, I'd noticed his jet-black hair, tan skin, and perfect green eyes, but this morning in the kitchen, when we were talking about my mom's art, the expression on his face, anticipation, gave me a little flutter in my stomach. That's why I called Veronica as soon as I left the house. I needed to admit to someone that I thought this new guy renting our spare room was hot, but that I was against everything he was trying to do in Creekstone.

I was so thankful when the end of the workday came around. I bolted from my desk and headed to the storage room, where I pulled out every tree stand, tree skirt, and random holiday decoration that I could find. I piled them onto a cart and brought them out into the library. Trent had put on a holiday playlist, and folks were arriving. Nick had taken over the circulation desk and was assigning each team a spot for their tree.

I brought the cart of extra supplies to Nick at the circulation desk.

"Good evening, Mayor," I said pretending to salute. "Here are the extras from last year in case a team needs a tree stand or skirt."

"Wonderful!" Nick said.

I spent the first part of the evening helping teams get their trees in the door, and the second part of the evening walking around appreciating everyone's creativity and holiday spirit. I decided to take photos of the teams as they decorated their trees. I laughed when I heard Ms. Patty was telling her team that too much tinsel was desperate, and Ms. Pearl was telling her team that the bow on the top of their tree needed to be bigger.

I headed toward the children's section to take a photo of the team that was decorating the tree in that area of the library. As I was turning the corner, I ran into someone. We really slammed into each other, and I started to fall backwards, but two strong arms wrapped around me and caught me. Surprised, I looked up to see William.

"I'm so sorry," he said. His face looked panicked. He helped me steady myself, and I couldn't help but notice that his hand lingered on my waist for just a moment longer than necessary. Our eyes met. I felt breathless.

"Kit, are you okay?" William asked. He said again, "I'm so sorry. I was just helping this team move their tree, and I didn't see you coming around that corner."

"It's okay." I was stunned, but then it occurred to me that William was here at the library. "What are you still doing here? Are you on a Christmas Tree Team?"

"Yeah, actually, when I was talking to Nick earlier this week, he mentioned this competition and said some of the nonprofits needed help this year, so I offered to help out," William said and then shoved his hands in his pockets, rocking back and forth on his heels. "So, I actually bought some decorations to donate while I was in Atlanta earlier this week for a team to use."

"Huh," I said. I crossed my arms. I couldn't help myself. "This seems like a lot of work to close a deal. Do you do this for every deal you work?"

"I'm not doing this for the deal," William said. "I'm trying to get involved in my community."

"Your community." That was rich. I rolled my eyes. Who did this guy think he was fooling? "You just moved here. It's your literal first day here."

William took a deep breath and tilted his chin back. He said slowly, as if he was having to exercise a lot of patience, "Well, you can question my motives all you want, Kit, but the truth is I live in Creekstone now. In fact, I live with you. So, if you're done giving me a warm welcome, I need to get the rest of my decorations out of my car."

I felt a surge of regret. What was wrong with me? Why was I being so rude to this guy? Just because I didn't trust him didn't mean I should be a different person.

"Wait, wait." I waved my hands in front of me to stop him. As he tried to walk past me, one of my hands touched his chest. I looked up and our eyes met. William raised his eyebrow the way he did when he was amused, but this time he wasn't smiling, and I pulled my hand back quickly. I took a deep breath and composed myself. "I'm sorry. I don't know why I keep being so rude to you. It's not like me. I'm going to be nicer."

"It's okay. I guess I just bring out the best in you," William said with a little smile and a wink as he walked past me toward the circulation desk.

Did he just wink at me? I rolled my eyes. He was handsome and charming, but I wasn't going to give in to this. I needed to see him for what he was: a businessperson trying to close a deal that could ruin our town.

I spent the next hour or so helping teams get their trees set up. Trent cranked the Christmas music up to pump up the holiday spirit, and several of the teams had brought holiday sweets and treats to share. When the tree decorating was done, Trent came to let me know it was time to lock up.

"Hey, Boss Lady. Everyone is done. Wanna come check out the trees with us?"

I followed Trent to the front where the last remaining decorators were lingering. Nick was there with his wife Melissa. She was still wearing her scrubs from her shift at the regional hospital, and she had festively draped garland around her shoulders like a feather boa. Nick and Melissa were canoodling by a tree. When she saw me, she broke away from Nick.

"Kit! Hey!" she said. "These trees look amazing! How do you like our team's tree?"

Melissa was on a team with local nurses. They had covered the tree in cute medically themed ornaments and garland made of gauze.

I stepped back and scratched my chin as if evaluating the tree. "The dangling syringe ornaments are a nice touch, especially the ones that look like they are full of green and red medicine."

Melissa clapped and giggled. She skipped over and hooked arms with me. "Let's go look at the other trees."

Melissa was about the same age as Nick. She was petite and cute, but what she lacked in size she made up for in personality. Melissa lit up every room she went into. They met when they were in elementary school and Nick had been devotedly in love with her ever since. Nick and Melissa were the quintessential high school sweethearts. When Nick moved away and went to the University of Georgia in Athens, Melissa stayed home, went to community college, and finished her RN degree. I got to know Melissa when she would come to the library in the evenings to study for her college classes. She would study until I closed, and then we would walk to The Pub together to get a late dinner.

Melissa pulled me along from tree to tree, singing "It's beginning to look a lot like Christmas."

"I love this one!" Melissa exclaimed at the Humane Society's tree. It was covered in ornaments of dogs and cats that were up for adoption.

"This one is my favorite," I said, admiring a tree covered in ornaments that looked like books and bookmarks.

"Shocker," Melissa said, wrinkling her nose. Then her eyes grew wide. "Oh, wow. Look at that one over there."

I turned to see where Melissa was pointing. Behind me stood a tall Frasier fir tree, decorated with long elegant ribbons, huge shiny bulbs, and the perfect twinkling lights. The tree looked like it had been decorated by a designer.

Melissa tugged my arm and we went toward the tree. As we approached, we saw Nick and William walking toward us.

Up close, I noticed the tree had silver tinsel that matched the perfect glowing star on top. I crossed my arms and frowned. Melissa noticed my frown and said, "What? You don't like it?"

"That's an understatement," I said under my breath. "It's awful. It's generic. It looks like it belongs in a department store. You can't even tell which team decorated this tree!"

Melissa looked at the tree as if she was considering what I was saying. "Yeah, I see what you mean."

"This tree sucks," I said.

"You don't like it," a familiar voice said.

I swirled around on my heel to see Wiliam and Nick standing behind me.

"Excuse me?" I tried not to look surprised to see William still here in the library.

"The tree," William said pointing at it. "You said it sucks."

"Well," I said, "It's just not in the spirit of the contest. It's generic. You don't get the essence of the team that decorated the tree."

William crossed his arms across his broad chest. He scratched his chin and tilted his head to one side. "I don't know. It looks pretty Christmassy to me."

"It is a beautiful tree," Melissa said with a polite smile. "The ribbons are so beautiful."

"An interior designer I work with hand-selected the ornaments for me from Ponce City Market in Atlanta," William said.

"Very nice," Nick said. "I talked to William earlier this week and told him about the tree contest. I mentioned that the Senior Citizens' Center's team needed some help with their tree, and he volunteered."

I don't know why I couldn't let it go, but before I could stop myself, I asked. "So, what's the theme?"

"The theme?" William narrowed his eyes and scratched his chin as he looked at the tree.

Nick nervously rubbed the back of his neck. "I think it's kind of an informal trend that most of the teams started doing over the years. They have a theme for their tree, but it's not mandatory."

My arms were crossed in front of my chest, and I was tapping my foot waiting for his answer. I tried not to notice how handsome William's face was as he was working through how to respond.

"Well, it's simple," William said, his eyes lighting up. "Classic Christmas."

"Classic?" I scoffed. "What does that mean?"

"The decorations are classic, like the senior citizens are classics," William said, the corner of his lip turned up in a triumphant smile. I hated that he was so handsome when he smiled, and I especially hated that he probably knew it.

I said, exasperated, "That's not a theme."

"Sounds like a theme to me!" William said. He slapped Nick on the back, and they turned and walked toward the door.

Melissa gave me a conciliatory smile. She shrugged. "It's not an ugly tree, but you're right. The lack of theme sucks. There's no way a tree with no theme will win."

I sighed. "Well, I guess we'll have to let the voters decide."

Melissa raised one of her perfectly groomed eyebrows, "What's bothering you? I've never seen you go at someone like that."

"I didn't go at him," I said defensively. "I just take the competition seriously. And don't you think having an interior designer decorate your tree for you is cheating?"

Melissa gave me a concerned but playful look as she hooked her arm in mine again and pulled me toward the door. "Okay, are you sure it's not that William is so sexy and he's living with you now? Maybe you're trying to create a little conflict to create a boundary between you and your hot housemate."

"Melissa!" I cried. "You're married." My face burned with embarrassment.

"What? I'm married, not blind." Melissa laughed. "I can say someone is cute! Now let's go. I promised Trent we'd kick his ass tonight at pool down at The Pub."

I rolled my eyes. Melissa was right about one thing: William was sexy.

4

William

Decorating the Christmas Tree had been more fun than I thought it would be. I mean, it wasn't NBA playoffs at Madison Square Garden fun, but I knew better than to compare Creekstone life to New York City life. I had to stay laser focused on the endgame which was getting into the C-suite in Atlanta, and the only path there was through Creekstone.

Nick called me earlier this week to help me get set up in Creekstone. I asked if there were any organizations that he recommended I get involved with so I could meet more of the community, and he recommended I get involved with a local holiday competition because it would allow me to rub elbows with many of the business and nonprofit leaders. Nick connected me with the Senior Citizens' Center and said they needed help decorating their tree. When I talked to the program manager, Rhonda, she noted that funding was always an issue, so I offered to purchase some ornaments and bring them with me. Rhonda was ecstatic. I met her and her team at the library, and we got to work putting the decorations I brought on the tree.

Everyone seemed to think the tree looked amazing, and honestly, it should've looked amazing considering how much those decorations cost. The only person who didn't think the tree was great was Kit Campbell. It seemed like everything I did annoyed Kit, but everyone in town loved Kit. I understood why. She was smart, beautiful, and friendly to everyone—except me.

After our tree was finished, I stuck around because Nick invited me to go out and get a bite to eat and a drink. Nick told me we should walk to a place called The Pub. He told me it was a good time to run into folks as they headed home. Nick was right. Most of the shop owners were closing up as we walked down the street. He stopped and talked to every single person and introduced me to each of them. I was beginning to see how Nick won this election. His friendliness opened a lot of doors for him.

As we walked down the street, I had to admit that Creekstone at night was charming. The air was crisp, the holiday lights twinkled and reflected off the wet pavement, and the darkened storefront windows caught the light in a way that felt magical.

When we reached The Pub, Nick opened the door for me. Inside, the brown walls were covered in sports memorabilia and neon signs. A jukebox played the Smashing Pumpkins' "Bullet with Butterfly Wings" from the corner of the room. Locals dined alone or in pairs at booths and tables. Televisions were strategically placed so that people could comfortably watch TV from any spot while they ate. A no-nonsense bartender washed dishes behind the long bar. There was a pool table tucked into the back corner of the room with a group playing pool.

As soon as Nick walked in behind me, the group at the pool table waved him over. Trent, the librarian, and Melissa were standing on one side of the pool table facing us as we walked toward them. It looked like Melissa told the other two people playing pool that we were heading toward them because I saw them both turn to look at us. I didn't recognize one of the women and the other was Kit.

I took a deep breath. I felt a knot in my stomach. I hoped that Kit wouldn't be annoyed with me the entire night, but I was determined to make this work. I smiled and waved, but Kit scowled and turned back around. Kit's annoyance was particularly harsh because, before she went to work at the library this morning, she had changed into a cute little dress, some tights, and a pair of black boots. She definitely looked the part of the sexy librarian.

Nick made a beeline for Melissa. She threw her arms around him and snuggled her face into his neck.

Trent introduced me to the fourth woman playing pool. "Sasha, this is William. He's new to town."

Sasha was tall like Trent. She had long blonde hair and wore a black Metallica T-shirt under an unbuttoned flannel shirt. She held a pool cue in one hand and extended the other for a handshake. "Nice to meet you. I'm Sasha. Trent's wife."

"Nice to meet you," I said.

"So, William," Sasha said. "Trent tells me that you just moved here from New York."

"Yep," I said. "I moved to New York for work. I was never there though. I travel a ton for work. How about you guys? Are you all from Creekstone?"

"Yep, we're all Creekstoners." Trent had walked around the pool table to hand Sasha her beer. He shook his head. "We don't get many folks moving into Creekstone. What brought you all the way down here from New York?"

"Well, my company has an office in Atlanta, and I hope to be doing less traveling and more regional work. I decided I wanted to try something different." I didn't want to go into it too much. "I came to Creekstone for work a few weeks ago and loved it. So, I thought I'd give it a shot."

I looked over to see if Kit was listening, but she leaned over the pool table to take a shot. I was transfixed by her. The scoop neck of her dress exposed her collarbone, and even though I couldn't see much else, my imagination was definitely speculating.

Nick and Melissa appeared at the high-top table next to me and interrupted my thoughts. He had beers and a basket of cheese fries. Nick had his huge smile beaming. "Pizza is on the way."

Trent joined us as soon as he saw food hit the table.

"So, Nick told us that you're going to help bring some new development to Creekstone," Trent asked as he stole one of Nick's cheese fries.

"Hopefully," I said.

"Hopefully, something cool." Melissa said with a laugh. Nick looked at her wide-eyed.

"What?" Melissa pushed Nick's shoulder playfully. "William gets it. Right, William?"

"I think I do, but what would you consider cool?" I asked. The truth was, I had done extensive surveys and market research to figure out what Creekstone needed so we could appeal to the community. What we found was that young people just left and never came back. And, just based on what I had seen at the library today and even walking into this pub, it was quite possible that I was talking to some of the only young people in all of Creekstone.

Melissa pushed her lips forward in a thoughtful pout. She rested her forearm on Nick's shoulder. Nick looked up at her like being her post to lean on was his purpose in life. "Well," Melissa started. "Restaurants, shopping."

Melissa was taking a sip of beer when Trent said, "We need more places to hang out."

Melissa's eyes got wider, and she nodded as if in agreement with Trent. "Yes! Totally! But also, practical stuff like doctors, dentists, beauty salons."

"So, like, everything," Kit said, walking over to the table and picking up a French fry. "Trent, your shot."

Kit followed Trent back to the pool table. I couldn't help but watch Kit walk away, and then I sighed, realizing I was focusing on the wrong thing again.

Nick and Melissa were canoodling as they ate their fries. I interrupted and said, "So, Kit might be right. It sounds like a little of everything."

Melissa tilted her head thoughtfully. "Well, we have some of those things, but they aren't really for us. You know? Like, they're really there for our grannies and gramps. Their style. And then just outside of town where the college is, there's a little strip of restaurants and bars that cater to the college kids, but really, who wants to hang out with college kids?"

I chuckled a little because Nick and Melissa were barely older than the average college age student, but I got what she was saying.

Kit and Trent returned when the bartender brought the pizza to our table.

"So how were the Christmas trees this year?" Sasha asked.

"So rad," Trent said. "There is a Dolly Parton themed tree." Sasha's face lit up.

Nick agreed. Sasha eyed Kit who had been quiet since I arrived at the pub. "What about you, Kit? What did you think of the trees?"

"Love them. All the trees are beautiful. Holiday spirit was at an all-time high," Kit said, smiling at Sasha. For a brief second, Kit and I made eye contact.

Sasha turned to Melissa and Kit and started chatting about the Christmas trees like it was the Met Gala. There was something markedly different about the look in her eye when she was talking with Sasha and Melissa. She seemed polite and agreeable, but the fierceness and sincerity was absent.

After the pizza, Nick, Trent, and I started playing a round of pool. Melissa herded Sasha and Kit over to the bar to get more drinks. We were a few shots into the game when I noticed three guys had walked over to the bar and started chatting with Sasha, Melissa, and Kit.

Sasha and Melissa were laughing at whatever the guys were saying. Kit was smiling politely.

Trent walked over to join Nick and me at the corner of the pool table, where we were standing and watching.

"Sasha loves to flirt," Trent said after taking a shot.

"Does it bother you?" I asked, taking a sip of beer. I couldn't help but watch Kit as one of the guys was telling her story. She had the same polite smile on her face.

"Nah," Trent said, turning to me. "It'll make her feel extra confident and then later she'll want to get frisky and watch out!" Trent howled. He looked over at the bar and as if realizing something, "Oh, but I must go bail Kit out. She hates it when people hit on her."

I tried to sound casual. "A lot of people hit on Kit?"

Trent shook his head. "Brother, all of the time at the library. Don't get me wrong. She can handle herself, but I can just tell it's an annoyance, so I try to be helpful." Trent trotted over to the bar.

I kept my eyes on them, and I saw the look of relief when Kit slid off her bar stool and slipped away. I swallowed hard as I watched Kit lean against the other side of the pool table. I wanted to join her and talk to her, but I didn't want to be another one of those guys bothering her.

I turned to Nick who was still standing next to me. He was watching Melissa patiently. Nick turned to see that I was watching him. He laughed and patted me on the back. "Never have to worry about Melissa. We're soul mates!"

I tried not to make a face. I needed to stay in good standing, especially with Nick, so I had to be respectful and personable, but I had to know, "You believe in soulmates?"

"Absolutely," Nick said, taking a big gulp of beer. "Without question. You don't?"

"I guess I haven't given it much thought," I said, shifting my weight from one leg to the other. Nick could see I wasn't a believer, though.

"Well, then you haven't met your soulmate yet." Nick laughed and then said with an almost cautionary tone. "But watch out. When it happens, you're in trouble. There's no turning back."

5

Kit

The next two weeks were just a steady stream of community members coming into the library and telling me how beautiful they thought William's team's Christmas tree was. This wouldn't have been so bad if William hadn't decided to volunteer as a tutor for the high school. He was meeting with students every evening to help them with math, writing, and SAT prep. So, he was there to hear the constant awe and wonder people experienced when seeing the tree for the first time.

Trent and I were at the circulation desk when Ms. Pearl came into the library. As she removed her mittens and reached into her satchel to pull a book out, she said, "Well, I hate to admit it, but I think that the Senior Citizens' Center tree is the most beautiful one of the year."

Trent didn't even look up from his computer. "Kit hates it."

"I don't hate it," I protested.

"She does," Trent said as he clicked through the books he was about to check back into circulation.

Ms. Pearl put the book she wanted to renew onto the circulation desk between us. "Why, dear? It's lovely."

Trent stopped clicking and turned in his desk chair to face me. "Yeah, Kit. Why do you hate the most beautiful tree of the year?"

I sighed. "I just like a theme. Okay?" I opened the book Ms. Pearl was renewing to scan the barcode.

Ms. Pearl looked curious. "Who decorated the tree?"

Trent pointed a thumb over at William. "The guy over at the tutoring table."

"Oh, I see," Ms. Pearl said with raised eyebrows.

"What?" I said defensively. "That has nothing to do with how I feel about the tree! Why isn't it believable that I just don't like the generic tree with no theme?" I pushed the book back to Ms. Pearl.

"Because that sorry excuse for a tree that Ms. Patty put up last year didn't have a theme, and you didn't object then," Trent said, turning back to his desk.

"Also, it's a Christmas tree, dear. Christmas is the theme," Ms. Pearl said, smiling at me as she took the book back.

As soon as Ms. Pearl left, I checked my watch. It was time to close. Trent stood up after logging out of his computer.

"Going to The Pub tonight?" I asked.

"Look at you, party animal," Trent said, smiling. I had made a point of going out more since Trent called me a hermit. "I wish I could, but I told Sasha we could have dinner together at home tonight."

"Sounds nice," I said with a smile.

I decided to head to The Pub on my own. Aunt Rita was working a late shift at the hospital, so I thought it might be nice to get dinner at The Pub. I loved walking through town at night during the Christmas season. The twinkling lights looked enchanting.

The Pub was busy for a weeknight. The Nirvana song "Smells like Teen Spirit" played on the jukebox. I decided it might be faster to eat at the bar, and I took a seat at one of the corners. The bartender, Ray, gave me a menu without a word and disappeared to fill drink orders. I ordered a glass of red wine and a steak salad. I had brought a book with me. I pulled it out of my bag and flipped to the page I had marked. Just as I started to sink into the story, someone sat down next to me. I looked up to see William.

William was looking straight ahead. He made eye contact with Ray who brought him a menu. "A Sweet Water IPA and a burger, please."

William turned to me and asked. "Any good?"

Ray appeared with my wine and William's beer.

"Charles Dickens' A Christmas Carol," I said, flashing the cover of the book at William. "I'd say it's known for being pretty good."

"Oh, a classic," William said, popping a peanut into his mouth with a mischievous twinkle in his eye. "Like our Christmas tree."

I rolled my eyes, but I bit my tongue. Over the last two weeks, I had tried not to let William get to me, but there was just something about him. I was known for being able to let everything roll off my back. I was known for being polite and considerate, but principled and determined. I took pride in this, but there was something about William where I just bluntly wanted to call out his bullshit. Unfortunately, this seemed to amuse him, and he never lost his composure.

"Agreed that A Christmas Carol is a classic. Disagree that your tree is a classic," I said opening my book back up as if I were getting ready to read.

"Oh, come on, Kit," William said. "When are you going to admit it? People love the tree because it's well done and, in fact, a well decorated, classic Christmas tree."

I shut the book and looked at him. I took a deep breath and said, "I don't think that. I think it's generic, and you cheated by having a designer pick out the ornaments." William nearly spit out his drink.

"Cheated? Because I bought the decorations in Atlanta? So what?" William said. I could tell I struck a nerve by calling him a cheater. He put his beer down on the bar. He sat back in his chair and looked at me. "I decorated that tree with three octogenarians and a very anxious middle-aged program manager. It was no small feat."

"What do you want? A medal for helping?" I said—then, before I could stop myself: "Or do you think by volunteering and working in Creekstone, everyone's just going to love you and sell you their land?"

Before William could respond, Ray put our food in front of each of us with another glass of wine for me and a beer for William. Ray gave us both a look like we'd need that second drink. I let out a frustrated sigh and drained my first glass of wine.

We sat silently for a few minutes. I was mixing my salad and cutting the steak into smaller bites when I looked up and noticed two women about my age talking to each other and giggling while making eyes at William from the other side of the bar.

"Do you know them?" I asked, pointing my fork over at the two women across the bar.

William looked up. "I don't think so," he said between bites of his burger.

I took another sip of wine as I watched the women whispering and giggling. Finally, one of the women, a tall, thin brunette, got up from her stool and teetered her way over to our side of the bar. She sat on the other side of William. The woman was wearing an impossibly short mini skirt and a tight sweater top that had a low-cut V-neck showing off her cleavage. She had her hair pinned back, which made her dramatic eye makeup more noticeable. I couldn't help but wonder if this was William's type. William looked at me out of the side of his eye before turning to the woman.

She gave him a seductive smile and said in a sultry voice, "Well, hello. This is kind of funny, but I think we matched."

"Excuse me?" William said, smiling as he took a sip of his beer.

"On the app, SingleMingle," she said, holding up her cell phone and shaking it a little with a coy smile.

I felt my eyes grow wide. I tried to look straight ahead, but I was dying of curiosity. I picked up my wine glass and took a sip. I lifted my book and stuck my nose in it to cover up the shocked look on my face.

"Is that so?" William asked. He got his cell phone out of his pocket and swiped a few times. "Well, it appears that we have." He looked down at his phone as if to check something and then back up at her. "It's a pleasure to meet you, SweetPeach706."

She held out her hand and giggled. ". My name is Katie."

"This profile picture simply doesn't do you justice." William shook her hand. He turned away from me so that I couldn't quite hear what he was saying. I leaned over as far as I could without falling off my bar stool.

Whatever William said, Katie found it hilarious, because she threw her head back and laughed. He leaned forward a little and whispered something else. I nearly knocked my salad off the bar trying to hear what he said.

Katie poked her bottom lip out in a pout and hopped off the bar stool. She put her hand on William's leg and leaned forward dramatically, popping a shoulder toward William and said, "Well, I understand. If you'd like to meet up some time, you know where to find me." She winked and trotted away.

William turned back toward his burger. He picked it up and took a huge bite. I watched as Katie took her seat back at the bar with her friend. She gave a little wave to William who smiled back at her. I hated that I thought he looked cute when he smiled like that.

"Did you match with that woman on a dating app?" I asked.

William put his finger up and pointed toward his full mouth. He took his time chewing his bite of burger and then took a long gulp of beer.

"Why, Kit? Were you listening in on my conversation?" William finally asked innocently.

"Um, everyone in the bar was listening in on that conversation." I was annoyed that William was pointing out that I cared. "Are you seriously on a dating app here in Creekstone?" I practically hissed the question. "Why are you dating women in Creekstone? You live in New York or Atlanta or wherever."

"First of all, I wouldn't call what people who meet on SingleMingle do dating," William said matter-of-factly. I blushed at the thought of William hooking up with that woman later. I let a puff of air out of my mouth because I hated that I had blushed. William turned back to his burger and picked it up. "And secondly, I live in Creekstone, Kit. I don't know what's so hard to believe about that, but I live here now—so dating or, in this case, SingleMingling in Creekstone is a perfectly logical."

"I just don't buy it," I said. "My friend who works in real estate in Atlanta knows all about your firm Braithway & Randall. She said it doesn't make sense for a big shot like you to live in a town like this long term. It seems like you're just trying to earn trust from Creekstoners like me, so your company can more easily push through its land purchases and development projects. You're going to ruin Creekstone, and I'm not just going to sit back and watch it happen."

William put his hands in his lap and turned to look at me. He let out a deep sigh, then said, "I'll tell you what, Kit. Let's make a little wager. If my team wins the Christmas tree competition, you'll stop accusing me of not really living in Creekstone, and if we don't win, you can continue to the think the worst of me and say those things about me."

"You know what," I nearly laughed at the thought of William's tree winning, but I held it together and said, "I'll take that bet. The community is going to vote for a tree that has real meaning—something that reflects the true spirit of Christmas and the team that made it. I know your tree isn't going to win."

William turned in his stool toward me. He leaned against the bar. "You're that confident?"

"Certain," I said turning my stool to face him. William cocked his head to one side, and the corner of his lip rose in a crooked smile that was incredibly cute.

William put his hand out as if to shake my hand and said, "Okay, deal."

"Deal," I said confidently. We shook hands but then held on a little longer than necessary. I looked up, and our eyes met. I felt a little flutter in my stomach, and I pulled my hand away. I swallowed a lump that formed in my throat and sat up straight so that I would appear confident again, and I said, "I can't wait for tomorrow's announcement."

William shook his head and turned back toward the bar. "I also can't wait for tomorrow's announcement."

Ray came to take our plates. "Want another round?"

I looked at William. The truth was I did want to sit there with him longer, but instead I said, "I really need to go home and get some sleep. Big Christmas Tree Competition announcement at the library tomorrow."

"One check?" Ray asked.

"Yes," William said.

"Two," I said at the same time as William.

Ray tried to hide a smirk. William said, "Just one. I got it."

"You don't have to do that," I protested.

"No, I really do. I ate all your breakfast bagels last week," he said looking at the bill that Ray had laid on the counter in front of him and pulling cash out of his wallet.

"That was you!" I cried. "I thought it was Aunt Rita. My name was written on those."

"I know. That's why I ate them." William chuckled. "I guess we're even now. Wanna walk home together?'

"Yeah," I said hopping down from the bar stool and putting on my jacket. I hated that I really did want to walk home with him.

I couldn't help but notice how the two women watched us leave the bar together, and I tried not to feel good about it.

As soon as we stepped out of The Pub, the cold air hit us. William pulled the collar of his peacoat up around his neck. I wrapped my scarf all the way around me and zipped up my long puffer jacket. The walk home was only about four blocks.

We were quiet for a block. William finally said, "I don't know if I'll ever get used to how quiet it is here at night."

I turned and looked at him. He had his hands jammed into his coat pockets to stay warm. I could see his breath as he blew air between his full lips. He looked down at me, his dark eyes twinkling, and I looked away quickly.

"I guess I lived in the city for too long. I got used to all the noise." He shrugged. "I like the quiet. It's just different."

"I get it," I said. "Growing up I spent every summer with my dad. He's based out of D.C., but he traveled a lot for work. He's a journalist, and every summer he took me with him no matter where he was on assignment. It was exciting to go to all those places with him, but when I'd get back here," I sighed. "I don't know. The silence and the darkness. I just feel at peace here."

I turned to see that William was watching me. I hoped he couldn't see me blush. He probably thought I was hopelessly corny.

We had arrived at our front stoop. William waited for me to open the front gate and he followed me up the walkway to the front porch. I hurried up the front steps and paused when my hand was on the doorknob.

"Hey, thanks for dinner." I turned to see that William was closer than I expected.

He was right behind me, looking down at me with his crooked smile. "Thanks for the bagels."

I chuckled, turned back around, and pushed the door open. A warm blast of air hit me in the face. I knew my face must be flushed and red from the cold. As I walked farther into the foyer, I saw that Aunt Rita and two of our renters, Aaron and Liz, were sitting in the front room.

"Hey, Kit. You're out late," Aunt Rita said. Then I saw her eyes go wide as William came in behind me. "Oh! Hi, William. We left a plate in the oven for you."

"Thanks," William said. "But Kit and I just had dinner. I'll eat it for lunch tomorrow."

I tried to play it cool as I hung my jacket on the hook and said to Aunt Rita, "Yeah, I thought you were going to be at work tonight."

Aunt Rita sat back, crossed her legs, and smiled. "Well, I got my days mixed up. I work late tomorrow."

"Oh, well, I have to get to bed. Big day tomorrow. Christmas Tree Competition," I called as I hurried up the stairs. "The library will be packed. Night!"

When I was halfway up the stairs, I looked back to see William taking his jacket off and making small talk with everyone. William looked up at me.

"Good luck tomorrow, William." I wasn't even sure he could hear me. I turned and hurried up the rest of the stairs, down the hall, and up the back flight of stairs.

I shut the door and leaned on it. I was a little out of breath. I stood there for a second. I could feel my heart pounding, and I tried to tell myself it was from hurrying up the two flights of stairs.

I crossed the room and sank into the sofa. Aunt Rita and I had converted the attic into a small two-bedroom apartment when we remodeled the rest of the house. It was modest, but it worked for us. Most importantly, we were able to rent out the oversized bedrooms for income.

I sat up and looked at a stack of bills Aunt Rita had left on the coffee table. I decided not to look through them then. It would make me feel too anxious to fall asleep. I headed to my room and got ready for bed.

The next day the library was busier than even I had anticipated. I offered to man the circulation desk, and Trent offered to set up in the meeting room to announce the winner. When Nick arrived for the announcement, he was followed by a photographer, videographer, and an incredibly hip-looking young person with a cell phone.

"Good morning, Kit," Nick said. "We're here for the announcement."

"I can see that! And who are these folks?" I asked, nodding toward the entourage.

"Oh, that's the media team William connected me with," Nick said. "They are helping the city tell our story on social media and the website. They're following me around for a couple of weeks to get some content. I thought this would be a good way to showcase the diversity of the community and different community groups."

Someone called out to Nick, and he waved. "I'll see you later, Kit."

I watched a steady stream of community members come into the building. I was busy helping many of them sign up for library cards and check out books. Trent peeked his head out of the meeting room and waved me over. I put up our "Away" sign on the circulation desk and headed over to the meeting room. I stood in the doorway and listened to Nick's speech.

"This year we had ten teams participate in the competition. More than ever before. This is particularly important because to participate each team had to raise money. All the funds go straight to the Boys' Lodge and the Girls' House here in town. Let's give all our teams a round of applause," Nick said into the microphone. When the room quieted down, Nick continued. "Now, the winner of the competition is selected based on popular vote. And I know we all have our personal favorites. Each vote costs a dollar, and people are allowed to vote as many times as they want. This year we raised more money from voting than we ever have before. So, let's give the Creekstone community another round of applause."

I had to admit; Nick was really stepping into the role of mayor. Nick continued through his speech. He took a picture with each team as they came up to get their participation plaque.

"And now the moment we've all been waiting for. Drum roll, please," Nick said, opening the envelope. "The winner of this year's Creekstone Christmas Tree Competition, raising a whopping $15,000 for the Boys' Lodge and Girls' House, is the Senior Citizens' Center!"

The program manager, Rhonda, jumped out of her chair and let out an excited whoop. The community room applauded and cheered. Rhonda and two of her staff members joined Nick at the front. It took me a minute to realize that this was William's tree. I couldn't believe it. There must have been some mistake.

As Nick was posing with the group and their trophy, Rhonda grabbed the microphone from Nick. "We just want to say thank you to Braithway & Randall. We couldn't have done it without their support. Where's William?" Rhonda scanned the crowd, then pointed. "There he is."

William was at the back of the room, clapping. When everyone turned to look at him, he gave a humble polite wave and then shoved his hands in his pockets.

My face must have shown how shocked I was because Trent nudged me with his elbow as he clapped for the winners.

"That's not fair! William's company bought all those votes!" I whispered to Trent.

"Just remember, Boss Lady, that's a lot of money for kids living in foster care." He whispered back from the side of his mouth.

I shook my head to break myself out of the shocked daze. "Oh right. Of course. So great."

I looked back at William, and he was looking right at me. He raised his eyebrows, and his crooked smile broke out across his face. I rolled my eyes and went back to the circulation desk. That would be the last time I made a bet after drinking three glasses of wine.

CHAPTER 6: WILLIAM

6

William

I scanned my work email inbox one more time. No new messages. I wasn't used to being so out of the loop. I knew that Mr. Braithway wanted me to focus on Creekstone, but I hadn't thought that he was serious about this being all he wanted me to do. I had only been in Creekstone for a month, and my division had almost completely transitioned me off their projects. Anytime I tried to jump in on an email thread to contribute or offer help, I would get a text message from Marla in the Atlanta office reminding me to stay in my lane.

My cellphone rang. I saw the name of my deputy division director, Meredith, pop up.

"Finally! Someone is calling me," I said, sliding my finger across the smooth surface of my phone to answer.

"Meredith, how's the Philly project shaping up?" I asked.

"Merry Christmas Eve to you, too!" Meredith's voice came over the phone.

"Oh, right." I looked at the date in the corner of my computer screen. It was Christmas Eve.

"Why are you on your computer right now?" Meredith asked.

"How do you know I'm on my laptop?" I looked around the studio apartment I'd been calling home for the last month, as if Meredith could see me.

"Your icon is green, showing you are active. And I just wanted to call and remind you to stop working and relax," Meredith laughed. "It's a holiday."

"Well, what are you doing on your computer?" I asked, sitting back and taking a sip of whiskey.

"Well, little-known fact, my boss—which is you—has been commandeered for a bizarre side quest by our CEO, so now I'm stuck doing two people's jobs. So, I am checking my email to make sure I didn't miss anything. I need to check-in on the status of that waterfront development's permit requests because my girlfriend, Addison, is dragging me to midnight Mass. Luckily, I know that one of the city's permit directors attends that church. I might see him at Mass, so I want to know the status."

"Is your plan to try to cut in behind him in the communion line?" I laughed.

"Something like that," Meredith retorted.

"That's why we pay you the big bucks, Mer," I chuckled. "I can't think of anyone better for this project than you."

"Where are you anyway?" Meredith asked.

"Atlanta adjacent," I said between sips of whiskey.

"Where?"

"Exactly."

"Sounds...swanky?" Meredith joked.

"Ugh, anything but. This town is lacking in pretty much every way possible. Really a hole in the wall."

"Speaking of job promotions..." Meredith said with a laugh.

"Who was talking about job promotions?" I questioned playfully.

"Me," Meredith said. "Everyone at the office seems to think the old man is finally going to give you the job."

"I wouldn't be so sure," I said. Anytime anyone mentioned a potential promotion, I felt the familiar nervous sensation in my stomach.

"No, no. This humble version of you won't do. You're not supposed to leave me alone in New York for nothing. You're supposed to move to Atlanta to accept the best job our company has to offer," Meredith said without trying to hide her annoyance. "What is this self-doubt? Don't tell me all the time and money you've spent on therapy and executive career coaching was a waste. My God, you could have bought a Mercedes with all the money you've spent on therapy."

"Well, Mer," I started slowly. "Therapy wasn't about winning a job."

"Oh, right." I can hear Meredith sigh on the other end. "Yes, yes. Right. Processing your grief and past traumas so you can make real connections with people and be less of a man-slut and thus have a more fulfilling future. Yes. That rings a bell."

"I'm so touched, Meredith. You have been listening all this time," I joked.

"Any chance you're dating someone wherever you are?" Meredith asked.

"Nah, I've decided to take a little break from dating. Focus on this project. Give myself some time to get my life together before I get involved with anyone. Why?"

"Well, I think it would help with some of the gossip going around the break room. People are already acting like assholes about the potential leadership changes. Charles in real estate already made some shitty comment about how having a bachelor for a CEO means more women will try to sleep their way to the top of the company, and he's even made snide remarks that some already have," Meredith said with a slight edge to her voice. She paused and said under her breath, "I don't need that."

"You slept with Braithway? He's in his 60's, I think! The Silver Fox strikes again," I joked, laughing.

"It's not funny, William," Meredith said seriously. "I've always loved hanging out with you and our friendship means a lot, but I don't want people to think that I am where I am in my career because I sucked your dick when we were in grad school."

I sat up and pinched the bridge of my nose. "Shit, Meredith. I think anyone who has ever met you knows that you are where you are because you're a ruthless and relentless genius who is an absolute deal hound. Not because of anything else. Charles is a dipshit. He's just jealous because you're out there expanding airports, transforming waterfront properties, and brokering million-dollar deals. None of that has anything to do with me."

I tried not to sound annoyed with Meredith, because it was Charles I was annoyed with. I looked up at the ceiling as I added more gently, "I'm not trying to minimize your concerns. They are valid. Women are treated unfairly in this business. But in our case, it's been almost a decade since we dated, and you've been with Addison for years now. You don't have to worry about those rumors. Charles is just trying to get to you. I'm not going to do anything to perpetuate those rumors."

Meredith knew all of this but needed reassurance. I knew her concerns about her reputation were real, and I felt some regret that I could be part of a narrative that might hurt her.

I tried to lighten the mood. "So, Mer. What did you get Addison for Christmas? Something expensive since you're working on Christmas Eve, I hope."

"Are you drinking?" Meredith asked.

"Why would you ask that?" I looked at my phone to make sure my camera wasn't on.

"You only call me Mer when you're drinking. So, I hope it's an expensive whiskey, at least." She took a deep breath like she was afraid to ask. "Are you spending the holiday alone?"

"No, of course not," I lied.

"Okay, good. Because you know, you're always welcome to spend holidays with Addison and me," Meredith said softly.

"What? And start that rumor mill? Adopted by my co-workers? No thanks," I playfully scoffed. Meredith laughed.

"Okay, I've got to go." Meredith said. "Merry Christmas, William."

"Merry Christmas to you, too."

I watched my phone light up and then go dim as the call ended. I sat back in my seat and thought more about my conversation with Meredith. This was not my first 'reality check' conversation with Meredith, and it probably wouldn't be my last. A lot of people didn't like Meredith because she was so direct, but our friendship had been one of the only constants in my life since grad school. Meredith's top priority was her career. I respected that Meredith knew what she wanted and that she could get it on her own. Meredith wanted the credit for getting to where she was in her career, rightfully so. I hated the thought that people might think otherwise.

I knew what I needed to bounce back from this work funk. I needed to eat real food. Rita had left me a note earlier this week letting me know that she, Kit, and all the other renters would be out of town until New Year's. She said she'd left some frozen dinners in the freezer for me if I wanted them. I decided I needed to eat something more substantial than potato chips tonight.

I took the back staircase down to the kitchen, and while I was rummaging around in the freezer, I heard something in the front room. I thought I was in the house alone. I looked around for something to defend myself with in case it was a break-in. I picked up the rolling pin off the counter.

Maybe this was someone breaking into the house because they thought it would be empty due to holiday travel. I quietly crept down the hallway, past the stairs, and into the foyer. I could hear someone rustling the boxes under the Christmas tree. I crept farther into the foyer and, before I could surprise the intruder, I heard gentle bells and then Mariah Carey singing about how she didn't want much for Christmas.

I peeked around the corner and saw the back of Kit singing and dancing around the Christmas tree to Mariah Carey's greatest hit. I leaned against the doorway to the front room and crossed my arms in amusement. She was really getting into it. Somewhere around the first key change at the bridge she twirled around, her eyes went wide, and she screamed as soon as she saw me.

I stood up and put my hands out. "Hey, I'm sorry. I didn't mean to scare you."

"What the fuck are you doing here?" she gasped. "You scared the shit out of me."

I couldn't help but laugh. She was wearing a knee-length pajama shirt featuring a picture of The Grinch and mismatched socks pulled up to her knees. Her hair, which was typically pulled back into a neat braid or bun, was in the messiest nest on the top of her head. And I was a little too far away to see from where I was standing, but I'm pretty sure she was wearing a retainer.

"I'm sorry," I said when I stopped laughing. "Rita told me everyone was going to be gone from Christmas Eve to New Year's Day, so I thought I was alone. Aren't you supposed to be at your dad's?"

Kit let out a deep breath that blew through her lips like she was calming down. "Yeah, I was, but when I got to the airport my dad called to tell me his flight from London to D.C. had been cancelled and he wasn't sure when he'd get home. So, I decided to just visit him another time."

Then as if realizing she wasn't alone and was standing in front of me in an oversized Dr. Suess-themed T-shirt, Kit shifted her weight, looking a little uncomfortable. She put her hand on her hip. "But what are you doing here? I assumed you'd be visiting your family or girlfriend or something, like everyone else?"

"Eh," I lied. "I needed to get some work done." I wanted to change the subject, so I offered, "I was looking for something to eat in the kitchen. Want to join me?"

"Yeah, that would be nice." Kit looked like she was finally relaxing. She started to walk toward me but then remembered something and said, "Oh, when I got home, there was a package on the porch for you." Kit pointed to a large crate sitting under the Christmas tree.

I recognized the wooden crate immediately. I felt some relief that I had something to offer. "Perfect!"

"What is it?" Kit asked curiously. I headed over to the tree and picked it up off the ground. "It's my annual gift from my boss. He sends me the same thing every year."

Kit followed me into the kitchen, and I put the crate on the large island. She looked curious as to what was in the crate, and I couldn't help but think how cute she looked, trying to peer over the top of the box as I cracked the crate open.

"My boss sends all his directors his favorite bottle of bourbon every holiday season," I said, pulling out a ridiculously expensive bottle. Kit tried to hide a look of disappointment. I smiled when I said, "But even better, he also sends his favorite red wine, and this year it looks like he sent two bottles of red."

Kit's eyes lit up in a way that let me know she was interested. I had noticed that Kit mostly drank red wine when she was at The Pub, so I guessed she would like this. She picked up the bottle and examined the labels. "Can we open one?"

"Of course!" I said. She moved across the kitchen to get a bottle opener. I pulled the rest of the contents out of the crate: a container of chocolate-covered pecans, gourmet smoked sausage, cheese wheels, and crackers. When Kit turned around and saw the rest of the gifts from the crate, her face completely changed from simply content to actual excitement.

"Want some snacks?" I asked.

"Yes!" Then with the most endearing look of excitement in her face, she cried out, "We can make a sharkcuterie board!"

I must have looked puzzled and before I could say anything she held her finger up, then bent down so that I could only see her hair bobbing around as she dug through the cabinet below. Kit eventually emerged holding up a large cutting board in the shape of a shark. "Sharkcuterie!"

Kit laughed at her own joke. "I never thought I'd need this again."

"Why do you have that?" I asked, reaching for the bottle of wine and the opener.

"Well," Kit said, placing the board on the counter, "every year my friends throw a pun potluck, and this year I brought sharkcuterie." Kit looked satisfied as she reached for the food to start arranging it on the board.

We agreed we needed to eat more than snacks and wine, so we put some pizza bagels in the oven. I poured each of us a glass of wine. Across the kitchen, Kit hopped up onto the counter to sit and wait for the pizza bagels. I leaned against the opposite counter with one hand in my pocket and the other holding my wine glass. Kit told me stories about past pun potlucks.

I liked seeing her like this. She seemed happier, less guarded, and definitely less annoyed with me. My expression must have shown that I was thinking about her because she shifted her weight the way she did when she was feeling self-conscious and asked, "What?"

"Nothing," I said, looking down at the ground. I was trying not to look at her legs. "I guess I'm just glad you're still talking to me after I won that bet about the Christmas Tree Competition."

Kit sighed and said, "Well, I am bound by honor to say nothing negative about your work."

I took a breath and said, "I know, but you really seemed to dislike me as much as you dislike my work, so I just didn't think you'd ever be this...friendly toward me." I chuckled. "I'm just glad I've finally figured out how to get on your good side."

"Oh, yeah." Kit raised an eyebrow. "And how is that?"

"Ridiculously expensive wine and snacks," I joked.

"Well, I do love sharkcuterie," she said with a coy laugh. "And I guess you're growing on me."

Kit jumped down from the counter and pulled the pizza bagels out of the oven.

She added them to the cutting board. I refilled our glasses and said, "Why don't we take this sharkcuterie into the front room?"

"Oh! Let's watch a holiday movie," Kit said, practically bubbling. I followed her into the front room. I had to admit that I was enjoying this friendlier side of Kit.

We put the food and drinks on the table. Kit set her cell phone down as she started putting logs into the fireplace. I asked, "Need any help with that?"

"I got it," she said and looked over her shoulder. "I didn't think city boys knew much about building fires." Kit finished putting wood in the fireplace and started the fire. She sat on the far end of the sofa from me.

I pulled the coffee table closer to us so the food would be easier to reach. I heard a familiar cell phone chime. I checked my cell phone, but I saw that it wasn't the one chiming. I looked at the coffee table where Kit's phone was sitting face up, and I saw the familiar SingleMingle icon pop up and another chime.

"Wait a second!" I said playfully. "After giving me such a hard time about SingleMingle, you're on the app, too!" I snatched the phone off the table before Kit could grab it.

I read the text alert banner out loud. "MountainMan2000 has winked at you!"

Kit's face looked shocked and then determined. She lunged at me to grab the phone from my hand, but I quickly held it above my head just out of her reach. "Oh, no. Give me back my phone!" She laughed.

Kit struggled to grab the phone from me. I liked how she brushed against me as she reached for her phone. I wanted it to last longer, but after a few seconds I finally gave it back to her. Kit settled back on her end of the sofa. She gave me an annoyed look, but she was still smiling. She swiped across her phone as she popped a few chocolate-covered pecans in her mouth.

"Well," I said impatiently. "Is MountainMan2000 cute or what?" I hated that I was feeling a little jealous of the interest Kit was showing in this app.

She tilted her head from side to side, as if she wasn't sure, then finally showed me. "I don't know. I guess he's cute." The guy in the photo was a little older than me. He was wearing a fishing vest, in a boat, holding up a fish. He wore a cap, sunglasses, and had a full beard.

"You can't even see this guy's face!" I said, "How can anyone tell if he's cute or not?"

Kit laughed, raising an eyebrow at me. I hoped she wasn't picking up on my jealousy.

"Well, was that woman from the bar the other night—what was her name? Peach? —was that woman your type?" Kit shot back.

"No, not really," I said taking a bite of a pizza bagel, then I realized something. "Hey, if we're both on this dating app and it pairs you with people you're geographically close to, then why haven't we matched?"

Kit scrolled through her phone and said, "Huh. You're right. You don't show up on my 'singles nearby' page." She took a sip of wine and curled up on her end of the sofa. "Oh, I bet it's because I don't have 'casual encounters' selected as something I'm interested in. I have 'looking for love' selected."

"Ah," I said, taking a big gulp of my wine. "That's it. We're not looking for the same thing."

We were quiet for a minute. I focused on eating my pizza. Finally, Kit asked, "But so wait. You just want to hook up with people?"

"Well, I think the positives of those kinds of arrangements are obvious," I said with a chuckle.

"You're not interested in, like, meeting someone? Or dating? Like you go out a few times, and then you hook up, and then you both just go your separate ways?"

"Eh, not exactly. There can be some low-commitment, repeat engagements. I believe colloquially called the booty call," I said matter-of-factly. "I take it you've never really been into casual hook-ups?"

Kit shrugged. "I've just had one or two relationships. I dated the same guy all through college, and I've been pretty single otherwise."

"So, no sex with any of these guys you're dating?" I couldn't help myself.

Kit cackled a bit and said, "I don't need a boyfriend to have an orgasm, William."

"Little Miss Independent!" I laughed and took a sip of my drink. "Casual hook-ups are overrated, anyway. I stay on the app out of habit really. To be honest, they're more effort than they're worth for the most part. I just fell into the habit because I traveled so much for work that nothing else made sense. I just didn't have it in me to put that much effort into a long-distance thing."

Kit nodded as if she understood. "I get that. I mean, not for the exact reason, but I moved back here and was so focused on spending time with my mom before she died that I just couldn't fathom making room for anything else."

"I haven't really had a chance to say this, but I'm sorry to hear about your mom passing away," I said.

"Thanks for saying that. It's been a little over a year. The holidays are hard." She looked down and sighed. "I didn't tell my aunt I came home when my dad's flight was cancelled. Aunt Rita would have left her trip with her new boyfriend to spend the holidays with me, and I didn't want her to do that." She raised her gaze and asked, "But what about you? You didn't want to see your family during the holidays?"

"Oh, my mom is in the Philippines visiting her family for a few months. She goes every year." I scooted forward and reached for some crackers and cheese.

"What about your dad? Where's he during the holidays?" she asked.

Without looking at Kit, I said, "My dad died when I was ten. Car accident. My American family, my dad's family, wasn't so accepting of my mom. She was just so different from who they thought my dad would end up with, and when my dad was gone, it was hard for us to stay connected to them. So, it's just been me and my mom since then."

"Oh, I'm sorry," Kit said softly. I could see the sadness in her eyes. I knew the kind of grief she was feeling.

I cleared my throat. "I'm glad I can do things for my mom like send her to the Philippines for an extended vacation though. She worked so hard when it was just the two of us, so now I try to provide everything she needs so she doesn't have to work anymore."

"You mentioned that you moved back to Creekstone when your mom got sick. Where were you before that?" I asked.

"Oh, I was living in D.C.," Kit said between bites of pizza.

"With your dad?" I felt curious about Kit and wanted to know more.

"Actually," She tilted her head and paused. "With my ex-boyfriend, Matt. I was completing a fellowship, and he was there getting ready for med school."

"What happened to Matt?" I asked, trying to sound as casual as possible.

"Eh," Kit sighed. "Nothing. Matt was fine. I just wanted to move home, and he was moving to Los Angeles. We tried the whole long-distance thing, but honestly, I just didn't feel like it was fair to Matt, so I broke it off with him."

"What was unfair about it?" I asked, then added. "I mean, don't get me wrong, I know long distance is hard, but what was unfair? Seems like there's more to it than the simple long-distance excuse."

Kit looked down at her wine glass in her hand. She licked her lips and bit the inside corner of her cheek like she was thinking.

"Was the sex awful?" I smirked. "Is that why you're so good at the solo act?"

She laughed and threw a small Christmas gift-shaped pillow at me. "The sex was fine. I mean, it wasn't the mind-blowing thing people talk about in the movies and in romance novels, but it was nice and sweet, and you know, exciting enough." Kit looked at me for confirmation.

I shrugged. I honestly couldn't imagine having just regular vanilla, routine sex with Kit, but I didn't want to make her feel weird. "Sure, I think I get it. Long-term things get routine."

Kit turned her head and looked at the ceiling as if she were contemplating that. "Yeah, routine. That is a good way to describe it. When Matt and I started dating, it was an easy decision. Our best friends were dating, so we just kind of made sense. Matt is this super smart, handsome doctor, and he wanted me to be his girlfriend. His parents seemed to be okay with him dating someone like me. Our best friends loved us together. I think I was caught up in being part of this big picture that worked for everyone." Kit chuckled at herself, then leaned forward to pick up another cracker from the board. "My dad says I'm a recovering people pleaser."

"What do you mean, someone like you?" I asked.

"Huh?" Kit asked as she popped the cracker into her mouth.

"You said, his parents were okay with him being with someone like you. What does that mean?" I asked.

Kit covered her mouth as she finished chewing her cracker and said, "Oh, Matt's family is just so rich. They're old money. When we were in college, I'd visit Matt during the summer in Charlston. I'd show up to their coastal mansion in my thrift store dresses and in my beat-up car. His mom and dad were so nice, but sometimes his mom would give Matt and me new outfits, and then Matt would insist we'd have to wear them out to dinner with them at their country club. I know it's just because they were embarrassed by my clothes," Kit shrugged. "But they really did try, and Matt's parents were not the reason I broke up with him."

I was having a hard time not being insulted on Kit's behalf. I think it triggered me because I knew so many people like Matt's family. I worked with them all the time. From what I could see, Kit was near perfect. She was smart, albeit a little stubborn. She was funny, interesting, beautiful, and sincere. Surely, they all could see that was worth so much more than expensive clothes. I asked, "Then, what was the reason you guys broke up if it wasn't his family?"

Kit's lips pushed down into a thoughtful frown. "When I moved home to be with my mom, Matt was in Los Angeles for med school. The time apart did us in. I was just here taking care of my mom, constantly thinking about how short life is. I realized I needed to start doing what I actually wanted and not what made other people happy. And I couldn't say for certain that Matt made me happy. I let the long-distance thing be the reason, but if I was being honest, I just couldn't picture myself with him." Kit looked down at her socks and picked some lint off them.

After a moment she said, "Everyone is just kind of waiting for me to get back with Matt, I think. Aunt Rita thinks that grief clouded my decision and my best friend, Veronica, thinks I just need to relax and let fun happen to me. I think she assumes I'll find my way back to Matt, so I don't know. Sometimes I doubt myself and I think, maybe what I had with Matt was being in love. Maybe I just put too much stock into the notion that love was supposed to knock you off your feet, not just work well logistically for everyone. You know? Maybe my hopes are too high about falling in love? Maybe I should just relax and let it happen." Kit sighed and shrugged.

I didn't know who this Matt guy was, but I knew he was lucky if a woman like Kit was going to be his foregone conclusion. I took a sip of my drink and watched her face. I liked that Kit was confiding in me. For the first time, I was seeing a side of Kit I really liked. She was being open, honest, kind of playful and funny, so I didn't say anything to rock the boat. "Sounds like you have a lot of people that care about you giving you the best advice they have."

"I have heard every kind of advice. The good. The bad. The ugly." Kit let a light-hearted laugh go. She looked up at me and asked, "What about you? You're serious about not being serious with anyone?"

I shrugged. "The New York dating scene is wild. It's like I only attract stage-five-clingers, women who seem to feed on drama, or women who have dollar signs in their eyes." I quickly added, "I'm not saying all women are one of those things. This has just been how it's been for me so far."

"You sound as jaded as me, but for a totally different reason," Kit said. "But that's focusing on the women. What about you? What do you want?"

I raised my eyebrows. It would have been so easy to deflect and crack a joke, but instead I sighed and looked at her. "It's actually kind of embarrassing."

"What is?" she asked.

Maybe it was the alcohol, or maybe it was her endearingly messy hair and mismatched socks coupled with the honesty in her eyes, but I said the most truthful thing I had ever said to anyone. "I'm scared to be in a real relationship."

Kit's head jerked up and she looked surprised. I immediately regretted being so honest.

"At least, that's what I've paid hundreds of dollars an hour to hear my therapist tell me over and over again." I laughed to lighten the mood.

Kit sat up a little and took a sip of wine. "What makes your therapist say that?"

"Well, I like to think it's because I haven't met the one, but according to my therapist and many angry ex-girlfriends, I have a pattern." I shrugged and took a swig of my drink.

"Which is?" Kit leaned forward, her eyes wide with curiosity. "Come on! Don't make me pull this out of you!"

"Well, I tell women up front that I'm not emotionally available. Like a disclaimer. I'm totally transparent. I tell them that I have issues from grief and that I don't want to put myself in a situation where I can lose someone again. And even though I tell them that, they still want to date me. Selfishly, I enjoy spending time with them. You know, it's nice to have someone to hang out with. But when they get attached, I remind them that I am not attached, a real commitment isn't what I want, and that I'm not going to be able to meet their expectations in the long run. I'm just having a good time. I'm Mr. Right Now, not Mr. Right. And apparently that makes me a huge asshole."

"Agreed. You're an asshole," Kit said without missing a beat, but she looked amused and not disgusted. which was somewhat of a relief. She narrows her eyes and points her wine glass at me. "But you must want to change if you're talking about it with a therapist?"

"Well," I said, picking up the wine bottle and refilling her cup. "It's more that I don't like hurting people, but I'm not sure I want to change. My mom would love it if I had a major change of heart about getting married and having kids. She's always offering to introduce me to one of her Filipina friend's daughters so I can just get hitched and have a whole pack of children for her to dote on."

"Is that what your mom wants? For you to marry a Filipina?" Kit asked. I looked over and saw that Kit was sitting up and more attentive, but she looked away when I made eye contact.

"Oh, nah. It's not that at all. My mom doesn't care who I am with," I said, shaking my head. "Are you kidding me? She moved to the states by herself and was working as a line cook at Morehouse College's cafeteria when she met my dad. Falling in love with a college student wasn't her plan at all. She described it as being struck by lightning, and my dad equally adored my mom. I remember that. So, she would never say no if I was in love the way she was in love with my dad. I'm just not sure that kind of love exists anymore."

Kit nodded with a slight frown. "Yeah, I don't know if it does, either."

I tilted my head to the side and said, "But I can tell you one thing. My mom is ready for a grandchild. And I don't think she cares how I get the child, but she is ready for me to have a kid so she can have a grandchild."

"Fair enough." Kit laughed, but then with a touch of sorrow, she said, "I wish I could have done it all when my mom was still alive. I think part of me was tempted to make things work with Matt so my mom could be there for my wedding and maybe even kids, and Matt would have done it. But I knew that if my mom wasn't sick, I wouldn't have even entertained the idea."

I turned and looked at her. "I get it. Them missing the big moments. It is so hard, and I want to tell you that it gets easier, but I think over time it just gets different—the grief. Expected, so you know how to carry it in a way that isn't out front, but it's always there. And so, in some ways, those big milestone moments, the graduations and birthdays and celebrations, you learn how to cope with their absence." I paused and looked at the wine glass in my hand. Normally, I would have stopped there, but something in me pushed through, and I opened up. "It's the little moments. The unexpected moments of missing my dad that get me. Wishing he had taught me how to shave or how to drive. Wishing he could have helped me when I was worried I was going to flunk out of college. Wishing I could have talked to him about the Dodgers winning the World Series or the ending of Sopranos. Wondering what his favorite type of whiskey was. Wondering if he smoked cigars. Wondering which side of the G.O.A.T. debate he'd be on—Michael Jordan or Lebron James. Wondering what he'd look like as an old man." My voice cracked. "Sorry." I cleared the lump in my throat that had formed. "Sorry to be a downer on Christmas Eve. This is usually why I spend the holiday alone. I don't want to ruin it for..."

I looked over at Kit. Tears were streaming down her face.

"Oh, geez. I'm sorry," I said. I instinctively slid over and reached for her. She folded into me, buried her head in my shoulder, and softly wept while I held her. I patted her on the back and tried to keep my hands in appropriate places. After a few minutes, she pulled away and looked up at me, her long lashes glistening with tears.

Kit wiped her eyes, and I scooted back a bit to give her space even though I wanted so badly to pull her back to me, cup her beautiful face in my hands, and kiss her.

Kit sighed and confessed, "My mom loved Christmas. That's why I get so into it every year. I think the artist in her loved the decorations. She called it a visual expression of spirit and community. She told me that well-done decorations meant something. It was a way for people to express their joy, hope, and love during the holidays. I think that's why I was being so critical of your tree, and I'm sorry I did that. My mom would have thought your tree was beautiful."

"Hey, it's okay." I tried to lighten the mood. "You know what I think we need?"

"What's that?" Kit asked, wiping her nose on the sleeve of her T-shirt nightgown.

"To open this second bottle of wine."

Kit let out a laugh and nodded. I went to the kitchen to get the corkscrew and a second bottle of wine. When I got back, Kit had turned the lights off so just the glow of the Christmas tree and fireplace lit the room. The TV was on.

"I picked out a movie for us to watch," Kit said, tucking her legs underneath herself as I joined her on the sofa.

I settled back in on my end of the sofa. I put my phone down on the coffee table, refilled our wine glasses, and said, "Okay, so what are we watching?"

"Die Hard."

"I thought you wanted to watch a Christmas movie."

Kit looked at me and deadpanned, "This is a Christmas movie."

"Wait, you said my team's Christmas tree didn't have enough holiday spirit and you think Die Hard is a Christmas movie. The nerve!" I joked.

Kit busted out laughing as she started the movie.

7

Kit

I woke up on Christmas morning on the sofa. A little hungover, I sat up, stretched, and looked over to see William on the other end of the sofa. I guess that wasn't a dream after all, I thought to myself. After we watched Die Hard, we immediately started Die Hard 2. I must have fallen asleep during the second movie.

William looked peaceful as he slept. I felt something stir in me as I watched him. William was handsome, objectively. He obviously knew that, and over the last few weeks, I had decided that even though he was handsome, he was a little too self-assured. I found that irritating.

But last night William was different, because for a brief moment he was honest and maybe even vulnerable. It was unexpected, and frankly, it was hot. What was even more unexpected was that when he opened up to me, it unlocked my own honest emotional response. I hadn't been prepared for that. I knew this could be trouble.

I thought about leaving William sleeping on the other end of the sofa and disappearing into my apartment for the rest of the day, but it was Christmas. It seemed wrong for either of us to spend the day alone if we could avoid it. I decided I needed to stop being silly.

I nudged William with my foot. William stirred but didn't wake. I nudged him again. He grumbled and made a smacking noise with his mouth as he slowly woke up

"Hey, Merry Christmas," I said softly as I nudged him again to make sure he was awake.

William sat up. "Merry Christmas," he said as he stretched. I gave him a minute to get his bearings.

"What do you usually do on Christmas?" I asked him.

"Well, normally, I'm just getting home from a work trip, and I usually meet my friends Meredith and Addison in Chinatown for some Chinese food," he said. "What about you?"

I shrugged. "The last three or four years have all been different because of my mom's cancer, but for the most part we've just been home, watching Christmas movies."

"Let's do that," William said decidedly. He seemed to agree that the two of us would be hanging out on Christmas Day. I liked the fact that I wasn't going to have to ask him.

We made our way into the kitchen and put together a decent breakfast of pancakes, eggs, and bacon. We made huge cups of coffee, and I bullied William into letting me add gingerbread cookie-flavored coffee creamer into his coffee. We made our way back into the front room and settled in for more Christmas movies.

As we watched, William and I both drafted and sent Christmas text messages to friends and family. Sometime during the second movie of the day, William's phone rang.

"Oh, this is my mom. I should answer this," William said. He swiped his phone to take the call. "Hi, Mom. Merry Christmas."

"Anak! Merry Christmas! Maligayang Pasko!" A voice loudly called from his phone. I tried to nonchalantly look over William's shoulder. I could see a small Filipina woman's face filling the screen. Her glasses sitting on the edge of her nose. "I'm sorry I didn't call last night. We were celebrating."

"It's okay, Mom," William said.

"Say hello to your cousins, Carmen and Junior," William's mom said forcefully. She pulled two younger cousins into the screen. They awkwardly waved. "Merry Christmas, po."

William was polite. "Merry Christmas."

Carmen said, "You have a nice Christmas tree." Willam looked over his shoulder at the tree in the corner of the front room. "Oh, thanks," he said.

When he turned to look at the tree, he moved just slightly so that his camera was focused on me instead of him, and his cousin Carmen asked, "Is that your girlfriend? She's pretty."

William turned on the sofa so I wasn't behind him anymore, and I was off screen. He looked up at me, and I mouthed sorry.

We heard the rustling of William's mom snatching the phone back from Carmen and her face filled the screen. "Are you with a girlfriend?"

William had a momentary look of panic, but he said calmly. "No, mom. It's just my housemate at my new place in Georgia."

"Oh, can I see her? Let me say Merry Christmas to your...housemate," William's mom said in a sing-songy voice. William looked up at me. I nodded and shrugged.

"Okay, Mom." William turned so that I was in the background of the video call. I waved politely and said, "Merry Christmas."

"Merry Christmas to you, too!" I could see his mom's face light up. Her eyebrows raised in the same way that William's did when he was amused.

"Mom, we have to go. Merry Christmas."

"Okay, Anak. Love you."

"Thanks for doing that," William said, tossing his phone on the sofa between us. "My mom is very persistent."

"No problem. Hopefully, she couldn't tell I hadn't showered in two days." I laughed.

"You look great," William said as he set his phone back on the coffee table. He raised an eyebrow as he looked over at me. "But I could have sworn you were wearing a retainer at some point last night."

I scoffed and hoped desperately that my face wasn't turning tomato red. "For your information, I was wearing my retainer, but I took it off when we went into the kitchen to make pizza bagels."

William laughed. "You might be the only adult I've ever met who still wears their retainer."

"Why wouldn't I?" I asked with a bit of a laugh, and I shrugged. "I guess I'm a bit of a rule follower. Your mom called you a name, anak? Is that a nickname?"

"Oh, ha. Yeah, it's a term of endearment for your child in Tagalog, my mom's language," William said.

"You look like your mom," I said pointing at his phone on the table.

"Yeah?" William said with an amused look. "You're really the only person who has ever said that. My mom is a five-foot-tall Filipina lady. I'm over six feet tall and a spitting image of my dad when he was my age...from what I can tell from pictures."

"Maybe it's more the expressions you two make," I said thoughtfully. "In that way, you favor each other."

He was quiet for a minute. Then he turned to me and said, "You look just like your mom. I mean, based on the photos I've seen around here."

I blew air from my nose and shook my head. "I wish. My mom, she was this free-spirited, artistic, effervescent person that everyone loved to be around." The corners of my mouth pushed down in a doubtful frown. "I might resemble her, but I've never been like that."

William sat back and shrugged. "I don't know, Kit. She's stunning. You look just like her."

I felt my cheeks burn red. I tried not to read much into what he had said.

I looked out the window. "It's going to be a quiet week."

"Yeah? What do you mean?" William asked.

"Well, everything closes here in town until after New Year's Day." I saw the blank expression on his face, so I explained further. "Like everything is closed. Library, schools, stores, banks. The only thing open is the regional hospital."

"Even chain restaurants?"

"We don't have any national chain restaurants or grocery stores in Creekstone. You'd have to drive to the next town for that." I saw the realization cross his face.

"Oh, wow. So, everyone just shuts down till January second? That's some real small-town shit."

"Pretty much." I smiled and tried not to be defensive. "It's one of the great things about living in Creekstone. Slow pace of life, but if you aren't prepared for it..."

"Huh," William sighed. "I had a lot of work I needed to get done, but I guess it's going to have to wait till next week."

I was curious about William's work. Even though I was against it in principle, I was also a realist and knew that even if we didn't sell our land to Braithway & Randall, other townspeople would. I wondered what William's company intended to do with the land. But I decided against asking about it. I had lost that bet, so I had to try and not to be mean about William's relocation and work in Creekstone. Even though I usually had no problem keeping my cool, something about this topic triggered me. Every time it was brought up, I ended up biting William's head off. It's like when I was with William, I just lost my filter.

I wanted to be nice, though, and Creekstone was completely shut down until after the new year, so I said, "Tomorrow morning I'm going to go for a run by the river if you want to go with me. You know, get out of the house a little."

William's eyes lit up. "Yeah, that would be great."

I smiled and tried to play it cool. "Awesome. Hopefully you can keep up."

We had just started the movie again when my phone rang. I saw Aunt Rita's face pop up on my screen. I had already sent the requisite Merry Christmas text message to her, so I knew she was calling because she must have talked to my dad. If I told Aunt Rita I hadn't gone to D.C. and that I was back in Creekstone, she would change her travel plans to be home with me for Christmas. I didn't want that. I watched the phone ring in my hand, and I let the call go to voicemail. Almost immediately after that I received a text from Veronica. Are you home alone? I can come up there.

Aunt Rita called back immediately. I was looking at my phone trying to decide if I wanted to answer it or not when William said, "MountainMan2000 must really want to talk to you."

I let a laugh out. "No, it's Aunt Rita. She must have just figured out I am home alone on Christmas."

"I'm offended!" William said, pressing his fingertips against his chest in an exaggerated gesture of shock. His sly smile spread across his face. "Just answer it. You're not alone." William casually popped a few of the leftover chocolate-covered pecans into his mouth.

William was right. I slid my finger across my phone to answer it. Aunt Rita's face appeared immediately. She looked tan...and pissed. "Kit, why didn't you tell me your dad's flight got canceled? I could have come home."

"I'm not alone," I said into the phone. "I am..."

Before I could answer, Veronica started calling me. I sighed. "Aunt Rita, hold on. Veronica is calling me too. Let me merge the call."

I tapped the circle that allowed Veronica to join our video call. Veronica's face popped into the screen, and she started in as if she knew what we were talking about already, "Kit! You should have told me that you were going to be alone for the holidays. You had to drive right past my house in Atlanta when you left the airport and drove home to Creekstone. Why didn't you just stop and stay with us?"

Aunt Rita and Veronica broke out into a clamor of agreeing with each other and scolding me. I let it go on for a minute or so. My eyes flicked up from my phone to William, who was sitting on the other end of the sofa. He had leaned back and crossed his legs comfortably so that one ankle was resting atop his knee. He had one arm sprawled along the back cushions of the sofa. He had clicked off of the movie to a football game he was watching on mute, completely unbothered. Perhaps he was even enjoying hearing me get scolded.

"I'm not alone." This brought the scolding to a screeching halt.

"What?" Aunt Rita said.

"Yeah, I'm watching Christmas movies with William," I said nonchalantly, as if this should have been an expected response.

"Who?" they said in unison, like a pair of shocked owls.

I tapped the button that allowed me to flip to the front facing camera. William was in their full view.

"William? But you ha..." Veronica cut herself off when she saw William appear on her screen.

"Oh, yes. Of course. Hello, William," Aunt Rita cut in with her usual sing-songy voice. "Merry Christmas!"

William looked over at me holding the phone up. He waved. "Merry Christmas."

"Merry Christmas," the two hooted in unison.

I flipped the camera to be back on my face. Veronica looked shocked and mouthed, He's hot.

Aunt Rita said, "Well, I left some food in the freezer. Please help yourselves!"

"Thanks, Aunt Rita," I said, "How's the weather down there?"

"Oh, just lovely, dear." Aunt Rita said. "Harold is like a fish, just out there snorkeling away."

"Harold? I thought you went with Roger? And what about Hank?" I said, laughing.

"Aunt Rita!" Veronica cried. "Get ya some!"

I made a face. Aunt Rita beamed. "Ladies, I must go. It's time for the poolside conga line."

"I have to go, too," Veronica added. "I need to tell Gus we don't have to drive all the way up to Creekstone and pick you up. Unless you want us to?"

"Nah," I said, my eyes flicking up at William who was still watching football. "I think I'm good here. I need some down time."

Veronica made a face, and I said, "Merry Christmas," before ending the call. She immediately sent a text that said, He's hot!

I texted back. Not happening.

I put my phone face down on the coffee table. "Thanks for doing that."

"Oh, well, we're even. You just participated in a call with my mom and extended family in the Philippines. I think I can handle being your alibi for being a poor communicator with your aunt and Veronica, who I'm guessing is your best friend."

I scoffed at William's annoyingly accurate assessment but, instead of getting defensive, I changed the subject. "You like football?"

"Yeah, I do." He looked at me out of the corner of his eye and then back at the game. "How about you?"

"Eh, I don't watch much NFL, but I do watch a lot of college football," I said. "It's pretty big down here in the South."

"Oh, yeah?" he said.

"It's hard to escape. Everyone down here loves it," I said. "Well almost everyone. Matt was never that into it. I always felt like I was dragging him to games, so we just never went."

"Really? Seems like most guys would kill for a partner to watch football with," William said in disbelief.

I shook my head. "Yeah, he was more of a golf and tennis guy. His parents were preparing him to be a doctor from day one, and I guess they just assumed those would be the right sports for a doctor."

William's eyebrow raised and as if he just realized something, he said, "So, wait, do you watch all the college football bowl games that are on TV between Christmas and New Year's Day?"

"It's the most wonderful time of the year," I said with a coy smile.

"This might not be such a bad week after all!" William laughed.

We watched football and movies for the rest of the evening. Then I headed upstairs to take a shower and sleep in my own bed. William seemed a little disappointed, but I didn't need to fall asleep on the sofa with him two nights in a row. I had to admit that I was really enjoying spending time with William. When he wasn't trying to buy up half the town, he was actually pretty charming and laid-back, but I knew there were dozens of reasons why it was a bad idea for us to get too friendly. There was the obvious reason that he was on the other side of a potentially huge business deal for Aunt Rita and me. Another reason was that I didn't want to catch feelings for a guy who had just told me he was only interested in casual relationships. I had just navigated five of the hardest years of my life emotionally, and I was far too familiar with the loneliness of losing someone. The last thing I wanted to do was to put myself into a situation that could be far worse than being lonely, which was dating someone who was entirely indifferent. Plus, in my gut I knew that William wasn't really going to stay in Creekstone, and I was definitely not interested in a long-distance relationship. I needed to stay focused on my priorities and to keep my boundaries.

8

William

Kit came bouncing down the back stairs the next morning looking totally refreshed. I had thought Kit looked cute on Christmas Eve with her messy bun and oversized sleep shirt, but this was another level. Kit looked hot. She had her hair pulled back into a neat braid, and she was wearing a loose-fitting zip-up hoodie over what appeared to be a spandex workout top and a pair of black leggings. I tried not to look at her butt and legs as she crossed the kitchen.

I swallowed my coffee, trying to be as casual as possible. "Hey, still okay if I join you for your morning run?"

"Of course," Kit said, getting a glass and filling it with water from the sink. "I'm surprised to see you down here this early in the morning. Usually, I don't see you until sometime in the evening. I don't think I've seen you before two p.m. since you moved in."

"Except for yesterday morning." I couldn't help but point out that we had woken up together on the sofa the day before.

I saw a slight upturn of the corner of her lips. She took a gulp of water.

Kit put the glass in the sink. "You ready?"

Kit told me the route as we stretched. "We'll run three blocks in this direction and end up at the edge of town. We'll cross the street into the woods where there's a trail. We'll take the trail until we reach the riverbank. Then we'll run along the riverbank for a bit, take another trail that loops us back to the main road, and run along that back into town."

I should have been tipped off by Kit's expensive running shoes and the whole stretchy running outfit that I was in trouble. Kit wasn't just fine, she was actually exceptionally fit, and it turned out she got that way by being a distance runner, something she omitted telling me the day before.

As we ran through town, Kit pointed out houses and told little stories about each family. She didn't even seem to be breathing hard. At first, I was fine. But by the time we crossed the street and started running the trail in the woods to the river, I was struggling to keep up. As we ran through the woods, she was completely unphased as she hopped around rocks and limbs.

Eventually, Kit led us up the trail which was on a slight incline to the top of a hill. When I reached the top, I saw that we were at the river. I stopped to catch my breath but pretended to be taking in the view.

"This is great," I said, trying not to sound too winded. How was it possible that she wasn't winded?

"Yeah, when I was a kid, I thought this was the most magical place in the world," Kit said, her hands on her hips. We stood there for a second watching the water roll by. My breath created white puffs in front of me.

I was so glad Kit had invited me on this run. It was an unexpected bonus that the route passed along the property that Braithway & Randall were hoping to buy. The land was perfect for a variety of uses. My mind immediately went to work as I surveyed the land.

"You played out here a lot when you were a kid?" I asked.

"Oh, yeah. In every phase of my life, I have spent time out here. As a kid, I thought the forest was an enchanted playland. As a teenager, my friends and I would bring tubes and float down the river in the summer. And then, when my mom was sick, we'd come out here together."

"Really?" I asked. I saw the sad look in her eyes, but I could tell she also wanted to share this with me.

"Yeah, let me show you," she said. I followed Kit down a path along the river until we reached a clearing. A wooden platform had been built a few feet back from the river's edge. There was a wooden picnic table on the platform. Kit jumped up on it. I joined her on the platform. We were close enough that I could feel the heat coming off her body, but we weren't touching.

"My dad came down from D.C. and helped me build this platform for my mom," Kit said. "When she was feeling up to it, we'd park on the road and walk out here. Mom would paint or take pictures. Sometimes she journaled."

"That's really amazing, Kit."

She turned and looked at me. I felt an uneasiness in my chest. "I can see why you'd want to keep this land. It must mean so much to you."

"Well, I do love it, but honestly, my mom loved to share it with people." Kit sighed and crossed her arms. "Aunt Rita says Mom would have sold the land if she'd had more time. Maybe to a conservation group or something like that. Just so people could get out there and experience this side of Creekstone, the part she loved." The corner of Kit's lips pushed down in a forced smile. She looked at the ground as she kicked some leaves with her feet. For a moment, I could see Kit retreating. I could see walls going back up, and I felt a sense of panic. In another situation, I might have leveraged this opportunity to pitch Kit. I would have worked to get her into a position to sell her land, but I just couldn't bring myself to do it. Not there. Not then.

I cleared my throat and said as gently as I could, "Kit, can I ask you something personal?"

She looked up at me with an anxious look and nodded.

"Did you run cross-country in college? Because you were kicking my ass on that trail run."

The sincerest laugh escaped from her lips, and her face transformed back to the Kit I had spent Christmas Day with. I felt relieved.

"I did," she said as she stepped down from the platform. "You look so incredibly fit. I'm surprised you struggled at all during the run."

"Okay, I'm going to tell you something, and you can't laugh at me," I said as I followed her down the trail.

"No promises," Kit joked.

"I've only run on a treadmill for the last five years. So this, real trail running, is brutal."

Kit laughed. "That explains it."

We started walking down the trail and back toward town. Kit was gracious and walked us home at a leisurely rate.

I asked, "So, why a librarian?"

Kit was watching the ground as we walked, maybe to avoid tripping on a root or a rock, but I could still see the corners of her mouth pull back into a slight smile.

"Oh, you know. The usual things," she said cryptically.

"Which would be...you love being among timeless stories and poetic verses?" I guessed.

"More like, I like being a sentinel of intellectual freedom and free speech, the pillars of democracy." She grinned.

"Ah, that ol' chestnut," I said, to which Kit chortled.

We spent the rest of the day together. As soon as we got home, we each showered before meeting back downstairs to make lunch. After lunch, we both brought our laptops downstairs, and I worked a little while we watched football. In the evening, Kit made a fire, and I made us drinks with the expensive whiskey Braithway had sent me. Kit convinced me to watch another Christmas movie, and when she started to fall asleep, I gently nudged her awake so that she could sleep upstairs in her bed.

Over the next week, everyday was pretty much the same. We got more into a routine, and we each began to relax. I looked forward to our morning runs, and it wasn't just because I loved seeing Kit in her tight running leggings, but also because I loved seeing Kit by the river. Every day she'd show me another spot in the woods that she loved. It was like seeing a part of her that she never showed anyone else.

Kit and I transitioned from watching Christmas movies to watching the best Christmas episodes from our favorite TV shows. I worried less and less about my empty email inbox. I started looking forward to our evening cocktail by the fireplace, and I dreaded when Kit's eyes would get heavy and she'd eventually tell me she had to turn in for bed. I felt a twinge in my chest, something chemical in my brain, everything she said and did just seemed fascinating. Normally, after spending two days with someone, I would want space, but I found myself plotting ways to keep her talking and to keep her close to me. It wasn't something I'd ever experienced before.

One evening it rained, so the next morning a thick fog had rolled in. Kit told me it wasn't safe to run when the fog was that thick and suggested we skip our morning run. I still went down early to get coffee and eat one of Kit's breakfast bagels. When I got downstairs, I heard some shuffling from the hallway. I peered down the hall to see what it was. The noise was coming from a utility closet.

I called out, "Kit, is that you?"

A loud clatter came from an open door in the hallway. I hurried over and opened the closet door. Kit was standing on a ladder inside the large storage space, and below her there were several fallen boxes.

I asked, "Do you need help?" I hurried into the closet with her and started stacking the boxes.

"I didn't think I needed help, but maybe I did," Kit said with a laugh. She got down from the ladder. "I wanted to put away some of our Christmas decorations today. I know a lot of people think it's bad luck to take down your Christmas tree this early, but honestly, if I don't take it down now, it will be up until Easter. Things get super busy at the library in January. Everyone makes a resolution to improve themselves, so our fitness and healthy living sections get a lot of traffic."

"Let me help you," I said, picking up the empty boxes.

Kit hesitated, then sighed and said with a slight shoulder slump said, "Thanks. I do need help. Usually Aunt Rita is here, but I just got a text that a storm is moving through the Caribbean, so they aren't even sure when they'll get home. They are talking about canceling flights." Kit moved a piece of hair that had fallen from her braid out of her face. "If you can just take those into the front room, I can start packing them."

I followed Kit into the front room with the first few boxes. I went back into the utility closet to get the rest. When I was moving the boxes, a wire art rack became visible. It was filled with canvases and framed photography. I looked through it. Some of the work resembled the work in the dining room. They were large and bold. I looked through each painting that was stretched on a frame, and I noticed a rack of rolled canvasses in the corner.

"Hey, are those your mom's paintings and photographs in the storage closet?" I asked, setting the last of the empty boxes down in front of the fireplace.

Kit looked up from the pile of ornaments she was making on the coffee table. "Yeah, my mom had some great pieces. Did you see the colorful river rocks paintings she did? She did several of those over the years. I love them. I always thought she should try to get them into a gallery, but she was really focused on what her students achieved. She said that was her real masterpiece.

"Really? Her work is amazing, so she must have had some super talented students."

"Even though her work was amazing, she'd go on and on about a student who had finally mastered shading or perspective. She loved it when her students invited her to their art shows or craft fairs. Not that we have a ton of famous artists coming out of Creekstone, but I do think people who took her classes felt very supported and inspired. A lot of them went on to pursue some kind of art. My mom said that was what she was the proudest of." Kit shook her head and went back to taking ornaments off the tree. "Sorry, I'm talking about my mom too much."

"No, no!" I said. Kit turned and looked at me. "I'm glad you feel comfortable sharing stories about your mom with me. And trust me, I really get it."

Kit smiled as I joined her at the tree. I liked standing this close to her. Over the last few days, I'd spent most of my time with Kit, and if I wasn't with her, I was thinking about her. And, unlike other women I spent time with, I was not just thinking about having sex with her. Although, I had definitely been thinking about that. But it was more than that. I just wanted to be close to her. I kept replaying that first night when I held her. Sure, Kit and I had touched before, mostly incidentally. I had felt some sparks. I'd dismissed it as basic sexual tension, but that night when I held her on the sofa, that was different. We connected. I had never felt that before, and I wanted more of it.

"It sounds like your mom had a fulfilling career," I said, as I carefully took the ornaments off the tree.

Kit watched me for a minute and then asked, "What about you? Do you like your job?"

I thought about it. "I do like my work. I started out doing this job because I wanted to find a way to create financial stability for my mom and me, and I think I've done that. I'm being considered for a promotion. If I get it, I'd be able to do a lot more for communities, and I'm excited about that potential shift in my role." I wanted to tell Kit more, but I didn't want her to know that my promotion depended on how well I did in Creekstone over the next month. I didn't want to give Kit a reason to distrust my motives. She had been so distant and skeptical of me when we first met, and now I felt like she finally trusted me and maybe even liked spending time with me. I worried that if she found out more about my job and my initial intentions, she'd never talk to me again.

"A promotion?" Kit said. "That's exciting. When will you know if you got the promotion?"

"Eh, with my boss, there is no telling." I tried to change the subject. "Tomorrow's New Year's Eve. Do you love New Year's Eve as much as you love Christmas?" I asked, although I didn't know how that could be possible.

Kit smiled at me. "I'd say New Year's Eve is my third favorite holiday."

"What's second?" I asked.

"Umm, Halloween, of course," Kit said, as if I'd just said the dumbest thing ever, and then she laughed a little. "How about you? What do you usually do on New Year's Eve?"

"Eh, nothing special. I can't stand the crowds in New York on New Year's Eve." The truth was, Meredith usually insisted that I join her at some impossibly swanky New Year's Eve party with whomever I was dating at the time. "What's fun to do here in Creekstone?"

"Well, Trent texted me earlier today and told me that The Pub is open tomorrow for a New Year's Eve party. They are going to show the televised peach drop in Atlanta, set off confetti poppers, and serve cheap champagne in plastic cups. Some highbrow shit," Kit said with a wry smile. "Wanna go?"

"Are you inviting me?" I asked. I was careful not to use the word date.

"I'm informing you of the opportunity," she said, trying to sound nonchalant. "And that we are all going to be there."

"I accept your invitation," I said, ignoring her deflection. It was the first time in a long time I was looking forward to going out on New Year's Eve.

9

Kit

I stood in front of the full-length mirror in our bathroom. I turned to see if I looked somewhat decent. I knew I was just going out to The Pub, but I did want to look cute, mostly because William had agreed to come. Over the last week, I had spent a lot of time with William. At first, I was just glad not to be alone on Christmas Eve and Christmas Day. I told myself that this was what I was feeling, but as the week went on, I started to think about William all the time. I started to wonder if he was thinking and feeling what I was feeling, and I knew that this could be dangerous. William had already told me that he only wanted casual relationships, and I kept having to remind myself that I didn't want that. I sighed.

I settled on the outfit I was wearing: a pair of bootcut jeans and a low-cut black top. I went back to my room and started looking for a pair of hoop earrings when my phone rang. It was Veronica.

"Happy New Year!" Veronica said. I looked down at the screen and Baby Preston's fat rosy cheeks filled the screen. He gurgled and cooed at the phone.

"Happy New Year, you cute little thing!" I cried, picking up my phone to get a better look at him.

"Why, thank you. Thank you very much!" Veronica said, flipping the camera back to her face.

I laughed. "Well, you look less cute, hot mama."

"Ugh, I wish. Preston gave us a terrible stomach bug, and it pretty much wiped-out Gus. It's not pretty over here. That's why I'm calling so early. There is no way I'm making it to midnight to say Happy New Year," Veronica lamented into the phone.

"Oh, I'm sorry to hear that!" I said as I propped up my phone on my dresser. I started clipping my hoop earrings in as we talked.

"Speaking of hot mama, where are you going? Your makeup and hair look great."

"It's not too much?" I asked, suddenly feeling self-conscious.

"Not at all. Are you getting this hot to meet a Creekstone townie?" Veronica asked.

"It's for me," I said with a bit of a righteous tone as I looked at myself in the mirror. Then I looked back at the phone and laughed. "I'm kidding. I just don't want to always look like a librarian. Trent said people think I've turned into a hermit."

"Uh huh." Veronica said. "So, this has nothing to do with a certain super-hot real estate developer who you've been spending your entire week of vacation with?"

Veronica's face radiated skepticism. I said, "Look, I'd be lying if I said I didn't think William was hot, but the guy told me he only dates casually, and I don't even think he likes me like that."

"Kit, this man has spent an entire week watching Christmas movies and football with you. He could have been anywhere this week," Veronica said.

"We're just friends," I said.

I thought I was pretty convincing, but Veronica said, "Honestly, I think you should go out and have the best time in the world. This might be the exact thing you need. You said you don't think William is going to stay in Creekstone, so maybe you should lean into this causal relationship thing? And since you loathe what he's doing for work, it will be even easier to cut him off when you're ready to move on."

"I don't know," I said hesitantly. "I'm not sure I can do casual."

"Girl," Veronica said with a flat voice. "You're doing it again. You always try to do things a certain way. Just relax and let fun happen to you."

I sighed. "Well, it's silly to even think about this. Nothing's going to happen. I don't think he likes me."

"You're delusional if you think you can look that good and any man isn't going to try something. If that happens, we need a refresher on how to run game, my girl."

"Thanks, I think?" I said with a chuckle.

"Everything doesn't have to be so serious all the time, Kit. You have permission to enjoy yourself just for the sake of enjoying yourself," Veronica said.

Preston started gurgling and Veronica said, "I have to run. Have a good time! Happy New Year's Eve."

Veronica was probably right. I had to admit that this week I'd spent a lot of time wondering what it would be like to kiss William. Maybe I could find out if I could just relax a little and let go of the pretense that every date needed to have the potential to lead somewhere.

I checked the time. I made my way downstairs. Instead of taking the back stairs, I went down the second-floor hallway, down the front steps to the foyer, and into the front room, where William was sitting, reading something on his phone. When I walked in the room, he stood up.

"Wow, you look beautiful," he said, shoving his hands in his pockets, the way he did when he was feeling a little nervous. I felt a flutter in my stomach when our eyes met. Maybe Veronica was right. Maybe William did like me.

"You look handsome, too," I said. William always looked handsome. When I first met him, I thought he only owned business casual clothes, but this week, I was able to see a different side of William. He was wearing a black A Tribe Called Quest T-shirt, a pair of relaxed jeans, and Converse. The shirt was tight across his chest and around his biceps.

He pulled on a black zip-up hoodie. "Ready to go?"

We decided to walk to The Pub. By the time we got there, it was already busy. The bar was warm, and William and I immediately shed our jackets. People were crowded around the bar ordering drinks. A DJ was setting up in the corner, and the many televisions were showing a combo of sports coverage and NYE countdowns.

Trent, Sasha, Nick, and Melissa were at a table at the back of the bar. As soon as we approached them, Melissa jumped down and gave me a hug. "Hey, hot stuff!" I could tell she had been drinking because her cheeks were rosier than usual.

Sasha and Melissa both bubbled the usual "Hello," and "How was your holiday?"

Before I could answer, I felt a hand press gently on my lower back, and I turned to see William holding a drink for me. "Thanks," I said. William smiled at me and joined Nick and Trent on the other side of the table. The place where he had touched my back still tingled with an electric hum.

When I turned back, Sasha and Melissa were both staring at me with wide eyes. "What's going on there?" Melissa asked.

"Mm-hmm," Sasha hummed with a smile. "Trent said he saw the two of you jogging together the other day."

"Just hanging out with my housemate. Just friends," I said.

Melissa chortled, "Friends with benefits, I hope!"

I shook my head and laughed, but I wondered if Melissa had a point. Maybe we could just be friends with benefits? I tried to change the subject.

"I love the decorations."

"There's a lot of mistletoe hanging around here tonight," Melissa winked.

I pointed to the DJ table. "A DJ? That's fun!"

"I heard she's great," Sasha offered. "Plays the perfect mix of pop, hip hop, country, and reggaeton music."

"Nick helped Ray find the DJ. It's part of the new push to attract more young adults to stay in Creekstone. I think your

friend, William, has been helping Nick start all kinds of programs," Melissa said with a grin.

Sasha, Melissa, and I played a few rounds of pool. Sasha was
an unbelievable pool player, so it was mostly just rounds of
Melissa and me waiting for Sasha to sink all her shots. Occasionally, I'd look up to see William listening to Trent and Nick.
Sometimes, he would look over and watch us playing pool. I felt
his gaze linger a little longer than necessary on me.

By the third drink, Melissa was sharing stories about holiday
ER patients. Mostly Christmas decoration mishaps and holiday
cooking gone wrong. Suddenly, Melissa's eyes widened and she
pointed at Nick.

I looked over to where Melissa was pointing. Nick was
standing between Trent and William. Nick looked like he was
giving a campaign speech. William had his arms folded across
his chest as he listened. He was nodding along as Nick talked.

"I can tell he's talking about work. Let me go and bail Trent
and William out." Melissa bounced around and over to Nick.
She shook a finger at him. "No work tonight! You promised."

Nick looked like a kid whose hand had been caught in a
cookie jar. Melissa tugged at Nick's arm. "Let's dance."

Trent and Sasha followed Nick and Melissa out onto a spot
where the tables had been cleared away for dancing. William
walked over to me, and he shoved one of his hands in his pockets. We stood awkwardly for a moment, and finally William
said, "Wanna dance?"

Maybe if I hadn't had three strong mixed drinks I would
have responded differently, but at that moment, all I could really think about was being close to William again.

William was a surprisingly good dancer. He struck the perfect balance of dancing close enough to me so that other guys didn't try to cut in, but far enough away that I wasn't creeped out. After a while, I was sweating, and I motioned to William that I was going to the bar to get a drink.

The bar was crowded. I waved at Ray behind the bar, and he gave me a nod. I leaned on the bar and turned to watch everyone as I waited for my drink.

A tall, skinny guy with a backwards baseball cap appeared next to me at the bar. "Hey, I was watching you play pool earlier. I'm Brett. What's your name?"

"Annie," I muttered.

"Annie. You wanna dance?"

I turned to see Ray bringing me my drink. Just in time, I thought.

"No, thanks," I said, waiting for the drink to arrive.

"Aww, come on," the guy said. He took a step closer to me, and before I could say anything else, William stepped behind me.

"I was looking for you," William said to me but looking directly at Brett, who stepped back and held up both hands.

William motioned to Ray to bring him another drink. I turned toward the bar and looked over my shoulder at William, who was watching Brett skulk off.

As soon as Ray dropped off William's drink, I said, "It's so hot in here." I fanned my face. "Wanna go out on the back patio?"

William followed me through the rear door of The Pub, which opened onto a patio area. Since people usually only ate outside on The Pub's patio during the spring and summer months, the tables and chairs were not set up. Strings of lights lit the area, giving it a warm, inviting ambiance. Outside was much quieter, but we could still hear the steady thud of music from inside. A handful of people were standing in small groups, drinking, and smoking.

I leaned against the wall and sipped my drink. William stood next to me. I said, "Thanks for deterring that guy in there."

"I'm sure you can handle it on your own. That kind of thing must happen to you all the time," William said, taking a long sip of his drink.

"Yeah, but it's nice to not have to deal with it, too," I admitted.

"That's what friends are for," William said, taking a spot on the wall next to me. I tried not to let the sting of the word friends show on my face. We were quiet for a moment.

William patted his pockets and pulled his phone out. It lit up from a call. I saw the name Meredith and a beautiful woman's picture glowing on the screen. Meredith? I had seen William's phone ringing and the missed text messages all week, but this was the first time I got a clear view of who was calling. Not wanting to gawk, I looked away quickly.

"You can take that if you want," I offered. If we were just friends, I shouldn't be jealous of someone calling him.

William slipped his phone back in his pocket. He looked down at me. His brow wrinkled. "What's wrong? You've got that look on your face."

"What look?" I asked, biting the inside of my lip.

"The look you used to always give me before...before Christmas when you didn't like me," William said with a frown. He pushed a piece of hair away from my face and the brush of his fingers on my skin, in such a tender way, took my breath away.

"I'm all right. Just a little cold," I said softly. I looked down and then said, "But for the record, I never didn't like you. I just think...I put up walls to protect myself." When I looked back up, William held my gaze.

William shoved a hand in his pocket and said, "Hey, I just wanted to say that I know you were supposed to be with your dad for Christmas and you had been looking forward to that, and I'm sorry that didn't work out. But for what it's worth, this has been one of the best Christmases I've had in years."

I felt a flutter in my stomach. "Me too."

"Let's go back in so we don't miss the countdown." William put out his hand and waited for me to take it. I looked down at his hand and then up at him. My heart skipped a beat. I put my hand in his and we headed back inside. William led us straight out onto the dance floor. Sasha was right about the DJ. As we got to midnight, the DJ started playing more upbeat dance tempos, and more people were coming out on the dance floor.

This time, dancing was a little different. The dance floor had gotten crowded, so we had an excuse to dance closer to each other. William kept one hand on my hip, but he kept just enough space between us. Occasionally, William would twirl me around. With each passing moment, I could feel myself being drawn closer to him, until we finally danced pressed against each other, the way couples do.

William pointed to the DJ table. Nick had taken the mic and called out to the crowd that it was time for the countdown. A large screen behind the DJ table was showing a split screen view of the countdowns in Atlanta, NYC, Boston, and Miami. We all cheered. I turned to face the table where Nick and the DJ were leading the crowd in the countdown. I felt William close behind me. I stepped back and pressed against William, and I felt his hand settle on my hip, sending a tingle through my whole body. I realized I hadn't felt like this in so long: not just desired but protected.

When the countdown reached zero everyone cheered. People all around us were blowing noisemakers, and someone shot off confetti cannons from the bar. Still standing behind me, William leaned forward and in a low, sexy voice said, "Happy New Year, Kit." I could feel his hot breath on my neck and his deep voice resonated through me in a way that set a chill down my spine.

A trap beat version of "Auld Lang Syne" played over the speakers. I spun around so I was facing him. I felt a gentle tug as William pulled me closer to him, both of his hands on my waist.

"Happy New Year, William." I couldn't help myself. I leaned against him, my hands on his chest. I saw his eyes search my face and linger on my lips. I let out a little laugh and said, "I think it's good luck if we kiss...since it's New Year's."

William pulled me closer to him, and I felt the rough stubble from his cheek brush my face before our lips touched. I reflexively closed my eyes, and savored the warmth of his lips against mine. I felt the pressure of one of William's hands against the small of my back, while his other hand gently cradled my cheek. Our lips parted and the kiss deepened.

I pulled back and looked up at William. A crooked smile spread across his lips. I felt out of breath, but I managed to say, "Maybe we should get out of here."

William took my hand and led me through the crowd. We finally made it to the door. When I got outside, I felt the relief as a cold blast of air hit my face. I held William's hand as we hurried down the sidewalk toward the house. I felt a little dizzy with excitement as I followed William's lead. I couldn't remember ever feeling that way just from a kiss.

It had been such a brief one, and the anticipation of the next kiss was just as exciting. As soon as we turned the corner off Main Street, William turned and pulled me toward him. I practically melted into him as we started kissing.

I took a few steps backwards and William pressed me against the brick wall. He kissed my cheek and said in a low whisper into my ear, "I haven't been able to stop thinking about you." As he kissed my neck, one of his muscular thighs pressed between my legs. The lower on my neck he kissed me, the more I pressed into his thigh. I felt his hand grab my ass to steady me against him.

Finally, I gasped and said, "Please take me home."

William took my hand, and I let him pull me along as we hurried the next two blocks home. Light with excitement, we rushed down the sidewalk and up the front steps. I had never felt so eager before. I fumbled to pull my keys out of my jacket pocket at the front door. He was behind me kissing my neck. I felt his hand slip around my waist and under my shirt. His fingertips traced the line where my waistband lay against my stomach. His palm lay flat against my stomach and his hand lightly skated up my abdomen, sending chills through me as his fingers reached the bottom lace of my bralette. I stopped and let him whisper how he wanted me in my ear. His deep voice reverberated through me and ignited a desire that I had never felt before. At that moment, I knew that whether it was just once or forever, I needed to be with William.

10

William

It simply had never felt like this. The build up to the moment, the sensation of our lips finally touching, the way her body responded to my touch. It all drove me wild. Before we kissed, I knew that I liked Kit. She was attractive, but it was more than that.

We spent so much time together. The sexual tension was perfectly primed. But once we kissed, something was unlocked, and Kit became my sole focus. I felt this urgency to be with her. I had simply never felt like that with anyone else before.

I kissed her long neck from behind as she pressed against me. She tried to reach for the door, but she paused, and I heard the hitch in her breathing as my thumb traced the soft skin on her stomach. I felt her press against my hips, and I whispered into her ear, "I want you."

Kit turned and looked over her shoulder at me. Her beautiful eyes met mine, and I knew she wanted the same thing. Kit bit her lip and nodded at me as if calling me forward. Kit turned to unlock the door, and as soon as she turned the key she froze. Her body went rigid, and I knew something was wrong.

Kit turned to me, eyes wide and said, "The door is unlocked."

I must have had a confused look on my face, because Kit repeated what she had said before. I blinked trying to process her words. Then I repeated what she'd said.

"The door is unlocked?"

"Yes, and I'm sure I locked it," Kit said in a whisper. The look of anxious worry and alertness washed over her face.

"Let me go in first," I said. I fully expected Kit to argue with me about not needing me to protect her, but she stepped aside, let me push the door open, and I led the way inside.

When we got into the foyer, the lights were dim in both the front room and office, but I could hear something in the kitchen. I pointed to the kitchen and Kit nodded. She pulled her cell phone out of her jacket, ready to call the police if we needed help.

We slowly crept down the hallway, pressing against the wall so that whoever was in the kitchen couldn't see us. I took a deep breath and called out as I stepped into the kitchen.

"Who's there?"

A man, in his mid-sixties, stood in the kitchen by the back door. "Hey," I said putting my hand out. "Stay calm."

The man froze; his eyes fixed on me. Kit was right behind me, and she managed to squeak out, "Leave or we'll call the police. We don't want any trouble."

"That's not what the doorbell camera said. Looked like you two were about to get into all kinds of trouble," a familiar voice said from the dining room door. I looked over and saw a tanned, smiling Rita.

"This is Harold, my travel buddy," Rita said. She turned to the man who was still frozen in the kitchen. "Harold, this is my niece Kit and one of our renters, William."

Harold relaxed and said, "Oh, nice to meet you, Kit. I've heard so much about you." Harold crossed the kitchen and put his hand out. I shook his hand and then he stood patiently and waited for Kit to do the same. Kit's cheeks were pink with embarrassment from Rita teasing us about the front porch.

"Happy New Year, Kit," Rita said, putting her arms out. Kit moved around me and Harold to give Rita a big hug.

"I'm so glad to see you," Kit said, her voice muffled as she hugged Rita. Kit stepped back and said, "I'm just surprised. I thought you said your flight was tomorrow?"

"Well, they told us we needed to either leave early or risk being stuck there for several days after the storm, so we decided not to risk it. Not that the resort wasn't lovely, but I have to work doubles and the nurses who covered me over Christmas would kill me if I didn't come into work," Rita said with a sigh. "And if there is one group of people you don't want to piss off, it's a group of ER nurses."

Harold and I exchanged a look. I made a mental note not to make any nurses angry, including Rita.

"I should be getting home," Harold said. "Nice to meet you all." Rita followed Harold down the hallway to the front door to say goodbye.

We were alone in the kitchen. I waited to see how Kit would react. She turned to me and laughed. "Wow, that went from potentially scary to just a touch awkward."

I felt the corners of my mouth push down in a smile. I nodded and shoved my hand in my pocket. I felt anxious because I wasn't sure what to do next. I took a deep breath.

Kit looked down and ran her hand along the kitchen island and sighed. "Well, I guess I'm going to head to bed. I probably won't be up for an early morning run." Her eyes shifted up and met mine. I so badly wanted to close the distance between us, but I could tell that she was on edge. She said softly, "But maybe I'll be up for a night run tomorrow." I felt my heart thud in my chest. Just the way her long dark lashes fanned as she looked down was more than I could take at that moment.

Rita cleared her throat as she came into the kitchen. "Well, kids. I'm probably going to hit the sack," she announced, walking through the kitchen to the back stairs. Kit followed Rita. When she got to the bottom stair, Kit turned and said, "Happy New Year, William."

The next morning when I woke up, I immediately thought of Kit. I wished we had spent the night together. Before I could give it too much thought, my phone buzzed. I rubbed my hand across my face and sat up. I exhaled a deep sigh. It was Meredith. It would be nice to see a friend calling on New Year's Day, if I thought she was just calling to wish me a Happy New Year, but I knew it was about work. I had been dodging calls from Meredith all week.

"Hey," I said, my voice still deep from sleep. My mouth was dry. I put my feet on the floor and rubbed my eyes as I waited.

"Hey?" Meredith's voice said thick with annoyance. "Hey? You were M.I.A. at the company Christmas party in New York, which I told everyone was because you were in Atlanta, but guess what, you weren't at the New Year's Eve soiree in Atlanta last night? I thought you were working out of the Atlanta office? Where are you?"

I went to my kitchen sink and filled up my one coffee mug with water. "Happy New Year to you, too."

"Don't be cute with me, William. I'm pissed."

"Why? And how do you even know that I wasn't at Braithway's Atlanta party last night?" I asked. I could feel a post-drinking-dehydration headache coming on. I went into my bathroom to get some Advil.

"Because I was there, William." Meredith didn't hide her annoyance. "And guess what—I had a front row seat to Charles licking Braithway's ass. It was awful. He was totally angling for your promotion, William. Why would you miss such an important opportunity to spend time with Braithway and the board?"

"You just have to trust that I'm doing exactly what Braithway asked me to do," I said after taking two Advil. I walked back out and leaned against the kitchenette counter.

"You mean, your little secret project to buy half of a small town and turn it into a model redevelopment site to prove Braithway's affordable housing theory?" Meredith said.

I looked up. "What do you know about that?"

"Give me some credit, William. I have been at this as long as you have—and believe it or not, I've helped you get to where you are now." She let out a long, annoyed sigh. "I know my name isn't even being considered for CEO, so I have to do the next best thing: make sure you, not Charles, the greatest asshole known to man, gets the job."

"Look, just trust me, Meredith. I'm halfway through phase one of this project. When I get to phase two, Braithway is going to make the announcement. Just give me a few more months." I tried to relax. At least, Meredith didn't know I was in Creekstone.

"A few more months?" Meredith scoffed. "In a few more months, Charles will be pregnant with Braithway's child. He's such an insidious kiss-ass."

"That was so unnecessarily graphic," I muttered. "Yeah, maybe two months, tops."

"I want to see your progress," Meredith said after a long pause.

"My progress?" I shook my head as I chuckled.

"Put your pride in your pocket," Meredith said. "You and I both know we've pushed each other over the finish line in multiple million and sometimes billion-dollar developments. Let me take a look. I can see what you're missing, so we can get this over with."

"I agree that you're a valuable director on my team. I couldn't do this job without you." I tried to sound confident. "But this kind of development takes time. There aren't any tricks that can be played to get us over the finish line faster. Trust me. I'm working all the angles."

"Show me now," Meredith said flatly.

"Show you now?" I asked.

"I'm outside," she said and hung up the phone.

I hurried over to the window and looked out. Meredith was holding her phone in her hand, looking up at my window, as she leaned against a Mercedes G-Wagon that was parked by the curb in front of the house.

I sighed. On the one hand, this was annoying. Meredith should be in Philadelphia preparing for a huge deal's closing, not micromanaging me. On the other hand, it was nice to see a friend, and Meredith was the best at closing out projects. Possibly because everyone was terrified of her. If anyone could help me get phase one of this project over the finish line, it was Meredith.

I texted her. I'll be down in five minutes.

I brushed my teeth and splashed my face with water. I slipped on a pair of jeans, a T-shirt, and a fleece, then headed downstairs.

When I walked outside, Meredith was still leaning against the vehicle with her arms crossed. Her straight leg jeans and black ribbed turtleneck accentuated her tall, thin frame, and she lifted her expensive, oversized sunglasses to get a better look at me as I walked closer.

"You look…" Meredith paused, as if trying to select the right next words. "Better than usual."

"Must be the mountain water," I said. I crossed my arms in front of me. "How did you find me?"

"I asked Marla a million questions last night. Then I went back to my hotel room and looked at every property our company has recently purchased until I figured out which one could be your project."

"We purchase dozens of properties every month," I said, narrowing my eyes.

"I guess I'm just good," Meredith said pushing herself forward, so she was standing up straight and not leaning on the car. "Let's go."

I held out my hand so Meredith could drop the keys in them. She did. Then she gave me a hug. "I've actually fucking missed you. Let's get this deal done."

"Missed you too, Mer."

We got straight to work. I drove Meredith from site to site. I airdropped her the folder of plans and permits I'd been working from, so she could see all the work I'd done with Nick and the city and county permitting departments to secure the infrastructure improvement approvals we needed. I then showed her the properties we had already acquired, which included several empty lots and dilapidated buildings in the downtown area. I told her that the wheels were already in motion to revitalize those buildings.

The last place I took Meredith was the river. I explained that two landowners owned almost all the riverfront, and once we were able to purchase the it, we could build a riverfront mixed-use development that would serve as a new social center for the town. The property would have new spaces for restaurants, shops, and even some housing affordable enough for nurses, teachers, and first responders.

"This is the only building on the riverfront," I said, pulling into the parking lot of an old flour mill. "We just purchased this property. I'm thinking we'll restore this building and file for a historical preservation designation. Maybe use the building as an event space or something like that. It would be a great asset for the community and bring new families to the riverfront." I put the car into park, and Meredith got out.

I followed her to the corner of the lot, overlooking the river. I pointed toward the undeveloped lot next to us. "The riverbank lots for the next two miles are owned by one family."

Meredith nodded. "They going to sell?"

I shrugged. "Too early to tell. They're against outsiders. That's what I'm doing here, becoming an insider."

Meredith didn't hide her amusement. She laughed the kind of soul-crushing laugh that only women from New York can deliver.

I said, "Well, it might be funny, but it's true. It's how Braithway told me to handle it, and he said if I can't get it done this way, then I might not be the right person for the job."

The mention of Braithway's name stopped Meredith's laughing. "You tried threatening to build godawful things around their property to scare them into selling?" This was a common tactic of developers dealing with stubborn landowners who wouldn't sell: buy all the property around them, and just build terrible shit like strip malls filled with liquor stores and check-cashing places—driving down the property value—so that, eventually, they have to leave.

"No," I said. "Braithway doesn't want it done that way."

Meredith rolled her eyes. "You tried offering them so much money they can't say no?" Meredith waited for me. When I didn't answer right away, she said, "I can call our bankers to see what we can pull together and what makes sense for a town like this." Meredith scowled as she looked around as if just remembering she wasn't talking about a corner of the Upper East Side.

Part of me believed Kit would never sell. Kit had made it perfectly clear that she wasn't interested in talking about selling land with an outsider, but maybe, eventually, she would at least consider it. And if not, maybe I'd have to use Meredith's strategy.

I nodded as if conceding something and said, "Yeah, call the bankers. Give me some more time to see if they're even willing to sell, and if they are, we should be ready to make this deal work for the seller."

Meredith checked her watch. "I have to head back to Atlanta. I left Addison with my credit card and told her to treat herself to whatever she wanted."

"Ouch." I winced as we turned and headed back for the car. "That might be the craziest thing you've ever done."

Meredith shook her head and admitted, "People do crazy things when they're in love."

11

Kit

I was on cloud nine when I woke up. Everything that happened last night was unexpected, but it was something I'd been dreaming about since Christmas Eve. That first kiss with William was absolutely amazing. I had never felt that much heat from a kiss. Even though we got interrupted and things couldn't go much further than kissing, I felt a warm sensation every time I thought about it. I could still feel where his hands had been around my waist and on my thighs. I wondered what would have happened if we hadn't been interrupted.

I immediately reached for my phone and texted Veronica. "Made out with William."

I didn't wait for Veronica's reply. I knew I really needed to get up and get dressed. I had promised Aunt Rita I would make a ham, black eyed peas, greens, and cornbread. It had been our New Year's Day meal every year since I could remember.

I stood up and walked to the window. I looked down at the street and my heart skipped a little when I saw William walking down the front steps, but then I noticed that William was walking down the front path to meet a woman. I blinked. Was I seeing this correctly? Was William talking to a beautiful, super-model-tall woman? Before I could fully process what I was seeing, the woman threw her arms around William. They hugged, he got in the car, and they drove off.

I turned around. My face felt hot. I felt dizzy. Was I really so off about what had happened with William last night? I thought it was something special, but clearly, I had misread everything. Not just last night, but all the time we had spent together over the last week. I had been vulnerable with William. I had opened up about my mom and my past relationship with Matt. And to be fair, William had been open and honest with me when he told me that he doesn't get attached. I just didn't listen.

I covered my face with my hands and collapsed back onto my bed. As if I had sent a best friend bat signal into the air, my phone rang. It was Veronica.

"Sorry it took me a minute to call you. I had to put Preston in his playpen. Tell me everything!" Veronica said excitedly. I sighed.

"Well, it was pretty hot. We danced all night, and then we kissed when the ball dropped at midnight. It was completely electric, so we left together and made out as we walked home. It was so hot, and we came home fully intending to take it further, but then Aunt Rita was here from her trip and in the kitchen with her travel boyfriend. So I just called it a night and went to sleep. Probably for the best."

"Aunt Rita totally cock-blocked you by accident!" Veronica cried. "Do you think you'll hook up next time?"

"I don't know." I hesitated. Maybe she had a point. I told Veronica about how I had just seen William drive off with a supermodel in a Mercedes.

"Oh, well, fuck him." Veronica declared.

Buoyed by Veronica's support, I let a puff of air pass through my nostrils and said, "It's no big deal. It's been fun hanging out with William, but time to get back to the real world."

"This isn't about William. This is about you. Plenty of fish in the sea! New year, new Kit. Time to make a new year's resolution to embrace fun and spontaneity and to get laid."

"Was your advice always this full of cliches?" I asked.

"Yes, absolutely. And sometimes it even rhymes if I've had some drinks." Veronica bragged.

"I don't know..." My voice trailed off. I heard Preston cry in the background of the call.

"Girl, I have to go, but I want some updates about how you've reactivated that dating account and you are getting out there! Send me screenshots. I need proof you're not going to hide in your protective shell!"

I fell backwards onto the bed. I blew air between my lips. I knew that I had glossed over my disappointment about seeing William with another woman this morning. I wasn't ready to be honest with myself about how I was feeling, so explaining it to Veronica would have been impossible.

Veronica was right. New year, new Kit. I picked up my phone and clicked on the SinglesMingle app. I navigated to the profile settings and tapped to toggle the button next to Casual

Encounters from off to on. I threw my phone on the bed and got up to take a shower.

By the time I came back from my shower, I had half a dozen messages from people in a sixty-mile radius. Well, at least I have this going for me, I thought as I scrolled through the messages.

I heard Aunt Rita stirring in the next room, and I joined her. We went downstairs to the kitchen and spent the day together. While I made lunch, she started another batch of cookies. It was a nice distraction to be with Aunt Rita. She always knew how to make me feel good. I was careful not to bring up William, but eventually Aunt Rita asked, "So, you and William?"

"Just friends," I said without looking up from the pan I was pouring the cornbread mixture into.

"Oh, okay," Aunt Rita said with a smile. I shot her a look.

"No really," I insisted. "We're just friends. Last night, we just got caught up in the New Year's Eve drinks."

Aunt Rita put her hands up. "Sure, I mean, far be it from me to poo-poo anyone's fun. I'm happy for you, Kit." I didn't respond, and I think she knew to drop it.

Aunt Rita and I leaned against the island as we waited for the food to finish cooking. She was showing me photos from their vacation when William came into the kitchen.

"Hey, William. Happy New Year!" Aunt Rita said. She gave him a hug. I didn't turn around. I felt my whole body get tense, and I tried not to let it show. William opened the fridge and got out a soda.

"Hey, Kit. Happy New Year," he said. He had come around to the other side of the island, so we were facing each other.

"Yeah, Happy New Year," I said, smiling. "We're making some food. There's so much. You should have some."

"Thanks," William said. He was searching my face. I could tell he wanted to talk to me. Aunt Rita must have sensed it too because she excused herself and went into the front office.

I decided to rip the Band-Aid off. "I know I mentioned I was going to go for a night run tonight, but I actually have a date, so I'm going to be out tonight."

"Oh," William's face fell and I could see him swallow hard. "Cool."

"Yeah, I guess I should thank you," I said a little coldly. "Everyone, including you, just kept encouraging me to relax, have fun, be more casual, and I realized this was probably what I was missing out on. It's my new year's resolution."

"Your resolution?" he asked.

"Yeah, my resolution is to just relax and have more fun. Not to take myself or anyone else too seriously." I shrugged one shoulder playfully and said, "The cornbread has about five more minutes, but the black-eyed peas probably need more time."

William stared at me blankly.

I tried not to read anything into his expression and silence. "I figured you'd be fine with just having fun, since you said you only want casual flings anyways. We're cool, Mr. Right Now?"

William nodded. "We're totally cool." He shoved his hand in his pocket and let a slow breath out. "I'm going up to my room. I'm wiped."

I smiled as I watched him walk out of the room. As soon as he was gone, I slumped over and laid my forehead on the counter. "This is going to be harder than I thought," I whispered to myself, but I was determined.

I did go out on a date that night with a nice enough guy from the next town over, but it didn't go anywhere.

In fact, I went on several dates over the next few weeks. Every time it was the same thing. Some flirty texting back and forth to set up the date, a pleasant first date, and sometimes even a second date, but then the inevitable first kiss. These kisses enlightened me to a few things. First, I was actually attractive enough that multiple people were willing to kiss me. Second, it was possible to have a nice time and no potential, and that was okay. And lastly, a pleasant kiss is nice but not comparable to a kiss that sets you on fire because the chemistry is so explosive.

I tried to force myself to go on at least one date per week. This is probably what I should have been looking forward to, but instead, I found myself anticipating Tuesday and Thursday evenings when I closed at the library. William would be there until close tutoring high school and college students.

At first, I thought it might be weird, but we fell back into a friendly rhythm. I found myself making excuses not to make dates on Tuesdays and Thursdays, and I always offered to close. I had started walking to work on those days, so I would have an excuse to walk home with William. Sometimes we would go to The Pub and play pool after work.

On cold days, we'd hurry home. If there was a fire in the front room, we'd hang out in there together. If not, we'd go into the kitchen to make a cup of tea. William would tell me stories about work, growing up with a spunky Filipina immigrant mom, and all the best places he'd ever traveled to.

I would tell him stories about quirky library patrons, and the funny stuff people used as bookmarks that we found when we reshelved the books. And because I wanted to convince us both that we were just friends, sometimes I would even share weird first date stories. William had convinced me that I needed to watch Game of Thrones. He was absolutely stunned that I had never seen it. We started watching it on Tuesday evenings, but I insisted we watch holiday movies and shows on Thursdays. I told him he was woefully behind on decades of Christmas movies and he really needed to try and get caught up before next Christmas. To my surprise, he agreed. I made a long "to watch" list that we started working through.

Sitting on the sofa with William, laughing, and playfully arguing, was the best part of my day. The worst part was when one of us finally threw in the towel and said that we had to go to bed.

I was putting on a good front with Veronica. I was giving her a steady enough stream of first date stories that she wouldn't launch into the whole "New year, new Kit speech," and I made sure not to mention how much time I was spending with William. I wasn't admitting to myself, let alone anyone else, how my feelings for William were growing instead of dissipating. Dating other people was just highlighting how much I enjoyed William compared to other people.

My mind regularly drifted to that night William and I kissed. At first, I tried to push the memory from my mind, but eventually, I decided it was harmless to fantasize about him.

I reminded myself that if something were to happen again, a kiss or maybe even more, that William probably would just be having fun. But maybe I could be okay with that?

By February, William had started a weekly lunch meeting with Creekstone's fledgling Chamber of Commerce. He invited me to join them, saying that it's nice to have city employees join the conversation. I went to the first few meetings. Nick always opened the meetings, but William led the networking activities before the lunch, and he introduced the speakers that presented during the plated lunch. I liked seeing the work side of William. He was charming and charismatic, but he never corrected or overtalked people. He always had control of the room. Seeing William's composure and professionalism was such a stark contrast to the memory of New Year's Eve. Part of me liked knowing there was a part of William that could be passionate and heated. Part of me liked remembering the way he couldn't keep his hands off me that night. I knew there was much more to William. I wondered if he still felt that for me.

At the end of each meeting, William gave an update on the town's redevelopment project. When William brought in some large renderings of the potential development and displayed them on easels, we could see the whole vision for a new Creekstone. At the conclusion of each meeting, I would hear business owners and community members comment on how excited they were about the redevelopment effort and how, for the first time in a long time, they felt hope. Ms. Patty and Ms. Pearl both commented that they loved the vision.

At the end of February, William brought in a speaker to talk about small business support. It was the woman I'd seen with him on New Year's Day, Meredith. She was as smart as she was beautiful, and I felt an inexplicable jealousy. For the last two months, I'd been going on dates and sometimes even telling William about them, and he had carried on as if we were just the greatest friend. And William brought Meredith to one chamber lunch to talk about resources for businesses, and I felt so jealous I could barely make it through lunch. I bolted as soon as it was over.

The next day William ignored any ice daggers I threw his way and continued on, just as a good friend would. He waited for me after closing at the library. Then he walked home with me, even though I was almost silent. When we got home, he followed me into the kitchen. William busied himself with making me a cup of tea. We sat in silence until the kettle whistled. Then as William poured the water over the tea bag, I blurted out, "Have you slept with Meredith?"

"Excuse me?" William coughed, nearly spilling hot water everywhere.

"Meredith. The two of you have worked together and seem so familiar with each other. I wondered if there was more going on." I looked down at my tea, acting as if watching it steep needed my full attention.

William pressed his lips together to prevent a smile and put the kettle down. "I have slept with Meredith. A very long time ago. In college. And we realized we weren't suited for each other and became friends."

I sniffed. "Oh, that's a shame. She's beautiful."

William's lips parted and his head tilted like he wanted to say more, but he stopped himself.

"Let's go watch the next movie on our Christmas list," I said leaving the kitchen. I heard William's feet padding behind mine, and we settled onto the sofa. We watched the movie The Holiday. William acted totally normal. He seemed unphased by the cold shoulder I had been giving him for two days. He seemed committed to waiting it out until things normalized, and I loathed and adored this about him.

12

William

I can't say how many times I replayed the conversation that happened on Christmas Eve. I couldn't remember ever telling Kit that she should casually date other men, and if I could travel back in time, I would tell myself to shut the fuck up, because Kit Campbell was the most amazing thing that ever almost happened to me, and watching Kit date other people was hell on earth.

The worst part was that Kit was perfectly happy dating other people. Apparently, the amazing New Year's Eve dancing, kissing, and near sex had primed Kit perfectly to go out and find someone else. Normally, I wouldn't have been deterred by this. I would have made a harder play to get with Kit again. But the reality was, I needed things to stay relatively uneventful between the two of us because I needed Kit to sell her land to Braithway & Randall. Not dating Kit simplified things tremendously, but even with this promotion on the line, I kept going back to that night with Kit in my mind.

I tried not to pay any attention to Kit's dating life. I tried to focus on just being friends, but then she started telling me about it, and sometimes she would talk about it with Aunt Rita in front of me, just nonchalantly, the way friends would. It was fucking terrible. But the absolute worst was when I'd see Kit's phone light up on the table and I'd see Matt's name would flash on the screen. Or when I'd hear Aunt Rita casually mention that Matt had sent her a note saying he was applying for fellowships in Atlanta. Even though Kit showed no actual interest in Matt, I felt jealous of him. I felt jealous of the history and pull he had in Kit's life.

Even though it hurt to see Kit happily navigate the world of dating, I couldn't fully cut myself off from her. I made an excuse to be at the library every Tuesday and Thursday night because I knew she'd be closing on those nights and would be walking home. Those short walks home were my favorite fifteen minutes of the entire week. When we'd get to the house, we'd warm up by the fire or make tea. I wanted to spend more time with her, so I insisted that she had to watch Game of Thrones with me, and the only reason I picked that show was because I knew it had long episodes and several seasons. She agreed to Tuesday Game of Thrones if I would watch holiday movies with her on Thursday nights. I agreed and tried not to show my delight when I saw the long list of movies and holiday themed-TV episodes she had put together. I was happy to see that she was thinking of spending that much time with me, even if it was just watching holiday movies on the sofa.

Being just Kit's friend was a double-edged sword. It was agony not being able to explore the feelings I had for Kit, but at the same time, spending time with her and being a regular part of her Tuesday and Thursday evenings gave me a purpose. I powered through long days of work on Monday and Wednesday so I would always be free on Tuesdays and Thursdays. I dreaded Fridays and Saturdays when Kit would go on dates with other guys. And, when Kit started going on second and third dates with guys, I found myself lying in bed, staring at the ceiling, and wondering not just when, but if, she had returned home from her dates. It was destroying me. I started finding reasons to be gone on weekends, so I couldn't sit around and obsess over it.

On one of the weekends, I went to Atlanta. I spent all day on Saturday in the office, and sometime around six p.m., Meredith and Addison appeared in the doorway, holding hands. Meredith was wearing flowy tan linen pants with a white top, and Addison was wearing a matching tea-length dress.

"What are you two doing in town?" I asked, leaning back in my chair.

Meredith leaned against my office doorway. "I'm in town for a deal. Marla gave us tickets to a show tonight. She left them on her desk for me. We stopped by to get them. I think the better question is, what are you doing here?"

"Just catching up on some work," I said, gesturing toward my desk. "It's a lot easier to get some of these things done with the big desktop screens."

"Uh-huh." Meredith seemed skeptical. She and Addison exchanged looks.

"We've actually seen this show before on Broadway. Why don't we skip it and take you out to dinner?" Addison suggested.

"No way!" I protested. "You can't let those nice outfits go to waste. Go to your show."

"William, please. Wherever we eat dinner will be nice; these outfits will be appropriate, and you will be woefully underdressed and potentially under-showered for it," Meredith scoffed. "We're not going slumming with you, my friend."

Addison stepped forward. "Do you have a button-down here you can change into?"

I did, and with a little more pushing, Addison was able to convince me to go into my office bathroom, splash some water on my face, and put on the emergency white shirt I kept at the office. Addison picked Nikolai's Roof, an upscale downtown restaurant on the thirtieth floor of an Atlanta high-rise. It was a stark contrast to The Pub in Creekstone. The white tablecloth restaurant was known for its panoramic view of Atlanta.

Meredith ordered a bottle for the table as well as starters, but waved the waiter away when they suggested the caviar menu. "This is an old friends dinner. No need."

Addison and I ignored Meredith. We were both used to her take-charge-no-bullshit persona.

"So, tell me," Addison started. "Meredith tells me you've been living in that tiny town, Creekstone, since December. How has that been?"

"Honestly, better than I would have expected," I said taking a sip of water. The waiter appeared with the wine and commenced pouring each of us a glass. I nodded as he set mine in front of me. "Thank you."

"Seems like land acquisitions have slowed down. What's the status of that last parcel by the river?" Meredith asked.

"Owned by two relatives. One relative has assured me she is interested in selling, but the holdout is the other relative. It hasn't been a hard no, and I'm working on it."

"This is boring." Addison said with a pout. "Have you dated anyone since you moved to Georgia?"

I ran my hand through my hair and shoved my hand in my pocket. "Eh, not really."

Meredith's eyebrows raised, and a huge smile broke out across Addison's face. She leaned forward. "I know that look. That's the look of a man interested in someone. Tell me all about her."

I shrugged with a chuckle. "There's nothing to tell. I've just been spending a lot of time with one of the women I live with. She's the librarian there in town. She's very dedicated to Creekstone. She is very cute, but she's not interested in anything serious, and honestly, she doesn't seem that interested in me."

"Impossible," Meredith announced. "You're what every straight woman wants. You're incredibly handsome, wealthy, and at the top of your industry. You're smart, funny, and come from humble enough beginnings that you're not entitled—you don't take people for granted. Of course she wants to date you. Unless..." Meredith paused and narrowed her eyes, "What did you do?"

Addison interjected. "I agree that you're a catch, so why wouldn't she want to date you?"

I sighed. "Two things. First, I was a little too honest about how I'm not known for committing to the women I get involved with. So, I think Kit saw that as a big red flag. And the second thing is that Kit doesn't like what I do for a living. She doesn't want Creekstone to change. So, she just sees me as a friend."

Meredith's eyes went wide and she nearly choked on her wine. "William, are you kidding me? Kit? As in Katherine Campbell?"

Addison looked back and forth between us. "Who's Kit? Who's Katherine?"

I took a deep breath. I was about to get it from Meredith.

"Have you lost your mind?" Meredith ignored Addison. She ran both her hands through her hair in frustration.

"Listen," I said putting out my hand. "Nothing has happened. We aren't involved. We're just friends. I can close this deal."

"William, I can't even keep up with the long list of women you've dated. There have been ballerinas, models, schoolteachers, lawyers, doctors, strippers, and now, a librarian. And none of them are your friends anymore because you break all their hearts. It's your pattern. And if you get involved with this woman, and she refuses to sell you that riverfront property, you can kiss that fucking CEO job goodbye."

Addison's jaw dropped. She leaned forward and said, "The plot thickens, my dear William. Have you two kissed?"

"Just on New Year's Eve. We got caught up in the moment."

"Holy shit. We're screwed," Meredith said, running her hand over her face, then dropping her hand on the table in such a way that the dishes clattered.

"Baby, you're getting all worked up and assuming the absolute worst," Addison said, rubbing her hand over Meredith's. "Use your steps, baby."

Meredith's nostrils flared as she took a deep breath and exhaled slowly. She kept her eyes locked in on me in a way that let me know that if Addison hadn't been there, she would have thrown the crabcake in my face. I tried not to laugh. Addison nodded encouragingly. "See? That's so much better."

"Meredith, listen." I smoothed the tablecloth in front of me. "Kit is the one who rebuffed me. If she wanted to get with me, she could have. I have been there this whole time. She goes on a date with a different guy almost every week, and she tells me about it. She just sees me as a friend."

Meredith's shoulders relaxed a bit. Addison tsked her tongue. "Oh, I'm sorry, William. Unrequited crushes are so hard. Maybe you could just tell her how you feel. Maybe she doesn't know? Maybe that would change things," Addison reached for my hand.

Meredith pinched the bridge of her nose. "Addison, baby. Read the room. We want William to stay away from this woman."

I smiled at Addison to show my appreciation for her. "Nah, Addison. I think she does know. I am just not her type, I guess." Admitting that out loud gave me a sick feeling in my stomach. I frowned. "Kit has had a hard time. She lost her mom a couple of years ago, and it seems like she's finally coming out of the grief.

She deserves this new happiness she's been feeling. I'm not trying to rock the boat." I looked up and saw Meredith's eyes were about to pop out of her head. "And I don't want Meredith to kill me, so I'm going to keep my laser focus on closing this deal."

The waiter appeared with a second bottle of wine. "A gentleman sent this for you. From the table by the window."

Meredith turned in her seat, and I craned to look. Braithway was sitting at the table with one of his daughters and a teenage boy. The boy looked sullen and uncomfortable as his mother fussed about his shirt collar being askew. Braithway waved at us, and I gave a little wave back.

Meredith turned back around, and whispered, "Is that his oldest daughter?"

"Yeah, and his grandson, the turd," I said with a chuckle. "I hope the kid has figured it out."

Meredith looked puzzled and I said, "It's nothing. Braithway just has a way of making people learn and grow. He puts them way out of their comfort zone, and sets an incredibly high bar." As soon as I said it, I realized the challenge that had been set before me and knew I could get this done. I just needed to continue to build trust and stay the course. The waiter had lingered to ask if he could take our order. Addison kept the rest of the dinner conversation light.

Toward the end of our meal, Braithway walked over to our table. I stood up and shook his hand. He gave a nod to Meredith and Addison.

"Good evening, sir," I said.

Meredith added, "Thank you for the wine, sir."

"Oh, you both deserve it. I've seen all the work you've put into your projects. Speaking of, William, I'd like for you to join me at the board meeting in a few weeks. Did Marla already tell you?"

"Yes, sir," I said. "I plan to be there."

"Yes, I'd like to hear an update about your work." Braithway pushed his lips forward.

"Of course, sir," I said. Braithway excused himself and Meredith gave me a wide-eyed look that screamed, See? I told you. I nodded.

When I returned home to Creekstone from Atlanta that Monday afternoon, Rita asked for my help. Kit's birthday was later that week. Rita and Kit's best friend Veronica were planning a surprise birthday party for her on Thursday, the day before her actual birthday. Rita knew that we were usually together on Tuesday and Thursday evenings, so she wanted me to be in charge of bringing Kit to The Pub at eight p.m. on the day of the surprise party.

The night of the party, I waited around for Kit by the front of the library like I usually did. When she came out to lock the door, she smiled warmly at me.

"Ready to go?" she asked. I felt myself smile a smile far too goofy for the moment. I shoved a hand in my pocket nervously. The weather was starting to warm up, so Kit was wearing one of her cute, short librarian dresses. It was black with small white flowers and a little lace around the collar. It had delicate pearl white buttons down the front, and it was flowy and tight in all the right places. She had her hair pulled back in her regular braid. I wanted to tell her how beautiful she looked, but I didn't.

"Want to go to the pub? Get a bite to eat? Play some pool?" I asked, as nonchalantly as possible.

"Um, yeah." Kit agreed and added, "But I found the best Christmas episodes of The Office for us to watch later."

I texted Rita to let her know we were walking toward The Pub. I wanted to give Rita as much time as possible, so as we walked, I said, "Hey, want to see something I've been working on?"

Kit looked up with wide eyes. "Sure, you never talk about work with me."

I chuckled. "You come to the weekly Chamber lunch. Everything I'm doing gets talked about there."

"Oh, well, at a high non-personal level." Kit scoffed. "I just meant, you've never, like, shown me anything one-on-one, or you know...confided in me about work."

"You're right," I admitted tilting my head to the side. "I thought you hated my job, so I just never mention it." The truth was I wanted to tell Kit everything, but it felt too risky. First, she thought my job was annoying and that the work I was doing was fundamentally going to ruin Creekstone. And second, I didn't want to lose any edge the company might have in negotiating a land sale with her family.

"I don't hate your job," Kit said, pushing her lips forward in a little pout. She added softly. "In fact, I don't hate anything about you."

"Are you sure?" I shoved my hands in my pockets as we walked. "You've been pretty clear that you don't like my work."

"Yeah," Kit shrugged. She looked up at the sky as we walked, as if she was trying to think of the right way to explain it. "I'm just protective of Creekstone...and my family...and I guess of myself."

"Well, now that I've spent a lot of time with you in Creekstone, I see that all those things are really special and worth protecting," I said. I couldn't quite tell because it was already dark outside, but I thought I saw Kit blush.

I stopped. "Okay, this is it."

Kit stopped next to me and turned to look at the empty storefront we were standing in front of. "The old shoe repair place? I think it closed down last year."

"That's right," I nodded. "We acquired the building, and we partnered with the local college and the chamber to start an entrepreneurship center and business incubator."

Kit looked unimpressed. "That's cool."

"Well, you told me before that no one sticks around because there isn't anything for a young person to do, and, well, we crunched the numbers and confirmed that it just doesn't make sense for a business to stay here. So, we developed this program that will help new businesses form and give them tax incentives if they stay here in Creekstone, specifically if they base their businesses on the east side of Creekstone to help redevelop that area. I'm working with a few professors at the business school to offer night classes here at the entrepreneurship center for folks who want to learn more about running their own businesses."

I could tell I was getting into the weeds, and maybe I was losing her. "Anyway, we reached a milestone with the planning of the programs this morning, and I felt kind of pumped and just wanted to tell someone, I guess." I looked down at the ground and took a deep breath.

Kit kept her eyes on the dark storefront, then nodded slowly as if she understood. Without looking at me, she reached out and took my hand. My heart started to pound. Kit hadn't let me get close enough to touch her since New Year's Eve. I licked my lips nervously. I laced my fingers into hers. Her hands were soft and smooth. I was instantly transported to the night we kissed. I remembered how amazing it felt to have her hands on my face and neck as I kissed her soft lips.

Her voice brought me back. She turned to me and said, "I'm so proud of you, William. Thanks for sharing this with me. Could I promote it at the library?"

My heart pounded, and I took a deep breath. I ran my free hand through my hair. "Yeah, definitely."

Kit let her hand slide up my arm and she wrapped her hands around my bicep. "Maybe we should go to The Pub to celebrate."

"That would be nice," I said trying to sound relaxed, but my heart was pounding as every part of my body registered the way it felt as Kit touched me.

I had to stay focused. I checked my phone; I had received the text from Rita saying they were ready.

Kit didn't seem to be suspicious about where we were going. She seemed to be in a bit of daze. I opened the door to The Pub and let Kit go in first. As soon as she stepped inside, voices cried in unison, "Surprise!"

In that instant everything changed. The quiet and intimate moment I had shared with Kit dissolved into the chaotic energy of a surprise party. Kit's friends and family circled around her. Kit was shocked. She looked back at me, but before she could scold me for not warning her, Melissa pulled Kit away from me. She put a sash over Kit's head that said "30 and Flirty" in glittery letters. The jukebox was playing "Island in The Sun" by Weezer.

Kit was greeting and hugging every person in the room. I was happy to see Kit being celebrated by so many of her friends. I noticed a tall handsome man moving forward in the crowd. When Kit saw him she jumped up, and he picked her up and twirled her around as he hugged her. I instantly felt my neck and face get hot. Who was this guy?

After the man put Kit down, he exclaimed loudly, "Happy Birthday, KitKat."

She threw her head back and laughed. "What are you doing here?" she cried.

KitKat? Who the fuck was this guy?

I must have been obviously staring because the man made a beeline straight for me. He grabbed my hand and squeezed hard. "My name is Matt. Kit's...Matt."

"William," I said, trying not to sound too short. Matt didn't let go of his overly firm grip of my hand.

Matt snapped his fingers of his other hand as if remembering something. "Oh yeah, William. You're that little Christmas movie friend. Kit told me about that." Matt gave me a knowing grin, then continued. "Rita told me you'd be the perfect dis-

traction so all her real friends could get ready to surprise Kit."
He patted my shoulder with his free hand. "Thanks."

Little Christmas movie friend? Is that how Kit described me
to people?

Kit joined us. As soon as she was near, Matt let go of my
hand and wrapped an arm around her. Kit managed to wriggle
out of his hold and said, "I think you just met Matt."

"We've met." I shoved a hand in my pocket and took a deep
breath.

"This is Veronica, my best friend from college, and her husband, Gus," Kit said, pointing to a tall, thin woman holding
hands with a man about my age as they appeared next to us.

"Nice to meet you both. I've heard a lot about you," I said to
Veronica.

"Happy thirtieth birthday, Kitty," Matt said playfully,
squeezing Kit again. I wanted to barf.

"I can't believe you all came out here just for this," Kit said,
looking up at Matt, Veronica, and Gus.

"I wouldn't miss this for the world, Kitten," Matt cooed.
Veronica and Gus agreed.

KitKat? Kitty? Kitten? I excused myself and walked away. I
couldn't watch this. I headed straight for the bar. I took a seat.
Ray looked at me and nodded. He brought me a beer.

Over the next hour, I stayed posted up at the bar. A few people came over to chat with me, but then Kit appeared next to
me. I could tell she had been drinking by how flush her cheeks
were.

"You can't just sit here all night. Let's dance!" she said,
pulling me off the barstool.

A group of Kit's friends had cleared a space and started dancing. Kit must have sensed my hesitation, because she never let go of my hand, even when we reached the dance floor. She gave me a sultry smile, and I couldn't resist her. I pulled her close to me. There was a mischievous sparkle in her eye. I let my hand find its way to her hips and she smiled up at me as we danced.

When the first song ended, I felt a hand on my shoulder. I turned to see Matt. "Hey, can I cut in?" He winked at Kit and looked back at me. "Do you mind?"

I stepped back and nodded. Kit had a surprised look, but I gave her a reassuring smile because, as soon as I stepped away, Matt stepped between us. I saw Kit try to peek around him as dancing friends closed in around them. I sighed and headed back to the bar. I was kidding myself if I thought I could handle being just friends with Kit in situations like this.

Soon after, Aunt Rita appeared in the middle of the crowd with a large cake that said "Happy 30th Birthday, Kit!" The crowd broke out into song. Kit was glowing as she waited for the song to finish so she could blow out her candles. The whole time Matt stood next to her with his hand gently pressed against her lower back. When Kit leaned forward and blew out the candles, Matt spun her around and hugged her again. I caught a glimpse of Kit's face, and she looked happy. Maybe this is what she wanted all along—to find her way back to Matt. The thought crushed me. It was more than I could handle. I turned and headed back to the bar, I asked Ray to close out my tab. When he brought me my bill, Ray, a man who almost never spoke, paused, and said in a gruff voice, "Have you thought about telling her how you feel?"

"Nah, man. It wouldn't do any good." I dropped bills onto the bar, nodded goodbye to him, and left without looking back.

I could feel myself slipping into a mood, and I knew I just needed to be alone. I didn't want to ruin Kit's night. I headed back to the house. When I finally got up to my room, I was surprised by how cold it was. Even though it was March, there was a chill in the night air, and this old house felt like an icebox. I changed into some sweat pants and a long sleeve shirt to try and warm up, but the room was still chilly. I sighed and went back downstairs to the kitchen to get firewood off the back porch.

I picked three logs off the top of the pile of firewood. When I got back into the kitchen, Kit was standing by the island waiting on me.

"Hey," she said softly. "Can I help you with that?"

"Kit, is everything okay?" I looked around to see if she was alone. "Why aren't you at your party?"

"Party was over." Kit shrugged. "We had cut the cake, done all that. I saw you leave. I wondered if everything was okay. Veronica gave me a ride home."

"Oh, what about Matt?" I tried not to sound salty. "You two aren't hanging out tonight?"

"Um, no," Kit said cautiously, as if picking up on my jealousy.

"I'm sure he didn't like that. He seemed pretty determined tonight." I shut the door to the back porch with my foot and stood at the bottom of the kitchen stairs.

"Maybe," Kit shrugged. "I talked to Matt. He does want to get back together, but he knows I'm not interested in anything serious right now."

"Got it," I said, trying not to seem cold.

"Want help starting that fire?" she asked. "It does get pretty cold at night."

Kit opened a kitchen drawer and pulled out a box of extra-long matches. At which point, I realized what Kit already seemed to know; I needed help starting this fire. I just shrugged. "If you want to."

Kit followed me up the back stairs and down the hall. I pushed my door open with my hip. The room was still dark. I crossed the room to put the firewood in the rack. I had only brought up a few pieces.

"It's really cold for March." Kit shivered as she knelt by the fireplace and suggested, "Maybe you could go get three or four more logs. I'll get these started." I listened to Kit. I needed the space. When I got back to my room, Kit was still kneeling by the fireplace. A warm, orange light flickered across the walls in the room as she adjusted the logs with a black iron stoker.

"Thanks, this is great," I said as I put the extra logs into the firewood rack. I leaned against the mantel. "I probably wouldn't have been able to get it started on my own."

Kit moved one of the logs onto the fire. We were quiet while we watched the bark on the log turn black then amber and eventually catch fire.

Kit shifted slightly. She kept her eyes on the fire and asked, "Is everything okay? You seem mad."

"I'm not," I said, rubbing my brow.

"Well, I just wanted to tell you thanks for helping make the surprise birthday party happen. I was really surprised," Kit said. She stood up and stepped closer to me. She looked gorgeous by the glow of the fireplace. When I didn't move away, she put her hand on my chest. I could feel my heart pounding. Kit making a move was something I had fantasized about since Christmas Eve. I wanted more than anything to kiss her, but instead I blew a little air out of my mouth and said, "Kit, I can't."

"You can't?" Kit's expression immediately changed to one of confusion. She stepped back.

I scrambled to undo the hurt. "I know you're enjoying not being tied down and casually dating, but I can't be casually involved with you, Kit."

"What do you mean? You can casually date everyone in town, but not me?" Kit huffed. She crossed her arms.

"That's rich. I haven't even been on a date since I met you. You're the one going out on dozens of dates," I retorted. Kit's jaw dropped. She turned to leave but I put my hand out and caught her. "That was out of line. I'm sorry."

Kit crossed her arms and looked down at the floor. Without looking at me she said, "I just don't understand. If you aren't interested in me, then why would you be so nice to me? What's wrong with me?"

I said softly. "Kit, look at me." I gently lifted her chin so that we were looking at each other. Her eyes were sad. I felt a pang in my chest. I took a deep breath and said, "The reason I don't want to have a casual thing with you isn't because you aren't wonderful. Kit, you're absolutely perfect. And it's not because you aren't beautiful, because you are the most beautiful woman I've ever known."

13

Kit

A surge of confusion outweighed my embarrassment and I demanded, "Then what is it, William. What's wrong with me?"

William's jaw tensed. I could see the flex in his jaw and neck as he tried to stay patient and calm. He shook his head. "Kit, it's not you. No, it's me."

"Oh my god," I cried. "This is what you tell every woman. And I'm so stupid because you even admitted to me on Christmas Eve that you tell women this bullshit when they get to be too much for you."

William shook his head. "No, it's not the same, Kit. I want you to get to do exactly what you want. If you're happy dating and not being tied down, that's what you should do."

I shook my head, angry that I could be so stupid. "I can't believe I was so wrong about this."

"What do you mean?" William's composure began to dissolve. "This is nothing like any of the other women I've dated in the past."

"You know what. You're right. I'm not like those women. Because I'm not a supermodel. Because you fucked those women in your oh-so-noble transactional and transparent way. But with me, you draw me in close and then push me away and act like I'm...I'm...not enough...and you're an asshole for doing that to me." My face was hot with anger and embarrassment. In any other circumstance, I would have apologized for calling someone an asshole. Actually, I would never have done that, but William brought out a side of me that was unknown before. When I was with him, all my feelings were supercharged, overheated. I lost my reason and composure. I let out a frustrated sigh as I twisted my body to shake William's hands from my arms.

"I'm sorry." William's face looked hurt. "I'm sorry that I hurt you.""I just don't get it," I said. "Why would you spend all that time with me over the Christmas holiday? Why would you kiss me on New Year's Eve? Why would you walk me home from the library every night when I close? Why would you offer to bring me to my surprise party, then disappear during the party, only to now tell me that you can't?" I turned my face away from him. "You can, William. You just don't want to." I started to leave but William caught my arm. I looked up at him.

His face had changed. Before I could storm off, William wrapped his arm around me. I felt his hand on my face, then the sudden press of his lips against mine. William kissed me hard, as if this was the explanation I needed, and I felt myself melt into him.

My hands spread across his muscular chest. William pulled his face away. His eyes dark and serious, he said with a low voice, "You're wrong about me. This is different. I can't be casual with you because every time I get to experience a new part of you, I want more. You're all I think about. I am constantly thinking about ways to be near you, closer to you. It scares me because I've never felt this way."

I gasped, at a loss for words. William's eyes searched my face. He pulled me closer to him. He said softly, "And, I'm scared because I know if we go any further, there will be no turning back for me, but if that's what you want, then I'm yours, even if it destroys me."

I pressed into him and William responded. He kissed me again, hard and eager. Hearing William's confession ignited something within me. The furtive longing I'd been harboring for him was now blazing inside of me.

William pulled away from our kiss. He pressed his forehead against mine. My heart was pounding. I felt his hands move from my waist to my ass, eagerly grabbing at me. "Tell me you want this," William said in a low voice, almost a growl.

My heart was racing. I nodded, still stunned and breathless, but every part of me longed for more.

William shook his head no. "Tell me, Kit. Tell me you want me."

"I want you, William." As soon as his name escaped my lips, he lifted me up. I wrapped my legs around his waist, cupped his face in my hands, leaned forward, and kissed him. William carried me to his bed and gently sat me on the edge of the mattress. The bed was high enough off the ground that he stood between my legs, our hips perfectly aligned. He held me close to him as his hand slid across my jaw, and he leaned in for another kiss. A warm longing started deep in my belly and spread throughout my body. William moved from my lips to my earlobe, then made a trail along my neck. His large hands palmed my breast through my dress. I let out a jagged breath as I buckled into him. I could hear William breathe a gentle moan against me as he felt my body.

William sat back with a hungry expression on his face. With one quick motion, he ripped my dress open. I gasped, and a crooked smile crossed his lips. I let the sleeves of my dress fall off my shoulders, and it crumpled around my hips. William quickly wrapped his arms around me again. This time he unlatched the hook of my bra, pulled it off me, and dropped it to the floor. My skin tingled at his touch. I tugged at his shirt, and William quickly pulled it over his head.

Shadows from the fireplace danced across William's muscular chest and abs. When our skin touched, I felt an electric sensation run across my whole body. A tingling that made me gasp softly.

William whispered into my ear, "You feel this, too. I know you do."

William pulled back so he could look at my face. I nodded. He leaned forward and kissed me softly on the lips. Then he laid me down on the bed.

"You're so beautiful," he whispered into my ear. His mouth moved across my cheek, to my neck, then across my collarbone. My body was eager to feel the pressure of his hard kiss again, but William's touch became soft and exploratory. The dramatic contrast from the passionate hungry kiss before made me realize that William was in control. A current of pleasure hummed through my body, surging where he touched me. My back tensed longingly as his hands explored my exposed soft middle with a light sensual touch, gently progressing up. I ached to feel him. Finally, William firmly cupped my breast, and I felt the hot wet pressure of his mouth on their crests—at first softly, then rougher and more insistent. I moaned as the sensation of his touch intensified. My hips pressed against his as my back arched, pressing me further into his mouth. His teeth grazed my nipples.

I wrapped my legs around his waist, pulling him against me. I could feel his hard arousal through his pants.

One of his hands skated up my thigh and under my skirt. I heard his satisfied sigh when he found the soft, silky fabric of my panties wet with my longing. William hooked my panties in his thumb and pulled them down. I lifted my hips so they slid off me. William raised himself up and stood above me. I felt his fingers gently stroking but not entering me. I careened under his teasing touch. He watched with a look of satisfaction as I twisted at every one of his light touches, but he never entered me.

Sensing that I was becoming desperate for a release, William knelt between my legs. My dress bunched around my waist obscured my view of him, but one of his hands pushed beneath me and grabbed my ass. The other hand gently pulled back my dress so that he had a clear view of all of me. His lips grazed my inner thighs. William touched and kissed every place except for where I needed him. I felt an earnest throbbing between my legs where I wanted him.

I called out his name, almost pleading. "William."

"You're so beautiful. More beautiful than I could have imagined," William said, kissing me softly on my mound. I trembled with desire. I saw William adjust just enough so that he could watch my face, see my expression. Then he finally pulled me to the edge of the bed and against his mouth. Pleasure surged through my body as William used an intensifying combination of kissing, licking, and sucking. An almost unbearable vibration of pleasure rippled through my body. I grasped at the comforter on the bed. William's hums and sighs resonated through my whole body, and I begged for more.

He started off with methodical and precise movements, but as I became more excited and more aroused, so did William. I could feel his fingers dig into my thighs as my cries excited him. My ragged breaths and moans told him I was close. Even though it felt unbelievable, my body tried to jerk away from the intense source of pleasure that was William. My hips rose off the bed as I neared climax, but William refused to let me move away from this release. Holding me by my waist, his hands tangled in my dress, William pinned me to the bed, to him, until I finally broke and climaxed. I gasped for air, my heart pounding.

My whole body was humming. I felt William hover above me, then I felt the bare skin of his chest against my breast. When he kissed me, I could taste myself on his lips. My hands traced down his muscular back. Then my fingers pushed past the waistband of his pants. I could feel the length of his arousal against me as we kissed.

"William, I want you. I need to feel you inside me," I whispered in his ear. He let out a grunt and soft groan as I stroked his erection. "Do you have a condom?"

William didn't waste any time. He pushed himself up off the bed and crossed the room. The lights from the bathroom spilled onto the floor as he rummaged around in his bathroom.

I got up off the bed and let my dress fall to the floor. My braid had gotten twisted, so I pulled my hair tie from the braid and let my hair fall loose across my shoulders and back. I felt a chill in the air as I waited for William.

I crossed the room and added a log to the fire to warm up the room. A smile spread across my face as I realized where I was and what had happened. My body was still singing from William's touch, but I felt something new rising up inside of me, a feeling that I had never felt before.

"Kit." I turned to see William. He had stepped out of the bathroom and was looking at me by the fire. "Your hair is down."

"Oh," I said, looking down at my hair that fell across my shoulders. "I guess it fell out of my braid."

"I've never seen your hair down." William's voice was almost a whisper. "You look beautiful. Absolutely perfect."

I stood up, in awe of his perfect form. William had shed his clothes, so his full erection was visible and impressive. He held up the foil-wrapped condom between his fingers. "I found one."

I quickly closed the distance between us and plucked the wrapper from his hand. "Let me."

William smiled, but the surprised look on his face when I dropped to my knees in front of him was perfect. I gently rubbed the tip of William against my lips, teasing him just as he had teased me. He shuddered and said in a hoarse whisper, "Kit, I won't last long if we..."

Before he could finish his sentence, I took the tip into my mouth. William groaned. I looked up to watch him. I moved one of my hands up and down his shaft. With my other hand, I gently tugged at William's balls. He moaned. I took his hand and guided it to lightly touch the back of my head. I looked up at him as if to give him permission to be in control, then I used both my hands and mouth to move up and down.

At first, William's touch was light in my hair. I could feel him playing with my curls, but then, as I took more and more of him into my mouth, I felt him pushing, guiding me. He groaned when he hit the back of my throat, and pulled himself out of my mouth. I looked up at him and saw the tight flex in his neck and jaw. I knew he was getting close. I unwrapped the condom and gently pushed it down his length. He pulled me to my feet and said, almost urgently, "Kit, I want you. I need to fuck you."

As if it took no effort, William picked me up and brought me to the bed. He placed me in the center and covered me with his body. I loved the feeling of his weight as he settled between my thighs. I felt his length against me but not inside of me. He kissed me gently and said, "You are so beautiful."

I let my hands run over his shoulders and rippling back muscles as he pulled me into a deep kiss. I pressed my hips against him and moaned as I felt his teeth on my lip. William's hand palmed my breast then slid between my legs. I felt his fingers between my legs. Then he gently parted me, touching my swollen clit. I moaned. And he whispered into my ear, "Baby, you're so wet for me."

"Yes," I gasped as I felt him push a finger slowly in and out of me as his lips nuzzled my neck and cheek. I reached down to feel William's erection and guided him closer to me. "Please, William. I want you."

I heard the quake of need in William's breathing, and he gently pushed himself into me. I whimpered at the pressure, and he pulled back so he could see my face. Our eyes locked, he asked, "Is it okay?"

I pushed my hips up into him to take more and William said in a soothing, low voice, "Slow, I want to take it slow. I need you, but I don't want to hurt you."

William kissed me softly as he gently rocked himself into me. My body released and took more and more of William until finally he was deep inside me. We found an increasing rhythm that intensified the waves of heat radiating in my lower belly. As the pleasure intensified, William's low, hoarse groans turned into moans. He growled into my ear, "You feel so good. Kit, you feel so good."

I moaned and felt such an intense pleasure explode within me that my back arched into William. I pressed my hands against his chest as my body suddenly contracted, squeezing around William as I climaxed. I felt the ripple of muscles in William's chest as he finished with me.

William's dark eyes searched my face, and he said, "Kit, are you okay? You're shaking."

I wrapped my legs around him, and he leaned forward giving me a soft kiss. I let out a deep sigh and said, "I've never come like that before. That was so intense. It was almost scary; it was so good."

William kissed me again and held me. "I've never felt anything like that either."

I closed my eyes as three words swirled in my mind, and I pushed them away. I felt a flutter in my stomach as William's hand cupped my face. An exhilarating chill ran down my spine as I heard him whisper into my ear. "You're perfect. We're perfect together."

CHAPTER 14: WILLIAM

14

William

I lay next to Kit on the bed. I nuzzled my face into her neck and hair. Kit smiled and rolled onto her side. I sat up on the edge of the bed, quickly removed the condom, and put it into the trash can by the bed. Kit sat up behind me and pressed her breast against my back as she leaned her arms against my shoulders. I smiled over my shoulder at her. Curls fell over her own shoulder. I liked the familiar and affectionate way Kit draped herself on me.

Kit said, "Well, I guess I won't be going on any more casual dates."

I raised an eyebrow, looked over my shoulder, and laughed. "And why is that?"

"I don't have anything to wear. You ripped the buttons off my best date dress."

I laughed and said, "Good riddance to the date dress then."

Kit's laugh filled the room. I turned and hooked an arm around her waist and pulled her into my lap. Kit squealed and threw her head back, laughing. I laid back on the bed, and Kit adjusted so that she was straddling me. She leaned forward and her hair fanned to create a curtain around our faces. She kissed me softly. I felt it rising up in my chest, a feeling I had never felt before. I wanted to say it, but it felt caught in my throat.

15

Kit

It hadn't been a dream. Watching William sleep next to me gave me a flutter in my stomach that was a mix of excitement and nerves. His handsome face was relaxed with a slight smile. I closed my eyes trying to slow my heart. Feeling William stir next to me, I opened my eyes in time to see his light up when he saw me lying next to him.

He pulled me toward him into a warm snuggle. "Happy birthday, Kit."

I smiled and sat up, the blankets falling away from me. A spark was in William's eyes as they moved across my body in a way that made me feel powerful and desired. I leaned forward and kissed him. "I promised Veronica we'd get breakfast before she heads back to Atlanta."

William nodded, "It's going to be hard to let you go, but I take solace in the fact that I get to watch you get up and walk across the room to get your dress." His crooked smile appeared. I felt his hands glide along my thigh.

"Would you like to join me for dinner tonight? Aunt Rita and I usually go out to some kind of dinner and movie," I said, trying to be nonchalant.

"I would love that," William said. "Maybe we could watch one of our shows after."

The way he said our shows gave me a little flutter in my stomach, and I jumped a little with excitement. It made me realize that even though last night was our first time together, that moment had been months in the making. "That's a great idea. I would love that."

William's eyes were wide and his crooked smile had spread into a full grin. "I'm sorry. I forgot what we were talking about. Your joyful...bounce was...distracting," William said as he pulled me closer to him.

We folded against each other and converged, touching and kissing. His muscular thigh pushed between my own and he pulled me against him. I kissed him again and sighed as he moved me against his thigh and hip in just the right way to ignite a warm pleasure inside me. I would have let William do anything at that moment, but my cell phone began loudly playing "Best Friend" by Saweetie.

When he pulled his head back from our kiss, he said with amusement, "Veronica has a cool ringtone. Do I get a cool ringtone?"

I laughed. "You must earn the custom ringtone," I said, hoisting myself up to get my phone before the song got to the second verse. "I can't spend ninety-nine cents for a ringtone on just anyone!"

William propped himself up on one elbow and as he promised, he watched me cross the room to find my cell phone, which I silenced before it broke out into the full female empowerment anthem that it was. I slipped my dress back on and gathered my bra and panties. I hurried upstairs to shower and get ready before another renter or Aunt Rita caught me in the hallway or stairwell.

Veronica was already at the diner when I arrived. I slid into the booth. "Sorry, I'm running a few minutes behind."

"No worries, Birthday Girl." Veronica beamed. "You're glowing."

"Must be that extra bit of spring sunshine," I said, opening the menu. "Where's Gus?"

"Oh, he and Matt went to play golf." Veronica looked at the menu as she pushed her lips forward. "I think Matt is going to head to Charlston later today. He's got an interview there and said it might be good for him to get there a few days early to prepare."

"That's great," I said. "He called me this morning and we talked. I'm sure he'll knock their socks off. So, how's it been going back to work?"

Veronica knew me well enough to know that I was changing the subject away from Matt on purpose, and since it was my birthday, she was going to let this go for now. We slid into our regular banter about work and gossip.

After we ordered, Veronica asked, "Any special plans for your birthday?"

"Well, this breakfast is pretty special," I said. Veronica pretended to give an elaborate curtsey from her seat in the booth.

I added as I took a sip of my coffee, "And I think I'm going to go to dinner with Aunt Rita and William later. William and I have been watching Game of Thrones on Tuesdays and my favorite holiday movies on Thursdays. We...um...missed watching our show last night." I smirked.

Veronica's eyes widened when she heard William's name. After New Year's Day, my pride had prevented me from admitting to anyone, especially Veronica, how much time I had been spending with William over the last few months. I licked my lips and tried to act cool as a cucumber.

"Well, I did notice that William was the one who brought you to the party last night. Aunt Rita said he would be the best person, which I thought was odd since you said he was literally the worst." She put air quotes around the words literally the worst.

"So, you're still going with the 'we're just friends' thing with William?" Veronica said, placing air quotes around friends.

"What's with the air quotes?" I joked.

Veronica ignored me. "Is he just one of your casual friends you've been hanging out with?"

"Um, maybe not after last night," I said quietly, looking around. I could feel my cheeks turn pink.

Veronica gave me a wide-eyed look. "He's so hot. Did y'all just like make out, or do it? Was the sex good?"

I didn't respond. My lips pushed down into a modest grin. Veronica read my face and body language. She laughed. "Okay, gurrrl."

I shushed her and we both looked around.

"Relax," Veronica teased. "No one is eavesdropping on the town librarian."

"Well," I said. "Maybe I need a few drinks before I loosen up enough to give all the details, but it was amazing."

"Why didn't you lead with this?!" Veronica demanded.

"I don't know. I just, I think it all just kind of hit me," I said. I paused, and then trying to temper my excitement, I said, "But it was the best sex I have ever had. Like for posterity's sake, I need you, as my best friend and life witness, to know that on the very last night of my twenties I had life-altering, mind-blowing sex."

Veronica laughed and gave me a high five. "That's what I'm talking about. Going out there and having a hot birthday sex hook-up!"

I paused and said, "Let's just get the elephant out of the room. Matt."

Veronica nodded solemnly and crossed her arms. "Okay, let's do this."

Ever since we were freshmen in college, we had our way of dealing with whatever questionable situation was the 'elephant in the room.' The one friend would ask a series of pointed questions to make sure the other had considered all the possibilities.

I nodded. "Okay, hit me."

"Do you still have feelings for Matt?"

"I love him as a friend."

"Do you remember that his family is loaded?"

"Yes, hard to forget."

"Do you remember that he is also a doctor, so he will have his own independent wealth?"

"It has been brought to my attention before."

"Are you considering the amazing olive-skinned, beautiful children you would have with Matt?"

"If he even has kids!" I pointed out. "He's on the fence about having his own children, and the kids would be cute because of me, not him."

"Fair."

"Do you realize that Matt and my dear husband, Gus, will still be best friends, so when Matt does settle down and get married, I'll have to hang out with Matt and his new partner? Like engagement parties, bridal showers, baptisms..."

"I promise not to hold it against you or get my feelings hurt, and I promise not to expect Gus to love whoever I end up with."

Veronica was quiet for a minute, and then turned and whispered, "But like they are so, so rich..."

I let out a little chuckle. "I know, girl. But I was never into Matt for the money. I hope he makes some nice lady so happy and so rich." I smiled at Veronica. "He is a nice guy, and honestly, the relationship made sense in college. But once you and Gus started the next phase of your lives, the big wedding and house and now the baby, I just realized I didn't really want to do those things with Matt. I always went along with what everyone else liked, and it was never a problem because I never made a fuss. I think, because of the timing, everyone thought it was about my mom, like grief made me blow up my relationship, but it wasn't just the grief."

Veronica's eyes shifted, and I knew she was listening. I sighed and continued as I stirred butter into my bowl of grits. "Really, it was like it was the last lesson my mom got to teach me. Because watching her die so young, I realized I needed to start living for me, the way she did. My mom died with no regrets. She lived her life exactly the way she wanted to. Being a single mom in a town like this was not easy, but this is where she wanted to be. So, I'm working on doing what feels right to me and on telling people the truth about how I'm feeling—not just telling them what will make hard moments easier." I took a deep breath. It felt good to unload that. I looked anxiously at Veronica to see how she'd react.

Veronica reached across the table and squeezed my hand. We were quiet for a moment. Then she clucked her tongue and said, "Wow, that was some good dick you had last night. Like better than five years of grief therapy." I let a laugh burst from my lips. Veronica shook her head chuckling. "But seriously, good for you, Kit."

We ate and chatted for a bit, then Veronica said, "Okay, are you ready for the next elephant?"

I wasn't sure where she was going to go, but I said. "Yes, shoot."

"So, you no longer think William is an obnoxious grifter?"

"Okay, I never called him a grifter, but correct. I don't think that anymore."

"How did this happen? I thought you had sworn him off after New Year's Eve. Like really iced him out."

I made a tsk sound. "Yeah, so I'm learning that I jumped to some conclusions about William and the lady I saw him with on New Year's Day. My bad. And even though I was an ice queen, he still walked me home every Tuesday and Thursday night to spend time with me."

"I see. I didn't realize you two were spending so much time together." Veronica had a playful glint in her eye. "And do you still think he's going to move when this redevelopment project is over?"

"I'm not really sure." I smiled slyly. "I think I'm okay not knowing that right now."

"Wow, major departure from the typical calculating, measured, and protective Kit approach." Veronica gave me a little smile. "I approve of this development."

"Thanks," I said, bopping my head back and forth in a celebratory way.

"So, last set of questions: What about the land?" Veronica raised her eyebrows. "How will this impact your negotiations regarding the land if you and Aunt Rita decide to sell? And if you don't sell, is that going to sour things between you?" Veronica paused and said carefully, "I think you're drop dead gorgeous and all men would love to be in William's shoes, so I'm sure he's attracted to you, but is there any chance he's doing any of this to manipulate you to sell the land?"

I knew Veronica was just pointing out the elephant in the room, but I wasn't ready to think about all these hard unknowns. It took so little for me to slip into a dark cloud of overthinking and anxiety, and I just wanted to stay in a headspace where I could enjoy what was finally happening with William. I shifted my weight in the booth. "I hadn't really thought about it. I don't think he'd try to manipulate me. I'm the one who initiated everything last night." I cleared my throat. I didn't want to sound naive, but I really didn't think William would do something like that to me. I said, "Really, William hasn't mentioned selling the land in months, but I'm more open to it now than I was last year," I admitted.

"Whaaat?" Veronica mockingly gasped. "Is it the huge price tag this river front property is destined to go for that has changed your mind, or the amazing sex?"

"Ha, no, it's actually been hearing the folks in town talk about how the changes William is bringing will help their businesses. I realized that if the old-timers can be excited about change, I should be too. He is doing a lot for the town. He's helping a group start an entrepreneurship center. It's really cool."

Veronica stirred her spoon in her coffee slowly and said quietly, "Okay, but if William screws you over in any way, in business or in love, I promise to start vicious rumors in Atlanta real estate circles that all his properties are roach and rat-infested."

I laughed and said, "I love you too, Veronica."

"Like the big roaches that fly at you." Veronica nodded solemnly. Then her lips curled into a smile. "Okay. But like, for real. Life-changing? Come on. You gotta give me the details." When I leaned forward and whispered a juicy detail to her, Veronica's eyes widened, and I laughed.

So far, my thirtieth birthday had been perfect. I woke up next to William and had breakfast with Veronica. I just couldn't imagine it getting better, but it did. I went home and took a nap, and Aunt Rita woke me up right before dinner. She was sitting at the foot of my bed when I fully woke. I stretched like a cat, and, still groggy, I said, "Oh! I'm sorry. Did I oversleep for dinner?"

Aunt Rita crossed her legs and daintily rested her wrist atop her knees. "Actually, my dear, as we speak, a very handsome man is downstairs making you a birthday dinner."

I felt giddy and couldn't hide my smile. Aunt Rita playfully pinched my legs. "I knew you two liked each other. What has taken so long?"

"I guess I just had to get out of my own way," I said with a sigh.

"Well, I'm not going to say I told you so..." Aunt Rita said, examining her nails cooly, "But I did tell you so."

I rolled my eyes and threw a pillow at her. I hopped out of bed.

Aunt Rita headed for my door. "William said dinner will be ready in fifteen minutes if you want to run a comb through your hair. I offered to leave you two alone for dinner, but he insisted I join. I invited a date, so I wouldn't be a third wheel."

"That sounds perfect," I said. "I'll be down in fifteen minutes."

As soon as Aunt Rita closed the door, I quickly undressed. I went into my bathroom and shaved places I hadn't thought about in five years. I found and put on a matching black bra and panty set, then pulled one of my sundresses over them. I looked at my hair in the mirror. Aunt Rita was right. My nap had created an interesting cowlick that I couldn't quite tame. I decided a loose braid would have to do.

As I examined myself in the mirror, I realized I hadn't given this much thought to how I looked since New Year's Eve. I hurried down the stairs. When I got down to the kitchen, I could hear Aunt Rita laughing. She was seated in the dining room. A man a few years older than her had his arm around her chair, and William was placing a platter in front of them. When Aunt Rita saw me, she announced, "Here she is. Our birthday girl."

William looked up. "Hey, happy birthday. You look great." I could feel myself blush. William pulled out a chair for me, and I joined them at the table.

"Kit, this is Vernon." Aunt Rita said. "He's a doctor at the regional hospital."

"Nice to meet you," I said. "William, this smells amazing. I had no idea you could cook."

"Yeah, I learned from my mom. She worked in a lot of different types of kitchens, but she primarily taught me to cook Filipino food." William explained to Vernon, "This is a chicken dish called adobo that you eat over rice, and these noodles are called pancit. You're supposed to eat them on your birthday for good luck and long life."

"And these are lumpia!" Aunt Rita said taking a bite of a slender fried eggroll. Vernon laughed as he did the same. "Everyone who has ever worked in a hospital with a Filipina nurse has had the pleasure of eating lumpia at least once."

"This is so nice. I really appreciate it," I said trying hard not to gush. William went back into the kitchen to get serving spoons. When he sat down in the chair next to me, his thighs brushed mine. He put his hand on my knee. I felt a charge run through my body and a warm, pleasant sensation begin to collect in my lower belly.

"Well, I'm particularly appreciative because I am so useless in the kitchen. A home-cooked meal is always a special treat," Aunt Rita said as she poured everyone a glass of wine, and we started dinner. Aunt Rita and Vernon carried the conversation with endless and entertaining stories about working in a hospital. I felt grateful because all I could think about were the occasional electrifying brushes of Wiliam's hand on my leg as we ate dinner. William was careful not to draw attention, but each time he touched me he pushed my dress a little higher.

When Vernon and Aunt Rita went into the kitchen to get dessert, I saw the flame in William's eye as I rubbed my thighs together in such a way that his fingers were brushed between them. He swallowed hard. When my aunt returned with slices of cake and scoops of ice cream, William pulled his hand back and draped it around the back of my chair. I had liked the flirty touch of his hand on my thigh, but I was surprised to find that the familiar and assuming way William put his arm around me gave me butterflies.

Vernon was right behind Aunt Rita, and he brought cups of coffee.

I exclaimed, "This is so nice. I can't remember the last time we had dinner together like this."

Vernon settled back into his chair. "So, William. Rita tells me you're a big part of the development around the regional hospital."

"That's right," William said as he sat up to eat his cake. His hand fell from the back of my chair and briefly pressed against the small of my back before he used it to pick up his coffee cup. Every time William touched me, I was so acutely aware that I hardly heard their conversation.

"Well, I know all the nurses and staff are excited about some potential housing options," Aunt Rita said. "We're simply priced out of most of the homes in Blue Ridge and Elijay."

"Yeah, Creekstone is uniquely positioned to provide affordable housing to young and middle-aged professionals," William said. "We've been looking at different parcels of land to build homes for nurses and first responders. We're even looking at programs to help seniors who might be interested in downsizing from their large family homes to a senior living community."

"How would that work?" Aunt Rita asked.

"Well, we'd start by building affordable senior living communities. The ones in Elijay and Blue Ridge cater to very wealthy retired individuals, and that's not really the demographic of the seniors in Creekstone. So, the first thing we'd do is build desirable homes for seniors who have a more modest retirement income. We'd help them with either the sale of their home or setting their home up to be a rental property so they could afford a senior living community."

Vernon nodded. "That would be great. It would create more demand for outpatient centers that serve seniors."

"That's right. We'd want to create an entire ecosystem around the hospital," William said. "And part of that is having affordable homes in a community that's inviting to young and middle-aged professionals."

William continued, "I'm working with the mayor of Creekstone right now to make some improvements to the schools because that's a big part of attracting families."

My ears perked up a little. "How would you do that?"

"Similar strategies," William said. "It's important to have high quality teachers, so teacher pay is a big issue—but so are resources. We're looking at proposing a local option sales tax to help fund both structural repairs and updated materials in the schools. The tax would target goods and services accessed by visitors so that locals wouldn't feel the burden of the tax too much."

"Of course, the hospital foundation is working on raising money for local schools as well. I just saw a message go out about making donations to help promote medical career pathways," Aunt Rita chimed in.

"Yeah," Vernon noted. "I sat in on a meeting with the college and high school staff about recruiting students as early as middle school."

"Wow," I said sitting back. "Is that really early?"

"Not at all. It's important to get students into STEM fields early so that they get a good foundation in math and science. It helps the students see where they could end up in the medical field. It makes it all feel more possible."

"Sounds like a lot of positive things happening in Creekstone," I said.

"Truly, for the first time in ages, it feels like we have momentum going in the right direction," Aunt Rita said. "Your mom would have loved to have seen this."

I felt William's hand on my back again, and I turned to see his comforting smile.

Aunt Rita said, "Vernon and I will put this food away. You two kids go on and enjoy your evening."

"Are you sure?" I asked.

"Absolutely positive," Vernon said.

"After we clean up the kitchen, I'm going to Vernon's to watch the new show, The Pitt. Everyone says it's as good as ER, but with better medical accuracy!"

William and I left the dining room and headed into the kitchen. I stopped at the fridge and pulled out two beers for us. We headed into the front room to watch TV. I sat on the sofa in my usual spot, picked up the remote, and navigated to my list of holiday shows. William sat in his usual spot on the other end of the sofa.

I turned. My jaw dropped. I gave a scornful look at the sofa cushion sitting empty between us.

Laughter burst from William, and he said, "I've been wanting to do this for months." He reached across the sofa, hooked an arm around my waist, pulled me toward him, and perfectly enveloped me between his chest and arm. I stretched my legs out so that I was comfortably propped against William.

I instinctively rested my head against him, and he leaned forward to whispered in my ear, "Last night was perfect, and I cannot wait to have you again." I felt the warm tingle in my lower belly as his low voice passed through me. I rubbed his thigh with my hand. He continued, "But this, Kit. Holding you just like this. I've never felt this before. I can't even begin to describe how good this feels."

I sighed. I couldn't have agreed more. I couldn't believe how amazing it felt to finally be in William's arms. I put my hands on his chest and looked up at him. He leaned forward and softly kissed me. "Happy birthday, Kit."

16

William

The next two weeks were like a dream. Kit and I spent every second we could together. Mundane tasks became exciting because they were spent with Kit. Everything from grocery shopping, meal prep, laundry, hell, even brushing our teeth, became something I looked forward to simply because Kit was there. My daily routine revolved around her schedule. I went with her on her morning runs. We made breakfast and went to work at the same time. Usually, I had lunch meetings for work. But every afternoon, I would stop by the library and bring her an iced coffee, just the way she liked it, ridiculously sweet, just to get to see her. Most evenings, I met Kit when she was finished with her shift, and we enjoyed a slow walk home together, soaking in the last of the daylight and warm spring air.

My favorite part of everyday was sitting on the sofa with Kit after dinner. It was the most familiar part of our day. Much like before her birthday, Kit and I would watch our shows, but now Kit leaned against me as we watched. I would drape my arm around her. While she watched TV, Kit would run her hand lightly over the back of mine, almost as if she didn't realize she was doing it. I especially loved the way she'd sit up slightly and turn her face to me whenever she had a thought she wanted to share. Every single time I looked down at her my heart swelled, and I wanted to kiss her.

I'd dated plenty of women, and while those relationships shared some of the same rhythm as what I had with Kit, they always felt like a means to an end. I always felt comfortable telling those women to take it or leave it when I decided to draw my boundary, and when they inevitably left, I felt some relief. But this was entirely different. I had gotten myself into uncharted territory. I wanted to go further, but I didn't know what that looked like. I didn't want to push Kit faster than she wanted to go. And this nagging voice in my head, eerily like Meredith's, kept reminding me this could all implode my career.

Meredith had decided to come to Creekstone to check on me before the board meeting. She called to say she'd meet me for lunch. I suggested we meet at The Pub. I knew Meredith was going to give me the third degree about the project and my relationship with Kit, but seeing her face when she walked into The Pub was well worth it. The Pub had its usual mix of a lunch crowd. The Blues Traveler song "Run-Around" played on the jukebox. Meredith slid her sunglasses down to the tip of her nose. I saw her chest rise and fall as she realized she didn't have a choice. I watched Meredith with her thin lips pressed together as she scanned the The Pub until she saw me seated at the bar. I gave her a little wave. She rolled her eyes and marched over. Meredith hoisted herself onto the barstool next to me and placed her bag in the stool on the other side. I gave her a moment to smooth her dress out and adjust her hair.

Ray appeared, handed Meredith a menu, and walked away without saying anything.

Meredith sighed. "Is anything edible here?"

"You'd be surprised. Don't knock it till you've tried it. You should order the steak salad," I offered. "It's my favorite thing on the lunch menu."

Meredith's lips were pushed down in a deep grimace as she looked over the menu and sarcastically muttered, "This place has a lunch and dinner menu. I guess I did underestimate it."

Ray appeared, and I ordered my lunch and a beer. I turned to Meredith who said, "I'll have the same. Thank you."

Ray reappeared with our beers and a bowl of pretzels.

Meredith waited for Ray to leave, then she picked up her beer and clinked her glass against mine as if we were in a toast. "Well, here's to almost being done with this project so you can get the hell out of here."

"Aww, come on, Meredith. It's not that bad. It's got endless charm and quite a bit of potential. Maybe I'll stay here," I said, taking a big gulp of beer. I looked at the beer and said, "That's refreshing."

Meredith turned and looked at me. She tilted her head to one side and said, "Have you joined a cult? Why do you still live here? This place is...is..."

I laughed. "Really, I like it, Meredith. I think Braithway was strategic in giving me this assignment. This project helped me plug into the community in a way that reminded me how important and impactful our work can really be. This fresh perspective will be important in my new role."

Meredith turned back toward the bar and mumbled, "Oh, I know you've plugged into someone, and that's why you really want to stay in Creekstone."

"Okay," I said with a bit of a warning tone. I didn't want to get into it with Meredith, so I said, "I have a plan. Just trust me."

Meredith looked genuinely curious as she turned, placing her elbow on the bar. "Please, do tell."

Meredith took a long sip of her beer, and I said, "I'm going to tell Braithway the truth."

Meredith spit out her beer. She started coughing dramatically. I patted her on her back, trying not to look annoyed. Ray appeared with our meals and raised an eyebrow as he sat them down in front of us. "She's fine. Wrong pipe. Could you get her some water, please?"

As soon as Ray returned with the water, Meredith took a sip and cleared her throat. She dabbed the water from the corner of her eyes.

"You okay?" I asked.

"Yes, yes. I just died a little." Meredith said, picking up her utensils and inspecting them for spots.

I rolled my eyes, and we ate in silence for a moment. Ray returned with two beers. I nodded, "Thanks, man." He nodded back.

Finally, Meredith said, "How exactly do you think it's going to work out when you tell Braithway the truth?"

I started to answer but then Meredith continued. "Do you think Braithway's going to be glad you couldn't keep your hands to yourself and had to go and mess around with a potential seller? Do you think that'll impress him somehow?"

I sat back and waited. Meredith continued, "Like, how is it going to look to the Board of Directors?"

When it seemed she'd gotten most of it out of her system, I said, "I'm going to tell him I've become friends and gotten involved with the family that owns the land in a way that presents a conflict, and I'm going to ask him to broker the deal for me."

Meredith put down her fork and picked up her cell phone. She started quietly scrolling on her phone.

"What are you doing?" I asked, trying not to sound annoyed.

"I'm updating my LinkedIn profile so that when Charles becomes the CEO and fires me, I'll already have some job leads lined up." She picked up her beer and took a sip as she turned her phone to show me her profile.

This time I didn't try to hide how annoyed I was. I rubbed my hands through my hair and sighed. "Meredith, I think Braithway will respect my honesty. Maybe it'll bite me in the ass in the end, but I am going to tell him just what I told you. I'm going to ask him to broker the deal himself, and more than likely, he'll appoint you or Charles to help me with it."

Meredith sat back. I could see her wheels turning. "Let's say you negotiate a deal yourself. Everyone will think you gave your girlfriend a huge break because, well, she's your girlfriend—and if you don't, she won't be your girlfriend anymore."

Meredith continued. "Now let's say someone else negotiates on behalf of Braithway & Randall. Are you really going to stand by and not help your girlfriend negotiate the best deal? Doesn't that conflict with your role at Braithway & Randall?"

I didn't respond. Meredith looked up at the ceiling before finally looking at me.

"This is a textbook case of conflict of interest, William." Meredith had a look of genuine concern on her face. "What's going on with you?"

"I don't know, Meredith." I sat back and watched Ray wiping down the counter space at the other end of the bar. I turned to her and said, "Did you know you're my best friend?"

I didn't have to look directly at Meredith to see she was taken aback. I kept my eyes fixed on Ray across the bar. "All I've ever focused on was my job and my mom. Everything in my life is wrapped up in my work, even my best friend. And for once, there's something else that feels more important to me than work. I know you understand this because I've seen the way Addison has changed you over the years; for the better, I might add." I looked at Meredith. Now she too was looking ahead at Ray methodically cleaning the bar.

"Okay," Meredith said, almost as if settling into her role as my best friend. "Just let me say this. If you and Kit are the real thing, I'm happy for you. I'm sure she's great. For me, as your friend," Meredith paused and swallowed. "As your best friend, I just want to make sure you have fully thought out the consequences this might have on your career. If you walk into Braithway's office next Monday and tell him this, it could change everything for you. Are you okay with that?"

I nodded.

Meredith sighed. "Is she your actual girlfriend? Have you two talked at all about if you're on the same page?"

The expression on my face must have been telling because she said. "Well, buddy. I guess you should start there." Meredith poked her salad with her fork and chuckled. "For the last fifteen years, you've actively avoided having this exact conversation with whoever you're sleeping with, and now you're the one sitting here, hearts in your eyes and butterflies in your stomach, wondering if Kit is in love with you."

Meredith patted me on the back. "Time to find out if this is limerence or love."

"Limerence?"

"You know? Sort of like an infatuation, a serious crush," Meredith explained between bites of salad. She thoughtfully waved her fork. "Clearly this is more than just lust for you. Someone as ruggedly handsome as you can get laid anytime."

I took a bite of salad. Did Meredith have a point? I had never felt this way about anyone, but truthfully, I didn't know what it meant to be infatuated or in love. How would I tell the difference?

Meredith must have noticed that I was worried because she said, "Look, normally, I'd say give it some time and just let it work itself out, but since your career is tied up in the outcome of this land sale, I feel like you need a clearer picture of where things are between you and Kit. It seems like you're pretty into it, but what about Kit? Has she ever been in love before? Is she the kind of person who would try to use her lady charms to manipulate you into giving her a better deal on the land?"

"Definitely not that kind of person," I said quickly and maybe a little too defensively. "But you're right, I do need to figure things out."

"Well, then I recommend doing something outside your normal routine. You're practically living together already. Do something besides playing house and having sex. Go on a trip. See Kit somewhere beside Creekstone. See how you feel about her then. See how she responds when you show or tell her how you're feeling." Meredith took a bite of salad.

"That's good advice," I acknowledged.

"I know," Meredith said as she looked down at her bowl and stirred the greens and steak. "This salad is really fucking good. You were right about that at least."

After we left The Pub, Meredith and I had back-to-back meetings with the city council and business owners. When we finished, I invited Meredith to stay for dinner, but she said she had to get back to the city because Addison was waiting for her.

I had taken what Meredith said to heart. Part of me felt like if something isn't broken, why fix it, but I also knew I needed more clarity. I'd been planning something special for Kit in Atlanta. Maybe I needed to move it up a little to get a better idea of where Kit's head was at.

I knew she was closing the library that day, so I met her there. She told me she had a few pieces of equipment to lock up and asked me to wait in her office. I sat in the chair by her desk. The office was small. There was barely enough room for a desk, two chairs, and a couple of filing cabinets and shelves. The mismatched furniture reminded me of library furniture from the late 1990s because of the mauve and beige colorway.

I noticed a letter on Kit's desk. It was addressed to her. I noticed an official seal from Harvard at the top of the letter, but I didn't get time to read it before Kit returned. She slid between me and her desk. Kit looked great that day. She was wearing a form-fitting button-down shirt and a pencil skirt. Her hair was pulled back into a bun. I stood up and kissed Kit. She took a step back, and I lifted her so that she sat on the edge of her desk. She pulled away from the kiss and whispered, "Library is all locked up."

"I wanted to ask you about something on your desk," I said, pulling back a bit.

"Is it this?" She asked between kisses as she slid my hands around her waist to her ass, which I gave a playful squeeze. When I didn't kiss her, Kit frowned.

"I love this," I said kissing Kit's forehead and squeezing her again, "But actually, I was wondering about that letter from Harvard that your cute ass is sitting on right now."

Kit's sly smile returned. "Are you reading my mail?"

"I suppose I would have if you weren't sitting on it," I admitted. Kit laughed and rolled all her weight to one leg. She pulled the paper out from under her and held it up.

"It's just the annual letter they send telling me I have remaining fellowship dollars and asking if I'd like to complete my fellowship," Kit said with a shrug. "I just have to write a letter back letting them know if I'd like to defer for another year."

Kit handed me the paper. I looked at it. I asked, trying to understand, "You're a student at Harvard?"

"Well, kind of. I had a graduate fellowship to do archives work through a national library foundation. It was interrupted when I took a sabbatical to come home and take care of my mom. Last year, I asked for an additional extension because our library didn't have another staff member to take over if I left, so they're wondering if I want to complete the fellowship during the fall semester."

"What are you thinking of doing?" I asked.

"I don't know. I'd have to give it some thought," Kit shrugged. She leaned back and rested her palms against her desk. "I guess Trent could step up and fill in for me while I was out."

"That's so impressive." I tried to sound neutral about the idea of Kit moving back to Washington D.C. "Would you stay in D.C., or would you move back to Georgia when you are done?"

Kit shrugged. "I don't know. These fellowships often turn into long term positions, but I haven't given it much thought."

I wanted to probe more but Kit was being so evasive. I didn't want to press her about the future, so I pivoted to something more present, "What are you up to this weekend?"

Kit turned her head to the side and said, "No plans. What about you?"

"I have a big meeting in Atlanta next Monday, and I was thinking we could head down together and spend the weekend there, then maybe come back on Monday together. I'd have to do a little work on Friday to prepare for Monday's meeting but otherwise we could explore the city together."

Kit perked up. "Like a weekend trip?"

"I think it's exactly like a weekend trip," I said, wrapping my arms around her waist again. She draped her arms over my shoulders and laced her fingers behind my neck.

"I would love that," Kit said. "Our first trip together."

I liked hearing Kit say first trip, implying she thought there could be second and third trips. The thought excited me. I pulled Kit toward me and she wrapped her legs around me. I leaned forward and kissed her soft lips. We kissed again softly and then again. I gently licked Kit's neck. I felt her shudder with pleasure, then she said in a breathy voice, "We've gotta get out of here soon or we're going to be acting out that sexy librarian role play fantasy everyone always asks me about."

I pulled back and smiled at her. "All my fantasies are sexy librarian fantasies now."

"Is that right?" Kit asked.

"Yes, but who are all these people asking you about this librarian fantasy?" I said protectively with a laugh. I pulled her closer to me.

Kit threw her head back and laughed, her hands still hooked around my neck. I leaned in and gave her a long hard kiss.

17

Kit

Veronica squealed as I opened the door to her SUV and slid into the front seat. She reached over the center console and gave me a hug. "I can't believe I'm seeing you twice in a month." She cried, "I'm so glad you're in town!"

"I know. I'm so glad it worked out for me to come to Atlanta with William this weekend," I said, closing the car door. William and I had driven into Atlanta early Friday morning. We checked into the hotel, then William went to work. Veronica and I made plans to go to a spa, and she offered to pick me up at the hotel.

"Yeah, William has a meeting on Monday morning, and he wanted to come down today to do a little prep work, so we thought we'd make a weekend of it," I said as I buckled my seat belt.

She turned her wrist to check her watch. "Oh! Our appointment at the spa is in thirty minutes. My mom agreed to watch Preston all day. Let's go. I am so excited for spa day."

Veronica and I spent the morning at the spa. After massages, we sat in the sauna. I had my hair pulled up into a bun, and Veronica was quick to tease me about a red mark at the base of my neck.

"What's that? A love bite?" Veronica said playfully.

Luckily, in the sauna, my cheeks were already red, and Veronica couldn't see how embarrassed I was. I said, "I think that's from the other night when we hooked up in my office."

Veronica's jaw dropped. "You're fucking kidding me. You got frisky in your library office?"

"And at the drive-in movie theater, and by the river, and in the elevator at the hotel this morning," I said, trying not to beam.

"Wow," Veronica said, leaning back against the cedar walls. "Now I get why you came with him to Atlanta for a business meeting. You two lovebirds couldn't be away from each other for one weekend."

"Also," I reminded Veronica, "I'm getting to see you."

"Um, you haven't been to Atlanta in almost a year, but Ol' Slick Willy wants to come to town and here you are," Veronica joked.

"Eww, never say 'Slick Willy' again," I begged.

Veronica ignored me and wiped the sweat from her brow as she said, "So, this is kind of fast. You two have been dating for two weeks, and you're already going on weekend trips together."

I shrugged. "I guess if we're being technical about it, then yes—it is kind of fast. But honestly, William and I were spend-

ing so much time together before my birthday, it's really been
months of us talking."

"Okay, well, if you're saying this isn't just a hot sex crush,
what do you like so much about William?" Veronica teased.

"He's handsome and smart. It seems like he's good at his job
and hard-working. He likes to help people."

Veronica propped her elbow on her knee, leaning forward
and resting her chin in her palm. "Go on," she said in a playful
voice.

"Aunt Rita loves him. He loves her. William takes care of his
mom. It's one of his highest priorities. He talks about his mom
all the time." I smiled, but then quickly added, "But not in a red
flag way."

Veronica got up to check the temperature of the rocks. I
continued. "He's funny. He likes to travel. He reads real books,
and he isn't overly impressed by podcasting bros."

"Ugh, thank goodness. Podcasting bros are the worst."
Veronica said, making the distinct yuck face.

"I know, right?" I continued. "William is willing to watch
anything I want to watch on television, even Christmas movies
in April. He listens. He isn't scared of the saddest and darkest
parts of me, like my grief. He lets me have it, I don't know,
like...helps me until it passes."

"Oh, my god." Veronica grimaced as she plopped back down
next to me. "Are you in love with this guy?"

Again, I was glad my face was already red from the sauna
because I was fully blushing as I asked, "It's too soon to know
that, right? Like, three months is too soon to know if I'm in

love with someone or not? How did you know you were in love with Gus?"

Veronica pushed her head back and raised her eyebrows. "We went on two dates, and I started wearing his favorite hoodie, and I just never gave it back. I'm pretty sure he's just sticking around until he can get that hoodie back."

I laughed and leaned forward to let the sweat drip down my face. "I know that I really, really like William. I am just trying not to get too far ahead of myself."

"Okay, what's the reservation then?" Veronica asked.

"I don't know. A few years ago, I was so against Matt moving to Creekstone to be with me. I pretty much broke up with him as soon as he mentioned me moving to Los Angeles or him moving back to Georgia when he could." I shook my head. "But with William, I'm dying to talk to him about the future, but I don't want to sound like ...like ..."

"A Psycho. Needy. Desperate," Veronica said, batting her eyes at me.

"I was going to say putting the cart before the horse, but yeah, those things, too." I sighed.

Veronica sat back on the bench. "Look, I say give it some time. But if you're feeling this strongly about him, I think it's okay to do a little temperature check. Maybe ask him how long he wants to stay in Creekstone."

I nodded. "I thought he was going to ask me about the future earlier this week. We were in my office, and he saw the letter from Harvard. He asked me a few questions about the fellowship deferment, then he just changed the subject."

Veronica scrunched her nose. "Was this right before you two had hot office sex?"

"Um, yes. Why?"

"Maybe he was distracted, sweetie," Veronica said with a chuckle and then more seriously she said, "But there's nothing stopping you from initiating the conversation. You don't have to wait on William or anyone to talk about the future. It's your future, Kit."

"It's scary," I admitted. "I'm afraid if I say the wrong thing William will lose interest in me."

"Kit, I don't know how to tell you this, but no one but you wants to watch Christmas movies in April. I think this man is in love with you," Veronica said matter-of-factly. Then more softly she said. "Look, you don't want to do what you did with Matt again. You don't want to just go along with things until you finally can't take it anymore. It's better to communicate how you're feeling so the relationship has a chance to go in the direction you want it to go in."

Veronica and I left the sauna and headed for our scheduled facials and other treatments. Instead of relaxing during the expensive facial and skin treatments, I worried about our conversation. I couldn't help but think about what Veronica had said about how I needed to handle this situation with William differently than I'd handled things with Matt. I realized she was right. Things with Matt were very nice in the beginning. We didn't have nearly the heated passion that William and I do, but I enjoyed dating Matt, and I just went along with the direction he wanted the relationship to go. I knew what I wanted with

William, but what direction did William want to take this relationship?

Veronica and I had a late lunch, then she dropped me off at the hotel because she had to pick up Preston from her mom's house.

When I got back to the hotel suite, William was standing by the window in the living room looking out as he talked on the phone. He'd gone to the barber at some point, and the new cut looked very handsome. William was wearing a tie, but no jacket. He wore a pair of slacks and a pair of leather dress shoes I had never seen before. He had one hand in his pocket and the other held the phone to his ear. He turned as soon as he heard me by the door, and his warm smile melted away the more serious look of concentration that was on his face as he listened to the other person on the call. He held up a finger, and I nodded.

I headed into the bedroom portion of the suite, put my bag on the bed, and let my hair down. William had talked about going out to a nice restaurant for dinner, and my hair was a wild mess from the spa. I combed my fingers through my curls wishing that they would lay down. I took off my earrings, put them on the dresser, I slipped out of my shoes, and started to undress to get into the shower. As I was pulling my dress over my head, I felt arms around my waist. I gasped a little as William's deep voice whispered in my ear, "Damn, you smell so good."

I giggled as my dress fell to the floor, and I looked at us in the mirror. William was much taller than me, but he was bent over so that his cheek nuzzled against mine, and his arms were wrapped around my bare waist.

"We're a handsome couple," William said, looking at our reflection. I felt my heart flutter a little hearing William describe us as a couple.

"I think we are," I agreed. I was wearing only a lace bralette and matching panties. As William held me, I pulled the soft lacy cups of my bra down and watched William's eyes flash as his gaze looked at my topless reflection. I kept my eyes on William's expression in the mirror as I cupped my own breast and slowly caressed my nipples until they were hard. William's lips parted, and I heard him sigh into my ear.

"Do you like that?" I asked.

"You probably don't remember this," he said as he gently rubbed his hands along the waistband of my panties, "But on Christmas Eve, you made a comment about how you didn't need a man to have an orgasm, and I have to admit I've fantasized about watching you pleasuring yourself so many times since then."

"Oh," I said licking my lips and keeping my eyes fixed on William's face in the reflection. I liked that William still thought about something I'd said in passing. The fact that it had stayed with him made me feel powerful and attractive. I slowly moved my hands down my stomach until they covered his. Then I pushed his hands so that they hooked into my panties and slid them down. My panties fell to the floor so that I stood naked in front of William. His expression changed from playful to longing. I saw him clench his jaw as he tried to show restraint.

"You waxed?" he said, his eyes on my reflection.

"I treated myself at the spa," I said nonchalantly. I pulled William's hands up my body until they palming my breasts.

"You're so beautiful," he said in a low voice. I kept my eyes on him as I pinched my nipples, slowly rolling them between my fingers, until William's hands moved over mine and he mirrored my touch. I pressed against him enjoying the way his fingers created pleasurable pressure that radiated throughout my chest.

18

William

Kit pressed against me. Her dark eyes gazing back at mine in the mirror. I watched as Kit's hand slowly rolled down her body until she reached her center. I couldn't take my eyes off her. I watched as her fingertip gently traced her crease. I wanted so badly to touch her there and feel how smooth was, but I had dreamt of watching Kit.

Kit gasped a little and gave a satisfied sigh as she pressed her fingertip against her pleasure point. I couldn't take my eyes off her hands. She pitched back against my chest as her hand started to move in slow, small circles. I felt Kit's chest rise and fall as her breathing changed from gentle sighs to more ragged moans. Kit braced herself against my thigh with one hand, parting her legs slightly to let her fingers move deeper and faster. She pressed against my growing erection as she rolled her hips and pressed against her fingers.

"You're so sexy, Kit," I whispered in her ears. I pinched the tan buds on the tip of her breast until she closed her eyes and cried out for more, her hand moving faster. "Seeing you like this is driving me crazy. Will you come for me?" I practically growled in her ear. She frantically nodded. I squeezed her nipples again as I watched her fingers work against her swollen clit. Her ass was now pressing directly into my erection, and her rhythmic rocking against me felt so good.

Kit turned around so that she was facing me. She stopped me from closing in on her by gently pushing her wet fingertips against my lips. I stepped back as I tasted her excitement. She pushed past me to the bed.

In a quiet whisper, she said, "I want you to see what I look like when I fantasize about you."

Kit moved to the center of the bed and slowly spread her legs. I had never wanted someone more. Without looking away, Kit slowly started circling her clit again, but this time, I had a full view of her. She licked her lips and pinched her nipples as she moved against her own hand. Her eyes met mine, and she said, "I thought about you after we spent Christmas together and again on New Year's Eve."

I nodded. "I know, baby. Tell me what you wanted."

And she did. Between gasps and moans as she touched herself, she told me how she wanted me, what she longed for. I couldn't take my eyes off her fingers as they moved around her pleasure point. I loved how her hips moved against her hand. My eyes moved up to her perfect breast, then to her beautiful face twisted with pleasure.

I commanded her, "Come for me, Kit. I want to see you make yourself come."

Kit locked eyes with me and nodded. She slowly shifted her weight and rolled onto her stomach. She spread her legs and slid one hand beneath her so that she could continue to play with her clit but now with more pressure. Seeing this view of Kit's beautiful body made me so hard that I had to stroke myself through my pants as I watched her hips circle in a slow rhythm. She lifted slightly onto her knees so I could see her fingers working against her clit, bending in a way looked like she was beckoning me to her. Kit's body tensed, then relaxed. I looked down at her swollen, wet crease and imagined how good she felt.

She gasped, "I'm coming." She threw her head back and cried out. She turned and looked over her shoulder at me as she pushed herself up, so that she was on all fours, and in a whisper begged, "William, please I want you."

I quickly moved to the nightstand to get a condom. Then I moved to the center of the bed so that I was behind her, placing one of my hands on her hips. Kit looked over her shoulder at me. She started caressing her pussy again. I could tell by how easily her fingers glided that she was ready for me. As soon as I had the condom on, Kit pressed her ass against me. She reached between her legs and guided me to her slick, wet entrance.

Kit turned and pleaded, "Fuck me, William. Please."

I had no restraint left. I grabbed Kit's waist with both hands and let my fingers sink into her juicy hips. I pushed into her with a full thrust. Kit cried out for more, and I moved against her repeatedly until we found a rhythm that was faster and harder than we'd ever done before. Kit moaned, her back arching. I moved my hand from her hip to her shoulder, then to her hair. I pulled Kit's head back so that I could see her perfect, beautiful face. I could see the need in her eyes, and I demanded, "Come on me, Kit. You're mine. Come on me."

She gasped, and I felt the spasms. I released her hair and held her hips, pressing deeper inside her as she clenched around me, over and over again, giving me just what I needed to finish with her. 📷

We collapsed onto the bed. She was on her stomach, and I was on top of her. I wanted to cover every inch of her. I softly kissed her cheek, then the spot on her neck just behind her ear. I slid my hands beneath her so that I could feel her breasts and said, "I have never seen anything so beautiful and sexy in my life."

We lay in bed for a while holding each other and kissing. Until finally, Kit and I got up to get ready for dinner. We got into the shower together. I quickly washed my body then hers. I watched the water create rippling streams over Kit's body. I made a soapy lather between my hands and rubbed her body. She pressed her back against me and practically hummed as my hands slipped over her breast and between her legs. Kit let me bring her to climax again, then turned and kissed me deeply. I loved the feeling of her wet body against mine. I dutifully rinsed the suds off her.

"I'm loving how attentive you're being." Kit smiled at me and then asked, "But what time is our dinner reservation? Do I have time to wash my hair?"

I've come to learn that Kit's curly hair care routine can take five minutes or five hours, depending on if she washes it—and that it's best not to make suggestions unless I want a lengthy university-style lecture on curl care. I stepped out of the shower and dried off.

"Our reservation is in an hour, but I can change it. We can go tomorrow. That way you can take your time getting ready," I suggested. "Maybe we could do something a little more casual tonight?"

Kit turned the water off and peaked around the glass shower wall. I handed her a towel. She was frowning. "I'm sorry. Did I cause us to miss our reservation?"

I laughed and watched as Kit tucked the towel into itself. "Kit, you just fulfilled my favorite fantasy. It's a helluva reason to miss the reservation! No reason to apologize. I'll just reschedule it for tomorrow if I can. And if I can't, there are plenty of amazing places I can take you in Atlanta." I kissed her forehead. "But for tonight, let's just go out and see where the night takes us."

I changed into a pair of shorts, a T-shirt, and some Jordan 1 lows. I sat on the sofa in the suite living room and clicked on the tv to see if the NBA semifinals were on.

"Ready to go?" Kit asked, appearing in the bedroom door-way. I looked up. She was wearing a purple sundress with a pair of low-top Converse sneakers. Her hair was pulled back in a low braid with a few loose curls around her face, like the first day I met her. I felt a now familiar warmth in my chest.

After heading down to the lobby, I called an uber. I gave the uber the address. Kit scooted in behind me and sat a little closer than necessary, which I loved.

"Where are we headed?" Kit asked.

"There's an art gallery I want to check-out," I told Kit. "It's a building in our portfolio. I heard about the gallery, and I thought it might be something you'd like."

"Your portfolio. Sounds so fancy. An art gallery, too?" Kit's eyes lit up. "I spent so much time visiting art galleries growing up. My mom, obviously, loved to visit galleries when we traveled, but really it was my dad who took me to the most galleries as a kid. Anytime we were in a new city, he'd take me to a museum or art gallery. I think that's how I became interested in archives, which, in a way, led me to my love of libraries."

"That's really cool," I said. I loved the way her face lit up when she told stories. "So, you like art galleries, then?"

"Oh yeah," Kit grinned. "I never have a bad time at a gallery. If the art is good, then it's an enjoyable visit because I got to see good art. But if the art is bad..." Kit laughed. "Well, sometimes that's even more enjoyable."

As we drove through Atlanta, I pointed out buildings that were part of projects that I had worked on. The car took us through the West End of Atlanta. I pointed out a red brick building as we passed. "This is where my dad went to college."

"Oh, this is where your parents met?" Kit said looking out the window at the college buildings.

I smiled. It felt nice for someone to know a little about my family's story. "Yeah, this whole area of Atlanta is rapidly changing," I said as we passed by a new mixed-use development.

"Do you think the changes are good?" Kit asked. I could see her eyes scanning the buildings behind me as the car made its way to our destination.

"Only sometimes," I admitted. "Neighborhoods change over generations. That's just part of how communities work, but the change isn't always positive. For a neighborhood like this one, with so much history, I think it's important for the right people to be part of the redevelopment and revitalization of the area. Otherwise, it's just gentrification."

I thought I noted a glimmer of relief in Kit's expression. "You seem to know a lot about urban development."

"It's kind of what I'm known for," I said. "I built my career on redeveloping cities."

"How'd you end up in Creekstone?" Kit asked, her brows pushing together.

I sighed. "The company answer is that we have a lot invested in the redevelopment of the regional hospital and all the surrounding areas, and Creekstone is part of that. But the real answer is that my boss, Braithway, wanted me to prove I could do more than these urban development deals."

Kit looked as if she was considering what I'd said. She asked, "Do you miss living in the city?"

"I love cities, but I've found Creekstone to be surprisingly good in so many ways." I put my hand on her leg and smiled at her. She smiled back, and it may have been wishful thinking, but I sensed a bit of relief wash over Kit.

Then the Uber driver pulled up to a row of warehouses. I thanked him as we got out and made sure to tip on the app. Kit walked around the car and looked at me a bit puzzled.

"Have you been here before?" I asked.

She shook her head. [OBJ]

"Welcome to The Candler Warehouse," I said. "It's an industrial park housing various artist collectives and galleries. At night, the galleries have parties and food trucks pull up."

"How fun!" Kit said. "I love all these things! Art. Parties. And food trucks!"

"I thought you might," I said with a chuckle. "I wanted to check out this one gallery before it closes for the night. Then we can eat." I looked up at the unit numbers above the doors as we walked.

We walked past several gallery fronts that had closed before I found the right one. "It's just over here."

The lights were still on. I opened the door for Kit so that she walked in before me. I could feel myself getting nervous. I had planned this gallery visit for Kit, and I wasn't sure if she'd like it or not. Suddenly, I felt an uneasiness in my stomach and worried this might be too much. Kit must have noticed because she reached for my hand and said, "What's wrong? You look nervous."

"It's nothing. I guess I'm just nervous you won't like this," I confessed.

"I'm sure I'll love it. This is such a cool space." Kit squeezed my hand as we walked into the gallery.

19

Kit

When William opened the door to the gallery, a cool blast of air-conditioning hit my legs. I felt the goosebumps as I reached for William's hand. The gallery was small but bright. The brick walls had been painted white. The floors and ceilings had been sprayed white as well, giving the space a clean aesthetic. The gallery had a few floating walls that divided up the narrow, formerly industrial space.

A young woman wearing a white tunic dress and white Doc Martens was sitting at a large white desk toward the back of the gallery. She nodded at us but didn't stand up to greet us. I turned to William and raised my eyebrows as I stifled a giggle. He smiled nervously at me, and I squeezed his hand. Before we walked in, William had told me he was nervous I wouldn't like the gallery, but I was sure this was going to be enjoyable. It was something different than what we would have normally done on a Friday night in Creekstone.

We walked over to the first piece. It was a large colorful abstract done with acrylic paint. It reminded me of sunflowers. I read the title card below the painting. It was called "Shine" and by an artist named Andy Ernest.

"I know him!" I said, surprised. "He was one of my mom's students. I remember his work from one of her student art shows."

I hooked my arm into William's and looked up at him. "Isn't that cool?

William nodded. "It's a nice piece."

We moved a few steps into the gallery and looked at the next large piece on the same wall. It was another piece by Andy Ernest. This one was titled "Shadow," and it had similar abstract shapes with dark blue and blacks.

"I can't believe this," I said. "I can't wait to tell Aunt Rita."

We moved on to the next piece. I stepped closer to it to get a better look. It was a smaller hand-drawn piece of a woman and a baby. The title card said that it was called "Professor" by George Cage. I spun around. "You're not going to believe this, but George is one of my mom's students, too."

William's eyebrows raised and his crooked smile slipped across his face. He shoved his hand in his pocket. "This gallery features local artists."

A cloud of confusion took over. I tried to figure out how that was possible. I looked around at the other paintings at the front of the gallery. I silently moved from painting to painting. I recognized some of the names, but some of them I didn't.

"This is unbelievable," I said, completely dumbfounded, turning to look at William. That's when I saw it. When I looked past William and toward the back of the gallery, I saw the large, oversized painting of river rocks that I would recognize anywhere. It was the large river rocks painting my mom had painted a few years before she died.

"William," I said quietly. I pointed toward the back of the gallery. I felt a sense of confusion that blended and crescendoed into excitement. "William, that's my mom's painting."

I pushed past him and walked to the back of the gallery. There they were. All my mom's large river rock pieces. I spun around to see William standing behind me with an anxious look on his face. I was completely astonished. I stuttered, "How is this possible?"

"Your Aunt Rita and I wanted to do something for you and your mom," William said softly. "I reached out to my contact here at The Met, and I worked out a deal to have the space leased for six months for a special exhibit. We wanted to honor your mom, so Aunt Rita picked out her favorite large works by her. But you told me your mom felt that the work of her students was what she was most proud of, so we contacted some of her students and asked to use their pieces in this exhibit."

"This is unbelievable." I felt the swell of emotion as a sob burst from my chest. There was a sting in my nose and eyes as warm tears streamed down my cheeks.

"Oh, Kit," William said. He pulled me close to him hugging me, and I cried into his chest. I sniffled, stepped back, and he handed me a tissue.

"Has Aunt Rita seen it?" I asked.

"She has. She was here earlier today setting up because she's one of the artists," William explained as we walked over to a set of black and white photos. "She said your mom taught her how to take photos. She has some on display over here."

The photos were all of my mom and me by the river. The first was me as a baby. My mom looked so young and beautiful as she held me up for the camera to see. The second was of me as a toddler splashing in the water with my mom. The next was a photo of us playing on a tree swing. There was a photo of us walking by the river after a fresh snow. Another one of me, maybe ten years old, holding up a fish I had just caught while my mom clapped. Another photo of me as a teen sunbathing and reading on a rock while my mom painted. There was a photo of us in a canoe laughing after one of us dropped a paddle. There was a photo of my mom and me on a picnic blanket when I was home from a college visit, and the last photo was of me sitting next to my mom as she painted. Her head was wrapped, and she had a heavy blanket draped over her shoulders. I was looking at my mom's painting, but my mom's glassy eyes were fixed on me. She had a slight smile as we held hands. The title card of the collection read, "A Perfect Love" by Rita Campbell. Hot tears rolled down my cheeks. I turned and buried my face in William's chest again.

William held me for a while before I stepped back. He cupped my face in his hands and smoothed away tears with his thumbs. "Aunt Rita is coming back tomorrow so we can all see it together. She said she thought you'd like to see it alone first, and that you wouldn't want to cry in front of everyone."

I looked up. "In front of everyone?"

"Well, we're having a private exhibit opening in the morning. Just some family and friends. A few of the artists." William looked nervous.

I lost it again. I cried so hard into his chest that a dark circle formed where my face had been buried.

When I looked up at William, he looked like he was going to be sick. "Do you hate this? Are you upset? We don't have to come tomorrow if you don't want us to. Aunt Rita said she could handle the opening alone."

"William," I squeaked. "I love it. I absolutely love it. I can't even really comprehend it. How did you do all of this without me knowing?"

William tilted his head thoughtfully, his arms still wrapped around me. "I just secured the space. Aunt Rita and your dad reached out to the students and college professors your mom knew."

"College professors?" I asked.

"Well, the exhibit will be here through the fall semester. Local college art education programs are going to bring students who are working on their art education degrees here to see the impact teachers have on their students and how their contribution shapes the field."

I felt the swell of tears again. "This is so unbelievable." I sighed as I wiped the tears from my eyes. "My mom deserves this. I can't...I just can't even..."

"It's okay," William said quickly. He looked uncomfortable.

"No, I want you to know that no one has ever done something so thoughtful for me," I said, looking up at him.

William pulled me to him, and I closed my eyes. I felt his soft lips against mine. I had wondered before, but at that moment, I was certain I was in love with William.

20

William

The relief I felt when Kit told me she loved the art exhibit could not be described in words. Rita and I had been planning to do something for Kit to honor her mom, and things just came together perfectly for us to create this exhibit.

I knew what it felt like to lose someone. II knew how grief created this pressure around all your memories and thoughts about losing that person, but when that clears, what has crystallized is often something imperfect, but beautiful.

Kit and I spent over an hour looking at the artwork that night. The gallery attendant, Janet, left me the key. I told Kit she could stay as long as she liked. I watched her happily moving from painting to painting. I took a few photos of her in front of her mom's work, and she texted them to Veronica and her dad.

Eventually, Kit took my hand, looked up at me, and said, "I could stay here all night, but I'm starving."

We closed the gallery. I locked the door and texted Janet to activate the alarm remotely. When we stepped back out of the gallery, it was dark, but lights and music peppered the hot humid air. We walked down the alleyway toward the music, holding hands. When we turned the corner, several of the galleries had their doors open, and the steady thump of dance music emanated from the doorways. Nearby, a row of food trucks was parked, serving late night food and drinks. A crowd of people filed between the trucks and the galleries.

Kit squeezed my hand and started pulling me toward one of the trucks. "A Korean taco truck! That's like a fucking dream come true!"

We ordered bulgogi tacos and Korean beers. We ate standing up. Kit was beaming. I had never felt so invested in someone else's happiness. I had always been so incredibly focused on surviving the next hurdle or challenge and getting myself and my mom to a feeling of security that I never slowed down enough to let someone else in. Yet, Kit was in. She was all I could think about. And standing there with her, watching her laugh and joke with me as we ate tacos, I felt like I could explode with happiness—just because she was happy to be with me.

Kit ran up to one of the brightly colored food trucks and ordered us two mixed drinks. She returned holding out the drinks and announcing their names, "This one is a Watermelon Drama, and this one is Squeeze the Day. I love punny things." I couldn't help but laugh at how cute she was. I chose the lime drink.

Kit's grin grew. "I wanted the pink one! Thank you!"

I smiled as I watched her sip her drink through the little cocktail straw. "What?" she asked self-consciously.

"You just look so cute and happy," I said, then took a deep breath. "I feel really glad to be here with you."

Kit's smile returned. She showed me the text responses she'd gotten from Veronica, her dad, and Aunt Rita about the exhibit. She was surprised to find out that Veronica had already been invited by Aunt Rita to the opening tomorrow. "I can't believe she didn't even let on that she knew," Kit exclaimed. "We were together all day!"

As soon as we finished our drinks, Kit grabbed me by my hand and pulled me toward one of the galleries to dance. This gallery was a much larger space. A DJ table had been set up in the corner. The lights were off except for strobing black lights that moved across the room, occasionally lighting up the art on the walls. The dancing bodies were hot, sweaty, and beautiful as they bounced and bumped to the thumping music.

Kit turned and tried to yell over the music. I leaned forward so I could hear her, and she said, "I love this song!"

We danced for what felt like hours, occasionally taking breaks for more drinks. Even though we were surrounded by people, it felt like the two of us were magnetically connected. It felt electric to be so in sync with someone amidst the dark chaos of the dance floor. As if truly in sync, Kit and I made eye contact, left the dance floor, and headed back into the alleyway with the food trucks.

We were both dripping with sweat. Her braid had fallen out while we were dancing, and Kit moved her head so that her black curls fell to one side. She looked up at me and said, "I'm ready to go back to the hotel."

The words instantly excited me. I pulled my phone out and called a car. Kit and I walked down the alley toward the street so the car could find us easily. The closer to the street we got, the darker and quieter the alleyway became. When we reached the end of the alleyway, Kit turned to me and placed both hands on my chest. I stopped, spellbound by her touch. I leaned down and kissed her softly, but the feel of her soft lips against mine and her sweet scent overwhelmed me. I put my hands on her hips and pulled her closer. I remembered how amazing it felt on New Year's Eve, after a long night of dancing, to finally kiss Kit and how incredibly turned on I felt kissing her that night as we walked home. The memory had replayed in my head a thousand times, and now all I wanted was to go back to the hotel and make love to her.

I felt the phone vibrate in my pocket and pulled away. "The car is here."

We took the car back to the hotel, and as soon as we were in the elevator headed up to the room, Kit pressed against me. I reached around her so that my hand was firmly holding her ass. She stood on her tiptoes, which caused her thighs and ass to flex in a way that immediately made me hard. I leaned down to kiss her as she laced her arms around my neck. I picked her up and she wrapped her legs around me as I pinned her against the mirrored wall of the elevator. I felt her grind against my hip, and she let out a little moan against my lips as we kissed. The sound of Kit in pleasure sent heat through my body.

As soon as the elevator doors opened, I carried Kit to our room while she kissed the spot on my neck that drove me crazy. I set her down as I hurried to get the key out of my pocket. She pulled at my belt and the button on my pants. By the time we were in the hotel room, Kit had unbuttoned my pants so that they effortlessly fell to the floor. We pulled at each other's clothes until we were both undressed. I picked Kit up again and brought her to the sofa. Our room was dark, but we had left the curtains open, so the city lights created a soft light that sliced the darkness of the room.

Kit slid onto my lap. Her curves were highlighted in the cool, grey light. I pulled her to me until her breasts were against my mouth. I worked my tongue against her nipples until they were hard enough for me to pinch with my teeth, and she cried out. Kit leaned forward and made a trail of kisses from my earlobe to my shoulder. My hand slipped between us, and I let the tips of my fingers caress her smooth, wet line.

"I want you," Kit whispered into my ear. The sound of her voice sent a tingle through my whole body. I felt her hands on my erection, softly teasing the length of me.

I was ready for more. I practically growled, "Should I get a condom?"

Kit and I had talked, and I knew she was on birth control. We had both been tested since the last time we'd been with someone else. Kit pulled back, her perfect brown eyes locking with mine. She rubbed my chest and said longingly, "I want you like this."

I nodded and watched as Kit raised up on her knees, her beautiful body rising in front of me and slowly lowering until

I felt the intense pleasure of Kit's wet arousal surrounding me. She lowered herself slowly, her breathing uneven and broken as she took more of me into her.

My hands instinctively held her hips. I closed my eyes and leaned my head back. Kit always felt amazing, but the intensity of her heat sent spirals of pleasure through me. I didn't know how long I could last. I felt Kit's body release as more of me slid into her. Kit moaned and said in a whisper, "You're so big. I love it."

My fingertips pushed into her soft curves. I tried to keep my hips still and let Kit be in control. She began rocking back and forth, slowly at first. I used one of my hands to rub Kit's swollen clit as she rolled her hips against me. She leaned back and moaned my name.

"You're so beautiful," I said. She rocked faster and harder against me. I could feel her body responding. The intensity was building inside me. I needed a release.

Kit shifted her weight, and I pressed a little harder against her clit. She grabbed my shoulder to steady herself as she pushed against me, and I felt her body seize in pleasure. The sound of her moaning my name as she came was electrifying. The fast, intense spasms of Kit's body brought me to climax, and I filled her. She collapsed against me, pressing against my heaving chest. I nuzzled my face into her hair and neck, and she hummed against me. "That was so amazing."

Kit sat up. Still inside her, I cradled her face with my palm. She looked so beautiful in the pale light and, before I could stop myself, I said, "Kit, I think I'm in love with you."

A sudden awareness washed over me, and I felt so vulnerable. Kit must have sensed this because she leaned forward and kissed me, saving me. She pressed her forehead against mine and said, "I love you, too."

I let out a relieved breath, and I carried her into the bedroom. We got into bed. Kit fit perfectly against my chest and, as I fell asleep, I felt happy in a way that I'd never experienced before.

The next morning when I woke up. Kit was already awake. She was smiling at me as she watched me sleep. I reached for her under the covers.

Kit said, "William, last night..."

I stopped her. "Kit, I meant it. Every bit of it."

watched her chest rise and fall as she took a deep breath. "I did, too."

I pressed my lips together and said, "I've never done that. Had sex without a condom."

"Really?" Kit looked shocked. She propped herself up on her elbow.

"Yeah," I shrugged. I turned on my back and looked at the ceiling. "I've just been super careful. I don't know. I guess...just knowing my mom and dad didn't plan to have me. I think they were in love, and I think we were a happy family, but no doubt my unplanned arrival completely changed the course of their lives. So I've always just been so, so careful." I turned to see Kit's eyes surveying me. "I've never felt like this about anyone. I used to able to exert more control during sex, but with you, I feel like I need you in a way I've never needed anyone."

Kit's eyes moved to the sheets in front of her. She asked, "Is it very different without a condom?"

"Yes and no. It's always amazing with you," I said. I turned onto my back and looked at the ceiling. "It felt intimate. I felt like we were both vulnerable and connecting in a way we hadn't before."

"I haven't been with that many people before you. Sex was so routine with Matt. It seemed like something we did to satisfy a requirement, but it wasn't something either of us..." Kit looked down at the bed again and blew air through her lips nervously. "He was pretty indifferent about sex, so I kind of worried I wasn't good at it."

"Kit," I said turning toward her. "Our sex is mind-blowing. You are an amazing lover."

She seemed relieved. I pulled her toward me and kissed her forehead. "I wish we could stay in this bed all day, but there are going to be people at the art gallery at eleven a.m."

Kit's smile spread across her face. "I'm so excited."

I ran down to the lobby and grabbed coffees and croissants while Kit showered. When I got back up to the room, she was just getting out of the shower. I took a quick shower, then got dressed.

Kit was wearing a different sundress with a white sweater, and I was wearing one of my button-down work shirts with a pair of slacks. She stood in front of the mirror as she was putting in her hoop earrings. I stood behind her and put my arms around her in front of the mirror, just like we had the day before.

Kit smiled at our reflection. "We're a handsome pair."

We headed to our car in the parking deck. As I drove us back to the gallery, I told Kit that the gallery owner, artists, and their families would be at the exhibit. Aunt Rita had invited Kit's family and friends. Everyone would mingle and enjoy the art. There would be catered hors d'oeuvres and drinks. Then the gallery owner and Aunt Rita would say a few words. I explained what to expect if any media were present and assured her she could decline to speak at any time. I'd prepared Rita and the gallery owner with speaking points.

When I finished going over the opening, I looked over at her, and she said, "Holy shit. You're no joke when you're in work mode."

I chuckled. "I just want this to go well for you and Rita."

Kit reached over and squeezed my thigh. "It's already perfect."

And Kit was right. The morning didn't just go as planned; it went perfectly. As soon as we arrived, Kit made a beeline for Aunt Rita. I saw the two of them talking, then Kit gave Aunt Rita a hug. They went over to Rita's photos, and I saw them hug again as Kit and Rita wiped tears away from each other's faces. Soon after, Veronica and Gus arrived with their son, Preston. Veronica and Kit went piece by piece through the gallery together. I made small talk with Gus as he tried to keep Preston happy. Aunt Rita appeared and offered to hold him so that Gus could join Veronica and look at the art.

The artists began arriving. Aunt Rita and Kit greeted each one and thanked them for participating. I noticed a tall, thin man in his fifties arrive. I didn't recognize him, but as soon as he walked into the gallery Kit's face lit up.

"Dad!" she cried. Kit ran over to him and gave him a huge hug. I felt a nervous lump in my throat. I didn't know Rita had invited Kit's dad. Kit and her dad spoke for a few minutes, then Kit brought him over to meet me.

"Dad, this is my boyfriend, William Philips," Kit said, giving me an encouraging smile. I raised my eyebrows and tried to temper the smile on my face. Kit had never called me her boyfriend before.

"William, this is my dad, Tom Dean," Kit said.

I shook Mr. Dean's hand and said, "I've heard so much about you."

Mr. Dean smiled and said, "I've heard quite a bit about you as well. I felt terrible when my flight from Europe was cancelled, but I guess it gave you and Kit a chance to get to know each other."

Kit blushed and said, "Dad, can I show you some of mom's paintings?" She guided him toward the back of the gallery. I couldn't take my eyes off Kit as she moved around the gallery with her dad. She looked so beautiful when she was happy.

"So, you pulled all this together in two weeks?" a female voice said from behind me. I turned around to see Veronica. The question itself was harmless, but something about Veronica's impatiently tapping foot and crossed arms were hostile and skeptical.

"Hey, I'm so glad you came," I said warmly. "Rita and I have been working on this for a few months. Rita wanted to have something positive for Kit to think about when her mom's death anniversary came next week, and we thought this kind of celebration would be something she'd really like."

Veronica's face instantly softened, but she quickly regained her defensive posture and she said, "Kit told me that the two of you are...very, very serious, and as her best friend, I want you to know that if you do anything to hurt her..."

I nodded. "I feel so lucky that someone as special as Kit would ever want to be with me, and I won't do anything to hurt her."

Veronica said, "Well, Kit said you have dinner plans tonight, but next time you're in town, Gus and I would love to have you over." She turned on her heel and marched away toward Gus and Preston.

I looked over at Kit, Rita, and Mr. Dean. Kit waved at me from across the room, and I waved back. The gallery owner called us all to the front of the gallery to say a few words. I stood in the back of the small crowd. As planned, Rita spoke after the gallery owner. She spoke about her sister's life's work and how much the exhibit meant to their family.

The next part was unexpected, Rita turned to Kit who stepped forward and said, "We'd like to give a special thanks to William Philips who helped pull this exhibit together. Thank you for honoring my mother and her work as both an artist and teacher."

I wasn't used to getting recognized beyond the pat on the back and a paycheck at work. I smiled and shoved my hand in my pocket when everyone turned around to look at me.

After the event, Rita was headed back to Creekstone, and Kit's dad was headed out for a two-week work trip. Aunt Rita agreed to take him back to the airport after the gallery opening. Kit frowned when she heard her dad wouldn't be staying longer.

Mr. Dean gave her a hug and said, "Don't worry, sweetie. I'll be back in Atlanta in a few weeks. Maybe we can meet here again and spend a few days together." Kit agreed.

Kit and I headed back to the hotel. We collapsed onto the bed together.

Kit groaned. "I have had such an amazing twenty-four hours, but I'm exhausted."

I rolled over on my stomach so I could see Kit's face, "Same," I paused. "Maybe we should just change into our pajamas, get into bed, watch our shows, and order in?"

"William, you're a genius, and I love you," Kit said with a cheesy grin. She covered her face with her hands and gushed, "I can't believe I can just say that now."

"Well, Kit, you're amazing, and I love you, too."

We ordered take-out and bottles of wine from room service. The rest of the day was spent in bed alternating between streaming shows and taking naps. It felt like the perfect afternoon.

21

Kit

The next morning, I woke up before William. I always did. He didn't realize this, but he snored a little, and sometimes in the morning his snoring would wake me. I don't know why I found it endearing that someone who looked as good as William also snored. When I teased him a little about it, he said he had no idea he snored. I was surprised no one else had ever mentioned it, and he told me he rarely spent the night with the women he dated. So even though the snoring often woke me in the morning, it felt intimate and special that I got a chance to hear it.

That morning, I watched as William woke himself up from his own sleep by snoring, and I tried not to laugh. When his eyes opened, I watched as his face registered where he was—and then saw the smile that formed when he saw me.

"Good morning," he said groggily. I put my hand on his bicep and snuggled against him. William stretched and exhaled a deep breath. "What time is it? Wanna try to get brunch?"

"Hey, William," I said softly. I'd been waiting for him to wake up all morning so we could talk.

He must have noticed my tone because he turned to me and asked, "What's up?"

"I talked to Aunt Rita yesterday, and we've decided we're ready to sell the land." My voice was slow and clear. I'd thought about this for weeks, and I finally felt ready to tell William.

His face turned serious. "Really? Are you sure? You were so against it before. Did you decide this yesterday at the gallery?"

I took a deep breath. "No, Aunt Rita and I have been talking about it for a while now. The truth is we can barely afford the property taxes. We have so many bills from when my mom was sick. If we didn't have renters, we wouldn't be able to get by. My mom and Aunt Rita probably would have sold the land already if my mom hadn't gotten sick. They just didn't have the bandwidth to think it through when my mom was in treatment, but now we do." I paused. "And the best thing for us to do is sell the land. We've known that for a while."

"Are you sure, Kit?" William said, sitting up so he could see my face. He took my hand and moved his head so that he could see my eyes. I swallowed and thought before I answered.

"Yes, I'm sure, and the truth is, I trust that you'll do the right thing in Creekstone. I can already see the positive changes you're making." I smiled slightly at him. "Veronica's going to be our agent and list the land. If your company is interested, you can contact her to negotiate the deal."

William pulled me toward him and said, "Kit, this is a big decision. How do you feel?"

I nuzzled my nose into his chest and sighed. Then I pushed away from him so I could see his face and said, "Honestly, I feel relieved. Aunt Rita and I need this. This will change our lives. We won't be paycheck to paycheck anymore. Aunt Rita will be able to retire early, and I'll be able to start a real nest egg."

Then I licked my lips, pressed them together, and said, "And I realized yesterday that Creekstone doesn't have to stay exactly the same to remember my mom. The gallery made me realize that there are so many ways to share her memory and even make new memories around honoring my mom. I can't thank you enough for helping me see that."

"That's really beautiful," William said as he pressed his lips against my hand. "I love you, Kit."

"I love you, too," I whispered.

William moved his hands across my hips and he pulled me closer to him. His hand slid between my thighs, and I adjusted my legs so he could slide his hand all the way to my center. William's fingers worked against me to create a warm arousal in my lower belly. I pushed into his hand for more, and he rolled me onto my back. I pulled William closer, craving the press of his hard, muscular chest against mine—then the tenderness of his kiss. I guided William into me. A gasp escaped my lips as I felt the pressure of his penetrating erection. William cradled my face with his palm. At first, we moved together slowly, but as my body responded, he pushed deeper into me. I moaned at the pleasurable pressure, and my hips pressed against him for more. William hovered above me so I could look directly into his eyes.

William and I had been having sex for nearly three weeks, and it had been exciting and pleasurable. The newness and the release of all the sexual tension had been unbelievably satisfying, but I felt that we were doing something entirely different now. William's movements were slow and deliberate. His eyes burned through me as he watched me arch beneath him. William used his hand to stroke me as he slowly moved his hips. His touch was pushing me to the edge, and he knew it. His eyes were full of desire.

William sat back so he was on his knees between my legs. He pulled my hips so that, in one perfect motion, he was deep inside of me. I cried out his name. This unlocked something in William, and he groaned and pushed us into a rhythm that brought me to a quick orgasm—then, soon after, his throbbing finish. William pressed against me again, kissing me softly.

"You're so beautiful. You're perfect," William said, stroking my cheek.

"I'm yours. All of me," I pledged softly and meant it.

"I will do anything for you." He promised, and I believed him.

22

William

"William!" my coworker Charles cried as he approached. I was sitting in The Pub waiting for Charles to meet me for lunch. A Sublime song, "What I Got" played on the jukebox. Charles had just met with Kit and Rita to sign the Intent to Sell and a Memorandum of Understanding. All that was left was the due diligence period. Charles and I had decided to get lunch before he headed back to Atlanta.

He gave me his typical 'up top" high-five, handshake, and pat on the back.

"What's good, Charles?" I said, as he settled onto the stool next to me. Ray appeared with a second beer and a bowl of pretzels.

"Ah, man. That closing was a breeze. I am surprised you didn't do it yourself," Charles said. He looked at the menu on the bar.

"Glad it went well," I said.

"So, I heard the board was deliberating a new transition plan that Braithway proposed," Charles said, holding back a grin.

I nodded. "Yeah, I've heard about that. What have you heard?"

"Well, I've heard your name is at the top of the proposed org chart. So, congrats on that, my guy," Charles said.

I shook my head and said, "Nothing's official yet. I haven't heard anything from Braithway all week, but I'm scheduled to go down there in a few days to meet with him."

"Nah, I know it's gonna happen. Braithway has always had a soft spot for you, but don't get me wrong. You've earned it. I'm happy for you, brother."

"Thanks," I said. I was a little surprised that Charles was being so supportive. I had assumed he had wanted this role for himself.

We chatted, mostly about work. Charles gave me a few updates about projects he'd been managing. Notably, he shared only the ones that were successful. Usually, he had a lot of stories that started out with him working and ended up with him golfing with a celebrity or going out all night with some hot girls. Charles punctuated the end of every story with, "But don't worry, I didn't use the company card for any of that last part." But today, Charles kept it all business and above board.

Charles was sharp, and he knew how to work the system. He graduated top of his class and came highly recommended. His work was stellar, and he missed almost nothing when it came to contracts. But Charles was an absolute tool when it came to his social life. Meredith couldn't stand him. She not only loathed his bro-culture persona, but she felt the way he was tolerated underscored the double standard in corporate culture. But as I listened to Charles give the PG version of all his work trips, it occurred to me that the C-suite had never seen that side of him. I was well aware that Charles wasn't the kind of guy that should be easily trusted.

"So, Creekstone is a pretty small town. Have you really been living here since December?" Charles asked, then took a swig of beer. "When I heard, you were relegated to this project, I thought it was a punishment, but what could the crime have been to deserve this?"

"Yeah, the business development work that needed to be done started from basically ground zero, so I had to be here to really move it along. It's how Braithway wanted it done," I said, picking up my beer. "But I like Creekstone. It's not all bad."

"I guess it's not all bad," Charles echoed me with a smirk.

I raised my eyebrow but didn't respond, so Charles chided me.

"Well, I saw the way you and Kit Campbell were looking at each other all week," Charles said a suggestive flash in his eyes. "You hittin' it?"

I was expecting this from Charles. I kept my cool. "I've grown close to Kit. She's a good person."

"I see. Mixing a little business with pleasure." Charles clucked his tongue on the roof of his mouth. "So, is this how you convinced her to sell her land to Braithway & Randall?" he hooted.

"I don't think it has anything to do with me," I said non-re-actively. "It was a good business decision for her family."

"Sure," Charles said, looking back down at his lunch. "I mean, keep telling yourself that. But what it looks like is you proposed a land sale in December. She said, 'Not just no, but hell no.' You moved here, got into her bed, and voila...she suddenly is interested in selling her land." Charles laughed, took a bite of food, and added, "Good for you though. She's a total smoke show."

I didn't respond. I felt a fury inside myself that Charles was making light of my relationship with Kit, but I knew I needed to keep my cool. Guys like Charles lived for the reaction. I took a bite of my burger.

As if something had just occurred to him, Charles gasped. He squinted his eyes and pointed at me. "Is this why Braithway sent me up here to lead the negotiations?"

I didn't want to respond, but I knew Charles could dig around and figure this out for himself. "I disclosed to Braithway and HR that I had a conflict of interest with this particular land sale. I rent an apartment from the family, and I've become close to them. I just wanted to keep everything aboveboard for the company."

"See this is why Braithway loves you. You're always keeping the company's best interest in mind." Charles frowned as if he was giving something serious thought. "It's just surprising. You're a hot commodity on the dating circuit. A lot of ladies are going to be disappointed you're off the market."

I didn't want to give Charles too much. I didn't want to tell him that I was madly in love with Kit and that I would abandon Braithway & Randall in a heartbeat for her. I didn't want to tell Charles that for the first time in my life, I felt safe and loved. I didn't want someone as crass and shallow as Charles to ruin it for me.

So, I just let a little chuckle out and said, "None of that matters, Charles. I just know I'm happy."

Charles shook his head. "Hey, this gives me hope. If a dog like you can find happiness, then maybe it can happen for anyone."

"Thanks, I think," I said with a forced smile.

Ray appeared with one check, which he handed to me without saying much else. Charles looked up at Ray and said, "This steak salad is fucking amazing."

When I finally got the confirmation about my job promotion, I couldn't wait to get back to Creekstone to tell Kit. I stopped and picked up a pizza before I got back to the house. Kit liked a white pizza with buffalo chicken and hot honey drizzle. It was her favorite. When I got there, Kit was curled up on the sofa reading a book. As soon as she saw me, she popped off the sofa and gave me a sweet peck on the cheek. She followed me into the kitchen. I put the pizza on the counter, and she went over to the fridge and pulled out a bowl of salad she'd made.

"I've been thinking about this pizza all day!" Kit said, pulling two plates out of the cabinets.

"What about me?" I said. "You haven't been thinking about me?"

"Well, you are the cutest pizza delivery boy I've ever seen," she said, smiling playfully at me. I was headed across the kitchen to scoop her up for a kiss when she said, "Oh, speaking of deliveries. Something just came for you."

Kit pointed to a crate sitting on the kitchen counter. It resembled the crate delivered on Christmas Eve. I walked over, popped it open, and pulled out a bottle of whiskey and a bottle of wine. Kit clapped and said, "Is that the same wine from Christmas Eve?"

I walked over to the cabinet, pulled out two wine glasses, and opened the bottle to pour us a glass of wine. "It is."

Kit started humming the song "It's Beginning to Look a Lot like Christmas" while spooning salad onto our plates. She stopped to ask, "Did Braithway send that? What's the occasion?"

I kept my eyes on the glasses as I poured the wine and I said coolly, "The offer's official. Salary negotiations are complete. I'm the next CEO of Braithway & Randall."

"CEO?" Kit said, her eyes wide with surprise. "Your promotion was to become the CEO of your company?"

I nodded. "I was too nervous to talk about it, but yes, Braithway is retiring at the end of the year, and I'll be working alongside him preparing to take over as the CEO."

Kit dropped the wooden salad spoons with a clatter and ran over to me. She threw her arms around me and gave me a huge hug. "That's such great news! Congratulations."

I kissed Kit's forehead, "Thank you."

We took our plates into the dining room. Kit looked down at her pizza and salad and said, "I'm still in shock! This is such a big fucking deal. Should we go out and celebrate? You didn't even pick out the pizza toppings you like!"

"Honestly," I said, "This feels perfect to me."

"Why didn't you call me and tell me the news?" Kit said, swatting at my arm and pretending to be mad, then laying her hand on mine.

I smiled, "Is it too painfully corny to say all I wanted was to see you and tell you in person?"

Kit smiled and straightened up in her chair. "Okay, a toast to you. Congratulations on your promotion. You're going to do such remarkable things."

Our glasses clinked, and I took a sip of the wine. Kit smiled as she picked up her fork and started to eat her salad. "Tell me all about it. This is so amazing."

The moment felt perfect. We chatted about the job and enjoyed the pizza. Kit refilled our glasses of wine. Then we decided to head upstairs to my room. Kit and I sat on the bed together, and I turned on the tv to stream one of our shows, but before I started the show, I said to Kit, "Hey, can I talk to you about something?"

"Sure," Kit said. She had brought a bag of chocolate candies up with her, and she was happily unwrapping the chocolates and popping them into her mouth.

"I wanted to talk a little about how my new job might impact us," I said softly. I saw the change in Kit's expression, and I felt a panic growing inside of me.

She looked down at the candy wrapper in her hand and said, "That's probably a good idea."

I took a deep breath and pressed my lips together. "Now that it's official, I will need to be in Atlanta most of the week, and I'll have to take work trips pretty regularly."

Kit was nodding but not looking directly at me. "So, you'll be in Atlanta permanently?"

"Yes, and I know the distance was a factor in your decision to break up with Matt. I wasn't sure how you'd feel about being in another long-distance relationship."

Kit didn't look up. She kept her eyes down and she said, "Okay."

I felt the nervous flutter in my stomach harden into a knot. I had worked so hard to get this job. It was the one goal I had laid out for myself, but suddenly, feeling like my relationship with Kit could be in jeopardy because of it, I was having serious second thoughts. I had never had a relationship talk with a woman in which I was asking her for more, and I was trying not to panic.

I said, "I don't expect you to change anything, and I don't want to promise you that I can be here as much as I have been over the last few weeks because I just know it won't be realistic. So, I wanted to tell you that next week I'm going to start looking for a place in Atlanta."

Kit licked her lips and kept her eyes down, she said softly, "Are you breaking up with me?"

Surprised, I leaned forward and gently lifted Kit's chin with my index finger. I saw the tears in her eyes. "No, hey. No. That's not what I want. I want us to stay together. I was going to ask you if you'd ever consider trying a long-distance relationship again."

Kit's eyes went down again, and I dropped my hand into my lap. She shook her head, and I felt crushed.

"I don't want to be in a long-distance relationship again," she said softly. "I don't think it works, and I think it would just delay the inevitable."

"Would you be willing to think about it?" I asked. I tried not to sound upset. I felt almost foolish for suggesting it because Kit had been so clear that she'd never want to be in a long-distance relationship. I swallowed the lump in my throat and leaned back against the headboard. I felt the muscles in my chest getting tight and took a deep breath. I looked down at my hands in my lap and said quietly, "What we have is rare, Kit. You know that. It's rare and special, and I don't agree it's a foregone conclusion that we would break up just because of a long-distance relationship. It feels like you're giving up without trying."

Kit slid her hand over mine. She said, "A few months ago, when you started talking about a potential promotion, I wanted to know more about what that might mean for you and for us. You told me talking about the promotion made you too nervous, so I haven't asked more questions, but I assumed that your new role wouldn't be in Creekstone. I've been afraid to bring this up because I haven't wanted to freak you out and scare you off, but I can't imagine us not being together now."

I shrugged and asked sullenly, "How would we stay together if you don't want to try a long-distance relationship?"

Kit pushed herself up and crawled into my lap so that she was straddling me. "I don't want the norm to be us living apart and seeing each other on occasional weekends and random weeknights. I don't think it would work in the long term. I think we should stay together."

The realization came suddenly. I had been so sure that Kit would never leave Creekstone that I had never even considered asking her to move with me. "Would you be willing to move with me to Atlanta?"

The surprise must have been all over my face because she laughed and cradled my face in her hands.

"Are you asking me to?" she asked, then gave me a sweet kiss on the lips.

"Yes," I said quickly, my lips still against hers. I closed my eyes. "Yes, I'm asking you to move to Atlanta with me."

I was stunned. "What about your job at the library?"

"I love the library, but I think I'm ready to think about what's next for me. Now that we've sold the land, I finally have a little room financially to take a break and think about what I want." Kit sat back and said seriously, "I know it's crazy. Maybe it's too much too fast, but the idea of doing anything else and potentially growing apart feels wrong." She laced her fingers into mine again.

There was a look of honesty but also fear on her face as she waited for me to respond. I pulled her to me, and we kissed, long and hard. I flipped Kit over onto her back and eased myself on top of her. I felt her hands rake over my body as we kissed. I whispered in her ear, "You are everything to me. Please come with me."

23

Kit

Selling property isn't a quick thing. We'd sign one stack of papers, then wait days or weeks for the next, and then do it all again. When Veronica told me the final papers were ready to be signed, I felt very ready for this process to be over. I was shocked to find out our land deal was done in what everyone considered to be an extremely short amount of time.

Veronica met Aunt Rita and me at the bank in Atlanta. We signed all the papers, then a banker told us that the money had been wired to our accounts.

Aunt Rita clapped and gave me a hug. With tears in her eyes, Aunt Rita said, "Kit, thank you. This is going to change everything for us. I feel so relieved."

"Me too," I said, squeezing Aunt Rita closer. "Thank you for being so supportive as I worked through everything."

Aunt Rita had to work the next day, and I'd planned to stay in Atlanta to meet William. Aunt Rita took the car and headed back to Creekstone, but Veronica and I decided to visit a nearby brewery to celebrate. Veronica had ordered us a flight of beers and a giant pretzel with cheese. We decided to take advantage of the spring weather, and we sat outside on the patio. Veronica pulled her stylish shades out of her oversized purse.

I was completely demolishing the pretzel when Veronica said, "So, can I just say I am relieved to see how well you're taking this? I thought this would be a much more emotional day for you."

"Is that why you got me an emotional support pretzel?" I asked, then stuffed a huge chunk of pretzel in my mouth before the cheese could drip on my shirt.

"Exactly," Veronica said, sipping her amber beer.

"Maybe the pretzel is just super effective," I said after washing the pretzel down with some beer.

"Really? You're feeling okay about selling the land?" Veronica asked.

I sat back in my chair with my beer in my hand. "You know, I really do. For the first time in a long time, I feel like a whole stack of worries have just blown away in the wind. I can pay off the debt. Aunt Rita will be able to retire early, and I think William's company and the mayor have a pretty good plan for the town."

"So, things with William are still going well?" Veronica asked. Her sunglasses had slipped down her nose slightly, and she was peering at me over the top of them. "The art gallery was amazing. That doesn't seem like something you do for someone unless you're really into them."

I nodded. "I think we're in love."

Veronica sprung forward and slammed her beer glass down on the table. "Are you two already saying the L-word?"

I nodded. I felt my face turn pink.

"This is a big fucking deal! You waited almost a year before you even considered saying that to Matt," Veronica said, still stunned. "You and William haven't even dated long enough for the moon to make one full orbit around the earth, and you two are already telling each other I love you."

"Okay, it's been longer than one lunar cycle," I said, rolling my eyes. "And I don't know if it makes sense to compare Matt to William. Being with William doesn't feel anything like it did with Matt."

Veronica asked, "Um, elephant in the room. Do you think William will stay in Creekstone long-term?"

I bit the inside corner of my mouth. "No, I don't think he will."

Veronica softened her voice, and she said, "Have you told him how you feel about long-distance relationships?"

I nodded. "We talked about it a few days ago. William is accepting a new job, and he'll have to move to Atlanta full-time relatively soon."

"Would you move? For William?" Veronica tried to hide the surprise in her voice by taking a bite of the warm pretzel.

I looked at Veronica and shielded my eyes from the sun. "We're actually going to look at places this week while I'm in Atlanta."

"Are you two going to move in together? Or are you looking for separate apartments?" Veronica asked, trying to find some sliver of a timeline she could approve of.

I shook my head, looking down at the beer glasses on the table. "I mean, we're practically live together now. It seems silly for me to get my own place."

Veronica scoffed. "Kit, you've been saying for years that you love living in Creekstone and that it's what you've always wanted. You wouldn't even consider moving before. And now you've been dating William for a month, and you're saying you're in love and you're going to give up your job and leave Creekstone for him."

"I didn't say that," I said looking ahead to avoid the sun in my eyes. "I just said..."

"Kit," Veronica cut me off. "You're moving too fast."

I shook my head. "I don't think we are. We're in a good place as a couple. I would rather move to stay near him than try to be in a long-distance relationship."

"Do you even know how he feels about marriage? Having kids?" Veronica said with an exasperated sigh. "Does he have a history of cheating? Have you met anyone in his family? Any of his friends?"

"Veronica, come on," I said. "I have time to learn these things. If it doesn't work out, I'll move back to Creekstone, or I'll figure it out."

"It's always fun in the beginning, Kit, but that's a huge sacrifice for someone you really don't know," Veronica said, crossing her arms and leaning back in her chair. "It just seems like you've changed your mind about a lot of things since you met William." [OBJ]

"Veronica," I said with a warning tone.

"Kit, I'm just worried about you. What happened to being more assertive and not just going along with what other people want you to do?"

"It seems like you're only okay with me doing that when you approve of my decisions," I said.

Veronica's jaw dropped. "What's that supposed to mean?"

"Come on, Veronica." I rolled my eyes. "I've seen your looks and the things you mutter under your breath. You say you're being supportive, but you're being judgmental. You still think I am going to get back with Matt, and I'm not."

"That's not fair," Veronica pushed back. "I've never said I think you should get back with Matt."

"Veronica, I know you don't get what's going on with William and me. It's not the same as Matt and me. It's not like you and Gus. We aren't college sweethearts. I'm not on some traditional cookie-cutter timeline with William. So, it might look wrong to you, but it feels good to me."

Veronica and I sat silently for a few minutes. We had fought once during college, and we'd never really argued again. I always let Veronica say what she wanted without calling her out, even if it bothered me. I felt like I had to because I didn't really have anyone else, but it was different now. I had William.

Veronica and I sat in silence until she finally spoke. She looked down at the floor and said, "I'm sorry if I was out of line. I just really loved having the old, happy Kit back, and the idea that you might get hurt again made me worry. But you're right—I don't need to add my commentary. No matter what happens, I'm here for you."

"Thank you," I said turning to Veronica.

She smiled and crossed her arms, "Besides, you moving closer to me in Atlanta is a win."

I gave Veronica a hug, and she squeezed me extra tight. After we left the brewery, I went with Veronica to pick up Preston from her mother-in-law's house, then she dropped me off at the hotel where William was staying.

When I got up to the room, William was already upstairs. He gave me a quick kiss on the lips. I went into the bedroom to kick off my shoes, then used the bathroom.

When I came out, William was sitting on the sofa smiling. "Congratulations on the sale of your land!"

I laughed and collapsed onto the sofa next to him. I tucked my head into the crook of his chest and bicep. I could smell his warm, musky scent. I looked up at him and said, "Thanks, I've checked my balance on my banking app like five times. My account balance usually has a three-figure balance, so it's a shock to see so much money. It's unbelievable."

William chuckled. "Hey, tonight Charles is showing a few houses to Meredith and Addison. They're thinking about buying in Atlanta since Meredith works out of the Atlanta office so often. Addison says she's tired of New York. Charles suggested I come along to get a feel for the market. Would you like to do that?"

"Sure," I said. "Were you thinking of buying? I guess I just assumed you were going to rent."

William tilted his head back and forth like he was weighing an alternative. "Well, you know my business is essentially property investment, so I try to avoid renting when possible."

"Oh," I said, my eyebrows raised. "That makes sense, but you rented in Creekstone?"

"Well, there were no properties to buy. Only rentals, and I wanted to be in the town," he said. "And looked how perfectly that worked out."

William and I got dressed so we could go out to dinner after we looked at houses. I didn't want to admit that I felt intimidated going to look at houses with Meredith, Addison, and Charles, but William seemed to think it would be helpful.

We drove to the first house. It was a 1930s bungalow tucked away on a quiet street in midtown. The house was small, white, and quaint. The garden was in full bloom, giving the house even more curb appeal. We parked on the street behind a Mercedes and an Audi.

"What do you think?" William asked.

"It's very cute," I said as I followed him up the pathway and through the front door. Charles was standing in the front room with Meredith. When he saw me, his eyes went wide, "Well, hello, Kit. I didn't realize you were in town with William or that he'd be bringing you to look at property.

Meredith seemed less surprised to see me. She gave a subtle wave as she listened to Charles. She was dressed more casually than usual, in a white button-down and a pair of bootcut jeans, but even in a simple outfit, she looked like she belonged in a Ralph Lauren catalog. She folded her arms across her chest as she listened to Charles give her the details of the house.

"Oh, hello, darlings," a tall thin woman said, coming into the room. Like Meredith, the woman was striking, but with darker hair and slight freckles across her nose. She wore a long white maxi dress with delicate black and white flowers embroidered across the hem. "You must be Kit. I'm Addison."

I gave a little wave. "Hi, everyone."

"Hey!" Charles said with a level of enthusiasm that surprised me. He pointed at William, who was standing right behind me. "Okay, Boss Man. I was just telling Meredith the details of this house."

Meredith rolled her eyes as soon as Charles said, 'Boss Man' and walked into the next room.

This house was different from our home in Creekstone. It was small and compact. I started to wander around the house, which was very charming. There was a decent-sized bedroom on the first floor and two smaller bedrooms upstairs. I wandered down the stairs and into the kitchen. It was a cute, small kitchen. There was a back door that led to a small garden patio overlooking a tiny but well-manicured backyard.

William came up behind me. "What do you think?"

"It's very cute," I said. "Small and cute."

He kissed my head and said, "Yeah for $800,000, I want more house."

I spun around, and my face must have looked shocked. "William," I whispered, "That's crazy expensive."

"It's the location. Close to the park." William's crooked smile spread across his face. "I know. For a house in Atlanta, we're going to spend at least that, but don't worry about the cost. Let's go see the next house."

Had William lost his mind? How could I not worry about the cost? That was a small fortune.

I followed Meredith, Addison, and William out to the curb. I heard Addison and Meredith talking about the property. "Too cute, but too small."

"Okay," Charles said. "Time to caravan to the next location. I've texted the address to you two in case we get separated in traffic."

William and I got back into his car. "Okay, what did you think of it?"

"Well, I liked it, but didn't love it," I said. "And that's way too expensive for a house. I started sweating in places I didn't know could sweat when you told me how expensive it was."

William laughed. "I agree. Not the right kind of house."

I took a deep breath and said, "Okay. So, what would be the right kind of house? Are you thinking of buying a house to live in for like a couple of years or are you thinking like...longer?"

I saw William's sly smile creep across his face, but he kept his eyes on the road. "Well, we're just looking right now, but I think I'd like to buy a house that's big enough for us to live in for the next five years. What do you think about that plan?"

My cheeks burned red, and I tried not to look flustered. "Oh. Well...I mean...I haven't had much time to think about it, but that's helpful. So, something big enough for you, me, and maybe a dog—if we decided to one. Or...something."

William whistled. "I do like the idea of a house we can expand into."

We pulled into a long driveway behind Meredith's Mercedes. The second house was a mid-century Craftsman style home. It was beautiful, with a lush green yard and stonework leading up to the front door. The inside of the home was perfectly done with built-in cabinets and archway accents above every doorway. The kitchen was large with enough room for a kitchen table, and the dining room had floor to ceiling windows that looked out over the back yard. The yard was much bigger than the last house. The upstairs had three decent-sized bedrooms.

Charles didn't try to sell any of us on the house. William had told me that he was just showing the houses as a favor to Meredith, and William had asked to tag along. Meredith loved the house, but Addison said she wasn't sure about the neighborhood.

We moved along to the third property, which was a condo in midtown. Meredith asked questions about the amenities. William asked boring real estate questions about the neighboring buildings. The condo was luxurious and grand with a rooftop pool and a concierge, but it wasn't somewhere I would want to live. As I wandered through the condo, I imagined schlepping all my groceries down the hallway every week and grimaced. I walked into the master suite. It had an amazing view of the Atlanta skyline. When I made my way into the master bath, I found Addison lying in the walk-in shower.

"Oh," I said surprised. "Sorry."

Addison sat up. She laughed, "No worries. I was just trying to see what could be accomplished in this shower." Addison laid back down. "Like if I want to lie in the shower and lament my own mortality while hot water scalds my skin, could I lie down fully?"

Addison turned on her side and propped herself up. "Seems like it would do the trick."

I let out a laugh. "Yeah, plenty of room for an existential crisis."

"Exactly, and it has a double showerhead," Addison said, hopping up onto her feet with surprising agility. "So, it is probably a great place for sex as well."

"Really a shower for the ages," I joked.

Addison giggled. She smoothed her dress as we both walked out of the bathroom. I asked her, "Do you like this condo?'

"Oh, darling," Addison said with a smile that had a hint of pity. "It wouldn't matter if I hated it. M loves it, so we're probably going to buy it. I'm just here for moral support." She winked at me.

"You're okay with Meredith deciding for you both?" I asked, trying to hide my surprise.

Addison frowned and looked at me. "Oh, darling. Don't think of it like that. It's not so bad. We have a good life. But I'm a piano teacher, and Meredith is the breadwinner. Meredith feeling happy is important. It helps her do well at work. So, in a way, letting her make this decision is a way for me to assure that she's comfortable and we're stable. It's part of the trade-off." I detected a bit of an instructional tone in Addison's voice, and I couldn't help but wonder what it would be like for William and me.

Addison and I stood in front of the floor-to-ceiling windows in the master bedroom, admiring the view. She looked at me and said, "Meredith mentioned that you might move to Atlanta with William. What do you do for a living?"

"I'm a librarian." I wondered how Meredith knew I was moving to Atlanta.

"Oh see, darling, you get it. William was doing well before, but now he's one of the top paid developers in the country, so I mean, you don't even really need to work, right?"

"Eventually, I'll go back to work." I stuttered. "I'm just not sure what I want to do. Besides, we're not married, so I'll need to work so I have health insurance and benefits."

"William adores you. Whether you're married or not, he'll take care of you."

I tried not to look surprised. It hadn't occurred to me that William might be rich. He'd never mentioned it before.

"Ready to see the last place?" Charles asked us. "I picked out this spot just for William."

The last home was in a historic neighborhood in the West End of Atlanta. I recognized some of the buildings William had pointed out to me a few weeks ago. The home was a large, brick two-story with a wraparound porch.

Charles was waiting in the driveway when we arrived. "Fully renovated. Beautifully done." He pointed down the driveway. "Huge bonus about this house is the garage. Most houses in these neighborhoods don't have covered parking."

We followed Charles into the house. The house reminded me of a smaller, slightly more modern version of our place in Creekstone, so I immediately liked it. I loved the warm wood floors and the sea salt color on the walls. There was a large staircase as soon as we walked into the foyer. A family room was to the left with a large fireplace.

William appeared next to me and put his hand on the small of my back. "This house is beautiful," he said into my ear. It sent a chill down my spine. Charles appeared next to us. "Check out what's in the back. You'll love this."

We followed Charles past the stairs and to the back of the house. The eat-in kitchen had a huge island bar. There were large windows that made the room seem brighter than the front of the house. Charles walked through the kitchen and opened the back door onto the deck. I followed him out.

"There's a small plunge pool out back in the garden and a pool house for guests," Charles said.

"This is amazing," I said to Charles.

Charles turned to me and smiled. "I know ol' William. He loves neighborhoods like this."

"He does?" I said, realizing that William and I had never talked about where he'd like to live before.

"Yeah, this has William written all over it. What about you?" Charles asked.

I shrugged. "Well, I have to admit this is pretty close to what I like."

"What's not to love?" Charles said, "This house would be a great investment. This neighborhood is on the verge of turning. So, buying now is what's up."

Charles followed me as I wandered through the house. "So, you plan on moving to Atlanta after William buys a house?"

"Eh, yeah. That's the plan." I tried not to sound overwhelmed. "We're still kind of discussing the timing."

"Well, I'm so happy for you two," Charles said. A mischievous look flashed in his eyes, and he added, "No one would have ever guessed William would settle down. One day he's being featured in The Ave Mag as one of New York's most eligible bachelors—out every Friday night with a different supermodel or socialite, absolutely slaying the city's social scene. Then he disappears for six months, and the next thing you know, he's house hunting with a new girlfriend no one's ever heard of."

"Charles," Meredith stepped into the room. "I thought even mediocre real estate agents knew not to hover around potential buyers. Buzz off and let Kit look around by herself."

Charles clicked his tongue. "What would I do without you to tell me how to do my job, Meredith?"

They scowled at each other. Meredith stepped aside as Charles walked past her through the door. Meredith looked over at me. "Was he being skeezy or just annoying...or both?"

My mouth pushed into a frown. "Just a little annoying but maybe illuminating."

"How's that?" Meredith asked, stepping into the room with me.

"He said that William was once named "Most Eligible Bachelor" by some magazine. Is that true?" I crossed my arms as I looked around the room.

Meredith laughed. "Yeah, I think those magazines are the worst. They don't mean anything."

"I guess there's a lot I don't know about William," I sighed. I wanted to change the subject. "This is a great house. Do you like it?"

"Yeah, it's not my style. Too much house for me. What about you?" Meredith asked. I was surprised by how personable Meredith was being. William had described Meredith as a force of nature, and she didn't strike me as the kind of woman who believed in small talk.

"I love it. It's the exact kind of place I'd want to live if I lived in Atlanta," I admitted.

"I guess Charles knew what he was doing after all," Meredith said, her lips twisting in disgust at the thought of Charles being competent. "My guess is William will like this house primarily because of the neighborhood and the guest house."

"The guest house?" I peered out the window overlooking the pool and guest house in the backyard.

"For his mom," Meredith noted as she peeked her head into the walk-in closet. I tried not to let it show that it bothered me how everyone seemed to know what William would want. After all, why should I be frustrated that he had friends who knew him? The truth was I was just frustrated that I didn't know him this well. Maybe Veronica was right. I felt a sick feeling rising in my throat.

"You okay?" Meredith asked. I looked up to see her standing a few feet away looking at me with concern.

"Yeah, it's nothing," I said.

Meredith pressed her lips together and said, "What are you and William doing for dinner tonight?"

"I don't think we have plans yet," I said, trying to shake off the feeling of anxiousness that was developing.

"Addison wants to try a new place tonight. You guys are welcome to join us if you'd like," Meredith said.

"That sounds nice," I said.

"Addison is always keeping me current." Meredith nodded. "I don't know where I'd be without her."

"You'd be a workaholic with very little social life," William said, stepping into the room.

"What do you think of the house?" Meredith asked him.

"I love it," William said with some excitement in his voice. "I love the neighborhood, and the guest house would be perfect when we have our family visit," William said to me as he put an arm around my waist. I responded by wrapping my arm around his so I wouldn't be standing there awkwardly.

I followed Meredith and William out of the house. I went to the car and immediately googled William's name and Most Eligible Bachelor. Nothing came up. I googled "Most Eligible Bachelor Ave Mag William." I clicked the link to the article and scrolled through the list of names and photos until I saw William's picture. He was walking on what appeared to be a red carpet. William looked like a fucking supermodel moving past a red velvet rope into who-knows-where. He wasn't looking directly at a camera. He looked as if he just effortlessly existed among this glitz. He was listed as Will P. from NYC.

How did Veronica miss this? I pressed the arrow to send her the link and added the message, "Check out Will P. from NYC..."

Veronica immediately texted back "Fuck me. Are you kidding?"

William and Charles chatted on the porch for a few moments, then William joined me in the car. "I really liked this one," William said. "Should we look at more houses tomorrow, or what do you think?"

"It feels so soon to make an offer," I said. I could see the disappointment on William's face, so I pivoted. "Look, if I wasn't in the picture, what would you do? Would you make an offer tomorrow?"

He shook his head. "No, you're very much in the picture. You're in all the pictures now. You're in all the future pictures. So, that's what I'm going to consider. What you think matters to me."

I pressed back into the car seat, and before I lost my nerve, I forced myself to say, "Do we know each other well enough to be moving this fast?"

William's head whipped around toward me, and I could see the concern on his face, but his voice was measured and comforting. "Hey, where's this coming from?"

I sighed and looked out the car window. "Veronica and I kind of got into it earlier today. She said we were moving too fast, and I barely know you."

He reached across the car console and touched my leg. "Kit, you can ask me anything, I'm an open book."

"Okay, when were you going to tell me you're one of this year's Most Eligible Bachelors in NYC?" I held up my phone so he could see the picture of himself.

"Well, technically, I was one of last year's most eligible bachelors," William said, tilting his chin up as if the distinction was important. "This year I'm one of the most committed and in love people in Atlanta." William didn't question how I had found the list.

I narrowed my eyes at him. "Your charm will not win you points. In fact, I think this is how you got onto this list."

William chuckled. "I am sure I got onto that list because Penny, in PR at our firm, wanted us to have a younger, hipper image to attract young-money investors—so she probably floated my name to the magazine editor over cocktails."

I let my head drop back and looked at the headliner of the car. "That doesn't make it any better, William."

He laughed. "Okay. Well, I'm sure there are lots of things about you I don't know."

"Um, not really. You lived in my childhood home with me for five months. You met all my friends and saw where I worked. You've seen me wearing a retainer," I retorted. "I think you have a really clear picture of who I am."

William kept his eyes on the road. "Okay, I'm not on any other lists that I'm aware of. Is there anything else bothering you?"

"Addison said you're rich," I blurted out.

William tilted his head to one side and said, "I wouldn't say I'm rich. It's not like I'm old money rich. I was raised by a single, immigrant mom. I'm not rich like Charleston coastal mansion rich—like Matt and his family—but yes, I'm not poor anymore."

"But you're rich enough that a house that's listed for over half a million dollars feels within your budget. Like you didn't even bat an eye when Charles told you the asking price," I said sharply.

"I'm sorry," William said hesitantly.

"I guess."

"Well, are you sorry?" I asked in a huff.

"I want to make sure I know what I'm apologizing for," William said cautiously. "I hear that you're upset that you didn't know how much money I was earning before and that it's news to you that I am in a comfortable situation financially."

"Yes," I let a frustrated breath out.

"Okay, I am sorry I didn't tell you that," William nodded. "I should have been more transparent about my financial situation. I can see how it feels lopsided because I've been privy to much of your personal and professional life by proximity, and you haven't had that same experience with me, but maybe we can change that."

"Humph," I responded, my arms crossed. I looked straight ahead.

"Just to be clear. I would not say that I'm rich by New York City standards. Some would say, I was barely making a living there. Now that I am a CEO, and I'm living in Atlanta with a lower cost of living, I'll be in a financial situation that's much more comfortable, but I don't know if I'll ever feel like I am rich. My upbringing will always have me worried about the other shoe dropping."

"Okay," I softened a little and added reluctantly, "By the way, the money you've spent on therapy has made you very good at apologizing."

"Thank you. I'll let my therapist know during our weekly session," William said with a quick nod.

"You have a weekly therapy session?!" I cried. "I had no idea!"

"Kit, come on." William laughed. "I haven't been hiding that. I have a therapy call every week at nine a.m. on Wednesdays. I just don't talk about it that much. I have a very high-pressure job. I have to talk through some of the dynamics I experience at work so I don't internalize all that toxic behavior. Therapy is great. Have you ever tried it?"

I snapped. "Of course. I went to grief therapy when my mom was sick and after she died."

"Well, maybe it's something you could try while we navigate all of these big changes in our lives." William's suggestion, albeit helpful, was ill-timed. He looked over at me and could see that I was fuming. "Hey, I'm not trying to make you mad. It's just a great resource."

William had parked the car in the restaurant parking lot. "Come on. What else do you want to know? I'll tell you anything."

I watched as Addison and Meredith got out of their car. "Maybe it's just that I haven't spent that much time with you and your friends. Maybe hanging out with Meredith and Addison will help. I've already learned a ton about you in one afternoon of house hunting with them."

"That's fair," William said. "Dinner with them will be fun."

It took me a few minutes to relax at dinner, but the drinks Addison ordered for us helped. Addison had selected a restaurant that had been recently added to the Michelin guide. I liked her. I could see how we might end up being friends. While I was very different from her, I appreciated her honest outlook on life, and I found her humorous truth-telling to be useful.

Meredith and William chatted and anytime they would slip into work talk Addison would gently cut in and scold Meredith. "Baby, no business talk at the table, please. You'll poison my sweet, innocent ears with all that war talk." Meredith took a deep breath and tried to pivot the conversation into something Addison would find acceptable. William hardly reacted to Addison and Meredith, so I assumed this was how they always were.

Addison said to me, "Are you excited about moving to Atlanta?"

I nodded. "It's going to be a big change for me, but I am looking forward to it."

Addison turned to William. "Darling, it'll be so divine to be in the same city again. We can start a game night."

Meredith chimed in, "I have never seen you play a board game, Addison."

"People are allowed to start new hobbies and interests," Addison said, narrowing her eyes at her fiancée before a grin spread across her face.

Our food came, and our conversation turned to how amazing the food was. The rest of the evening was Meredith and William sharing stories about their graduate school days. I knew William was making it a point to invite the reminiscing conversation so that I could hear more about him from someone who knew him well. Meredith didn't hold back. She told amazingly embarrassing stories about William during graduate school. She said it was like watching a blooper reel of an actual graduate student.

The next day we looked at a few more houses with Charles, but none of them compared to the place we'd seen with the guest house in the backyard. We decided William would make an offer, then we'd just see what happened.

We hadn't decided on a definite timeline, but it felt important for me to make a clean break to move to Atlanta. I worried I'd have one foot in the door with William in Atlanta and one foot back in my old life in Creekstone, so I pushed myself to make the change.

After looking at houses in Atlanta, I headed back to Creekstone to start telling folks I was moving. Aunt Rita and I had talked a few days earlier about me moving to Atlanta. She was happy for me. She gave me a hug and asked dozens of questions about where I'd be living and working, but generally it was all in an excited and 'I'm happy for you' way and not in a 'I'm judging you and worried about you' way. Even so, I couldn't get what Veronica had said out of my head.

Next, I had to let work know I'd be leaving. I called and asked Nick if we could meet to talk about my position at the library. In addition to being the mayor, Nick was the Board Chair for the Creekstone library.

We decided to meet for lunch. The next day, I headed to The Pub. I told Nick I wanted to take a leave of absence so that I could spend more time in Atlanta with William.

Nick sat back in his chair and nodded. "I anticipated this. Do you think Trent could take your place while you're gone?"

"He's definitely the best person for the job," I said. "I hope you'll consider hiring another full-time staff person to help him."

Nick leaned forward. "Actually, William helped me write a grant for additional funding for county employees, so the city council has just approved two new full-time employee positions at the library."

"That's great news," I said but then went back to something Nick had just said. "Did you say you anticipated this?"

Nick laughed and his big smile emerged. "Kit, you two are perfect for each other. I knew before I saw the two of you dancing together on New Year's Eve."

"Oh yeah?"

"Yeah, I knew when I saw the way you talked to each other during our very first meeting together. You're a consummate professional, always polished, and your feathers are never ruffled, but with William!" Nick hooted. "Boy, the sparks were flying. You told him to shove it where the sun doesn't shine and stomped out of the office. I just knew it was love."

I laughed and said, "That's not exactly how I remember it."

Melissa walked up to the table and waved a little. "Is it okay if I join you two?"

"I'm so glad to see you," I said, sitting up in my chair. "I wanted to talk to you."

Melissa took a seat on Nick's side of the table. Nick excused himself to say hello to a few business owners who had just sat down for lunch.

"He's a really good mayor," I said as I watched Nick wave to Ms. Pearl and Ms. Patty at a nearby booth.

"He's trying." Melissa's forehead crinkled and she said, "Is it true? Are you moving to Atlanta?"

"Word travels fast!" I cried. I sat back in my chair and said, "Yes, I'm going to move to Atlanta, but I'll be up here visiting Aunt Rita all the time, and I'm going to stay on the library payroll so I can sub for Trent and the new librarians, anytime they need help."

Melissa sighed and sat back in her chair. "Well, we're going to miss you here in Creekstone, but I'm happy for you."

"You are?" I asked.

"Of course!" Melissa cried. "Why wouldn't I be happy for you?"

I frowned a little and said, "When I told my college best friend, Veronica, she made it seem like I was making a huge mistake. You don't think I'm moving too fast with William?"

"Are you kidding me?" Melissa threw her head back and laughed. "You and William moved slower than molasses. I swear, I thought you two would never get together. Sounds like Veronica was just being an overprotective best friend."

"Yeah, maybe." I chewed the inside of my lip.

"I've had a front row seat and watched this whole love story unfold," Melissa said with a smile. "I know if Veronica had seen the way the two of you look at each other, she'd be singing a totally different tune."

I let a huff of air out and nodded, trying to believe her.

"Girl. The two of you are clearly in love, and if you don't mind me saying so, you have been since Christmas," Melissa said sweetly. "And don't look so worried. It's a good thing. Don't let other people rain on your parade. If you and William are happy, then that's what matters."

I took Melissa's advice to heart. I decided to focus on what I knew to be true between William and me and to block out all the rest. That made the next few weeks feel like a dream. Things were falling into place for me to leave Creekstone. I was spending more time in Atlanta with William. Veronica and I had gotten into a lovely routine of seeing each other a few times a week when I was in Atlanta. I'd started looking at different jobs and even ways I could complete my fellowship in Atlanta. Instead of just being content with what was safe, for the first time in a long time, the possibilities for my future felt endlessly positive and within reach.

When we got the call that our offer on the house in Atlanta's West End was accepted, William and I were watching television in his apartment in Creekstone. As soon as he hung up the phone, I jumped into his arms and squealed as I hugged him. We collapsed onto the bed hugging, and he pulled me so that we faced each other, laying on our sides. I draped my leg over his hip.

"The house is my dream home," William said.

"You don't say?" I joked as if we hadn't been over this a million times. "What makes it so special for you?"

"I love that it's in a neighborhood where my dad spent time when he was a young man. I love how the house has been restored. I love that there's a guest house for when Mom or Aunt Rita comes to visit. I love that it's close to your best friend. And I love that it's a family house."

My eyes grew wide at his last sentence. That was a new detail. "A family house?"

"You know, in case you want to adopt a family of dogs." William laughed.

I rolled my eyes and pushed William away, but he pulled me back to him. I left my hand resting on his hard, muscular chest, and he said in a whisper, "But it would be a perfect house to start a family someday."

I went still in his arms. I was quiet for a moment, then I said, "Is that something you'd want someday? A family?"

William nodded and said seriously, "I would very much like that."

I smiled. "You'd make an excellent father."

"Is that something you'd want?" William asked. I saw the look of anticipation in his eyes. We'd never really talked about this before. It felt like a big step.

"My mom was a single mom, and I just know how hard it was for her. So I think, in a perfect world, I would like to have children—but I'd want a partner."

William gently pushed a fallen curl from my face and let his finger linger on my cheek. He said, "So, what about marriage? Is that something you'd want to do someday?"

"Yes—neither of my parents ever married. Not just each other, but anyone, ever. They both said they didn't believe in it. But I always thought having a forever partner could be wonderful." I swallowed and held my breath. "Would you ever want to be married?"

"Yes, I like the promise of a forever partner." He stroked my cheek and there was a serious look in his eye. "Kit, sometimes I think about if we could be forever."

"Oh?"

He tilted my chin up to him, and his warm, full lips pressed against mine. He pulled my thigh further over his hip and he pressed into me. With my eyes closed, my lips still grazing his as he asked, "Is that something you think would make you happy, if we were forever?"

"Yes, I think about it all the time," I said, as his fingers traced my hips. I opened my eyes to see that William looked visibly relieved. I laughed. "Were you worried that I didn't feel the same way?"

William squeezed my waist and said, "I hoped, but I needed to hear you say so because what makes you happy is the most important thing to me now."

Without saying much else, we both started to undress. It was as if we both knew at that moment, we needed to be even closer and more intimate. I pulled at William's shirt, and he obliged by sitting up and taking it off. He gently pulled at my dress and removed it as well. I pulled at his jeans, and as I removed them, he took off my bra and hooked his thumbs into my panties. I lifted my hips as he pulled them down my body. The feel of the fabric and William's soft touch as they skated against my legs sent chills through my body, then I lay on the bed before William. His eyes took me in, and I wanted to be his.

We kissed tenderly at first, then the kiss deepened, and I felt the familiar throb and the warm sensation radiating from my center. He kissed my neck and whispered in my ear, "Kit, you're all I think about."

His hand slipped between my legs as he made a trail of kisses from my neck to my collarbone. He whispered, "I can't stop thinking about buying this house for us, for you. I think about coming home to you after a long day of work. How good that would be." His fingers teased at my slick crease. I moaned softly as he teased me, then, in a low growl, he said, "I think about our first Christmas in the house. I think about making love to you in front of the tree and the fireplace." I smiled. I loved the thought of that. William kissed my forehead sweetly. The pressure from his fingers increased slightly.

I gasped when he pushed the pad of his thumb against my swollen clit. Then he started making small circles around it, sending pangs of pleasure between my thighs. I whimpered as he whispered, "I have fantasized about making love to you in every room of that house." William watched intently as my back arched beneath his touch.

"You like that." His deep voice sounded rougher as it rumbled against my body. He gently pinched my clit between his thumb and pointer finger. A sharp sensation on the verge of pain shot through me. He released my clit, then used his fingers to stroke my wet crease. He alternated between the intense pressure I longed for and soft touches to tease me. I let out a jagged breath. "Please. I need more. I need you."

William slid a finger inside of me, then said, "I think about what I'll do to you in that swimming pool. In that shower. In that garden tub. Your beautiful body wet, slick as I fuck you in all those places." I moaned. I wanted that and so much more. I pressed against William's palm. I was close to climax and William knew it, but he was in control, and he wasn't ready for me to climax.

William moved to his knees and flipped me over so that I was on my belly. He whispered in my ear. "All I think about is making you happy. Keeping you safe," I heard him sigh as his dick grazed my thighs.

William gently lay on top of me. He slipped his hand between me and the bed. He pushed his fingers against my clit, and I couldn't help myself. I began moving against his hand. I could feel his erection pressing against my bare ass. I could hear William's excitement in his breathing. His deep voice in my ear sent chills down my spine as he said, "Do you like that?"

I nodded almost frantically as I gasped. The warm pleasure in my center had grown into a full-blown blaze. I needed more. I was begging for more. I ground against his hand. I heard the change in his breathing as the rocking of my hips rubbed his erection. William changed positions and flipped me over so that he was kneeling above me, straddling me. My hands immediately grabbed his huge cock. There was a hitch in his breathing as I stroked his length, and he moaned. I watched as his eyes moved from my lips to my breasts. I stroked him with one hand and pinched my nipples with my other. He didn't take his eyes off me.

"You're so beautiful, Kit. I can't believe how beautiful you are." I moved my hand down my body from my breast to my clit. I slipped two fingers inside myself and watched as William's eyes flashed. I let out a sigh and said, "You are everything to me."

I could see that he was starting to lose his restraint and that he needed more. I began to sit up to take him into my mouth, but he pushed me back down onto the bed and shook his head. "I just want your wet pussy," he growled. "I need it."

He lowered himself onto me, and I felt an intense pressure as he thrust into me. He groaned and buried his face in my hair. I wrapped my legs around him, pulling him deep inside me. My body opened to him, and I felt an intensifying heat as he began moving his hips, slowly at first, and then faster and deeper. I moaned for more. The waves, small at first, built into powerful surges, crashing through me with overwhelming pleasure. I couldn't quiet myself. I cried out, "William. I'm yours. Forever."

The word forever unlocked something in William. I could see it in his face. He pushed himself up so that he knelt before me. He pulled me to him until my ass was pressed against his thighs, holding me at just the right angle. When he thrust his full length deep inside of me again, I screamed his name, arching my back. I grabbed at the sheets and begged for it harder and deeper. William didn't hold back.

"You're mine," he said. "Forever."

"Yes," I cried as I climaxed, experiencing the sweetest release I'd ever felt. William thrust deep and hard until he knew I'd finished, then I felt him throbbing and pulsing inside me. William collapsed. I could feel him tremble slightly. I ran my fingers along his back. I kissed his temple and tasted his salty, sweet sweat.

"I love you, William. I'm yours forever."

24

William

We were sweaty and perfectly sticky. Kit ran her fingers across my back and arms softly and told me that she loved me. It was the perfect moment. During sex, I had been in control, giving Kit pleasure and then taking my own, but in that moment, Kit was in control. I was putty in her hands. The way she was glowing after our sex. The way she became tender and sultry. Her eyes dreamy and the corner of her lips curled into a slight smile. The way she smelled. The way she tasted. I knew I just couldn't live without it.

We cleaned up, then got back into bed. Kit pulled up our house listing, and we scrolled through it together. We started talking about what we wanted to do in each room. It was the most engaged Kit had ever been in talking about our future. It was the most open and excited I'd ever seen her. I felt like a door into Kit's trust had been unlocked for me. Kit's willingness to move to Atlanta had made everything so much better. Not just because it would be so much easier to live in the same city, but because it meant Kit was as serious about me as I was about her.

Later that night, I told Kit I had to head back to Atlanta the next day for work, but I asked if she would join me on Friday for a work happy hour. There was a company-wide leadership retreat on Thursday and Friday. My promotion created a domino effect within the company. Leadership musical chairs had happened, and the leadership retreat was where all the subsequent job promotions were being announced. Friday night the company would host a happy hour, and we were encouraged to invite our spouses to attend. I knew Kit didn't want to go to a corporate happy hour, but I promised her we would spend all day on Saturday at her mom's art exhibit and visiting niche bookstores in Atlanta.

Our project managers had invited several of their key community partners to the happy hour, so I was making my way through an endless lineup of introductions. During one particularly drawn-out introduction, I saw Kit walk into the bar. I couldn't help but smile. I'd offered to go back to the hotel to pick her up, but she assured me she could find her way to the bar on her own. She wore a cute summer dress. Her hair was down. Kit pushed her sunglasses back onto the top of her head, and I watched as her eyes adjusted to the dark lighting in the bar. I patted the shoulder of our project manager, and I said, "Hey, guys. I need to catch up with someone really quick. It was a pleasure chatting with you."

The bar was crowded. Mostly with people from our company. A sea of business casual was between us. Her face was serious as she scanned the bar looking for me. I would pay money to see the smile that spread across her face again when she finally spotted me in the crowd. I made my way toward her. She stood on her toes and gave me a quick peck on the cheek. "It's so crowded here."

"I know," I said looking around, "The company's picking up the tab, so everyone from the Atlanta office came."

"Well, hello! If it isn't Kit Campbell," a voice interrupted us. We both turned to see Charles approaching us. "I can't imagine that this is a coincidence." I rolled my eyes. Charles received the bad news that he would be promoted within his division. I had talked to him about how more retirements were expected in the next two years. I felt confident that, with his work record, he'd be next in line for a promotion—but I could tell he was upset, especially since Meredith had been promoted to vice president. Kit said something polite to Charles, then looked up at me.

"We'll catch up with you soon, Charles. We're going to the bar to get a drink for Kit." I hooked my arm around Kit's waist and walked her to the bar. I could feel her body relax the farther away from Charles we got. Kit never told me exactly what Charles had said that night when we looked at houses, but Meredith mentioned walking up to Kit and Charles having a conversation, and Kit had looked uneasy. As we made our way to the bar, half a dozen people stopped me to say hello.

At the bar, we ran into Braithway. I introduced them. Kit was her normal charming self. She shook Braithway's hand. I couldn't quite hear their exchange because the bar was getting crowded, but Braithway nodded with a laugh. I felt his hand on my shoulder. He leaned in and said, "William I need to introduce you to a couple of guys who are about to leave."

Kit gave me a reassuring nod and a wink. She turned to order herself a drink. I excused myself and headed toward the door with Braithway.

25

Kit

The happy hour wasn't terrible, but this was nothing like playing pool after work in Creekstone. Everyone wanted to talk to William. Various people approached us and pressed their palm into William's as they gave congratulations and playful jabs about his new role. William was in good spirits and worked the room well. Mr. Braithway had taken William to meet someone across the room. William crossed his arms, nodding as he listened intently. I knew that look. William was in the work zone. The drink I had ordered arrived. I leaned against the stool and watched William as he examined something on the man's cell phone.

That's when I heard it. Someone said my name. I turned and looked over my shoulder to see who was talking about me.

A woman was laughing. "I think her name is Kit. How provincial is that?"

A group of three women were standing clustered together around the bar. I took a step closer to the woman talking but turned my back so I could hear without them seeing my face.

"Alissa, tell Jenna what you just told me," one of the women said.

The second woman immediately obliged. "I heard Braithway would only give William this job if he could get a land deal done in north Georgia, and there was this one holdout—a woman."

"Of course, she has some choice riverfront property that Braithway wanted," the second woman chimed in. "Braithway said if he didn't close the deal, then he wouldn't get the promotion."

"Right." The first woman chortled. "The woman refused to sell, so William used his secret weapon. He started dating her, fucked her, and had her totally under his spell. She agreed to sell her riverfront property to Braithway & Randall."

The second woman said, hooting, "And get this. Her name is Kit or Cat or something basic like that."

The third woman said, "Oh my God! Where did you hear that?"

"Charles, of course, he was running his mouth," the first woman said. She put her hand on her hip. "But can you believe that? William convinced some poor country mouse he's interested in her to trick her into selling that land. And I'm sure after that once the deal's done, he'll dump her. You know William. He can't stay with one woman for too long."

"Unfortunately, I do," the second woman said with a scoff.

"Can you imagine William with someone like that?" The third woman shook her head.

The sound of the women laughing felt deafening. My cheeks burned. I instantly felt sick. I ran toward the bathroom.

Once in the bathroom I hid in a stall. I fished my phone out of the tiny purse I was carrying and texted Veronica a two-paragraph summary of what had just happened.

She immediately texted back. What the fuck? What are you going to do?

I sat my phone in my lap. My eyes blurred with tears. Could that be true? Could William be so calculating that he'd work me like some kind of real estate mark? The thought made me feel sick, but then why would he go to such lengths to make me think he wanted me to move to Atlanta with him? How cruel was he?

"Kit," said a familiar voice. "Kit, is that you in the last stall?"

I sniffled as I saw expensive heels approach my stall. It was Addison. "Will you unlock the door? What happened?"

"I can't." As soon as I spoke a sob escaped my lips.

"Oh, Kit." Addison's voice sounded sincere. "What happened? I'm not going to leave until you at least tell me you're okay."

I contemplated how long I could stay in the bathroom. I wished I could just disappear.

I heard Addison jiggling the door handle, then she said, "Kit, it's unlocked. Is it ok if I open the door?"

"Yes," I murmured.

Addison joined me in the stall. She shut the door behind her. Addison squatted in front of me. "What happened?"

We both heard voices come into the bathroom. I was silent letting tears roll down my face. Addison waited until they left the bathroom, and she said, "Did someone say something to you?"

"I overheard some women talking about William."

"Uh-oh," Addison said. "What did they say?"

I wiped my face with the back of my hand. Addison handed me a bundle of toilet paper to blow my nose.

I straightened up and sighed. "It doesn't matter what they said."

Addison said gently, handing me another wad of toilet paper, "Well, you seem upset. Is there something I can do to help?"

"Did you know that a condition of William's promotion was me selling my family's land?" I blurted out.

Addison's eyes grew wide, her head drew back, and her back straightened. She didn't have to say anything. Her expression told me it was true.

I shook my head. "I thought this was real, but he was just after the land. I'm such an idiot."

I stood up and Addison shook her head rising from her squatting position with me. "No, I don't think it was that simple, Kit. I think there is a lot more to it than that."

"It's okay, Addison. You don't have to sugarcoat this for me. I overheard three women talking about it. Said they'd heard it all from Charles, and you just confirmed it."

I straightened my dress. "It's better that I find out like this."

"No, Kit. I think you might be misunderstanding the situation." Addison looked panicked. "You really should talk to William about this later. I'm sure he can clear things up."

I scoffed. "I'm sure he can."

I gave Addison a weak smile and marched past her, back out into the brightly lit bathroom. I checked my makeup in the mirror and straightened my dress.

Addison crossed her arms in front of her chest with a worried look and asked, "What are you going to do, Kit?"

I sighed. "I don't know yet." I turned to Addison. "I'm not interested in a lot of drama, but I've got to get out of here."

26

William

Kit texted me that she wasn't feeling well and needed to go back to the hotel. She said I should stay and mingle. I tried to call her, but it went straight to voicemail. I looked down at my phone to text her back. Suddenly, Addison and Meredith appeared. Addison looked worried. In a hushed whisper, she recounted what had happened in the bathroom. Meredith assured me that she'd set the women straight who were gossiping, then she'd let Charles know what he'd done. I couldn't have cared less about that, but I knew she meant well. I patted her on the shoulder and headed for the door.

When I got there, Kit had changed. She was wearing a pair of jeans, her hair pulled back into a tight braid, and any remnants of makeup removed from her face. She had a bag on her shoulder.

"I'm heading to Veronica's," Kit said softly. She perched on the arm of the sofa without looking at me and said, "You know, I'm a recovering people pleaser, so I hate conflict." She seemed to be talking to herself more than me as she stared off into the corner. "But with you, I've never been afraid to tell you what I think. It was...refreshing...I thought."

I didn't like the distant and sad expression she had on her face.

"Kit, Addison told me what happened. Let's talk about this." I reached for her. When she turned to look at me, I could see a seriousness in her.

"William, was your job promotion dependent on me selling our riverfront property to Braithway & Randall?"

I froze. "Can I explain?"

"Answer me," Kit said coldly.

"It's not that simple. A lot of things had to be accomplished for me to get that promotion. Purchasing your land was not the only thing," I said. I tried to move close to Kit on the couch, but she stood up. I quickly said, "I was tasked with doing what's best for the community, and I believe the development potential of that property will completely revitalize Creekstone, change it forever, in a really positive way."

"Some women were gossiping at the bar, and I overheard them." Her voice was shaky and angry. I had never seen her like this. "They knew the whole story—which, according to Charles, was that I didn't want to sell in December. So you dated me, convinced me to sell, and then as soon as I sold, you got the promotion." Kit let a puff of air out and muttered, "I can't believe you let me believe..." Kit's voice cracked and she looked away. I stood up and tried to close the distance between us, but she stepped away, so I stopped. "I feel like such a fucking fool."

"Kit, I don't know what you think, but you offered to sell the land on your own. I didn't pressure you," I said hoping that I could make a case, hoping that she could see it from my perspective.

"Don't do that," Kit cried. "I should have known someone like you wouldn't be interested in someone like me. You made me think all of this was real, but you just wanted to buy the land."

"Kit, how could you say that?" I couldn't believe what I was hearing. The accusation hurt, and I could feel myself getting angry, defensive. "I love you. You know that. If you hadn't sold us the land, I would have been fine with that. If I hadn't gotten this promotion, I would have been fine as long as we were together. You're all I care about." I let out an exasperated sigh. "Kit, I asked you to move to Atlanta with me. I wouldn't have done that if I didn't love you."

"Correction. You asked me to be in a long-distance relationship. I'm the one who suggested moving." Kit shook her head, then said bitterly, "You used me to get what you needed. How long were you going to string me along?"

I took a deep breath. I needed to de-escalate the situation. "Kit, I want you to stay so we can talk this out."

"There isn't anything to talk about. We could have talked about this months ago, but you weren't honest with me about what was at stake for you. Any reasonable person has to wonder why you'd hide that sort of thing from me."

I shook my head. "No. Kit, I didn't hide it from you," I stuttered. "I just. I just..." I felt like the room was closing in on me. I could feel her pulling away.

"You just. You just...hid it from me." Kit mocked me. "Hiding something from me. Not telling me the whole truth. That is lying."

She sounded certain of herself, and she looked scornfully at me. "I already feel stupid, but now I am worried I made a huge mistake—and everything's going to get fucked up in Creekstone because I listened to your bullshit."

"Just stop." Something in me snapped. I felt anger rising inside of me. "Just stop. Okay. I didn't lie to you. I didn't pressure you. Kit, you knew I was working toward a promotion. If you didn't put two and two together, that my job performance would be tied to my promotion, then I don't know what to say."

"Oh, so this is my fault." She shook her head and rolled her eyes. "I just hope you and your company don't screw up Creekstone. I won't be able to forgive myself."

"Oh, come on," I snapped back. "Stop hiding behind Creekstone."

"Excuse me?" Kit said, her eyes going wide.

"You know what? Maybe I was the stupid one to believe you," I grumbled.

"What are you fucking talking about?" Kit scowled.

"All this talk about 'doing what's best for Creekstone' is just your defense mechanism so you don't have to take real risks," I said. I knew I was getting upset, and I should have just walked away, but Kit's scornful laugh stoked my anger.

"Please." Kit rolled her eyes, still laughing. "Spare me the regurgitated therapy words? I can't take someone seriously who isn't honest. Everything you said to me has been to a self-serving end. Do you expect me to believe anything you say?

Who knows what else you're hiding from me, Mr. Most Eligible Bachelor."

I let air blow through my lips. "You're so full of it, Kit. Do you expect me to believe that you care more about what's best for Creekstone than you do your own family? That you love that town more than you want love for yourself? Well, I don't buy it."

I could feel my chest heaving. My face was hot. My fists were balled at my side. "You have everyone thinking you're some giving, kind person. But you're just afraid to put your real self out there. That's why you adopt these noble causes and make them your whole personality, so when things get hard and you get scared and walk away from something, you have someone else to blame. But it's you. You're the one who puts yourself into situations you don't really want to be in, and that's why it's so easy for you to walk away. From Matt. From your fellowship in D.C. From Creekstone. From me."

Kit's face fell. "You're a fucking asshole. You don't know what you're talking about."

"I'm sorry I said that." The moment I saw the hurt on Kit's face, I stepped toward her. "I'm sorry you felt deceived, and I'm sorry that I wasn't more transparent, but can we please talk about this?"

Kit shook her head. "I...I... can't. I need to go."

"Maybe we could talk tomorrow," I said, looking down and pinching the bridge of my nose.

"No," Kit said softly as she walked toward the door. "No, I need space."

"Kit, this isn't fair," I said. I felt a lump rising in my throat. "Please. Tomorrow after we've had a chance to cool down. Can we meet somewhere and talk?"

Kit stood at the door looking at the floor like she was thinking it through, and she finally looked up at me and said, "I can't." Tears streamed down her perfect cheeks. "When I broke up with Matt, we stayed friends. He called and talked to me, and everyone tried to help us get back together. It was easy for me to ignore it all because I didn't want it. But I know..." Her voice broke. She took a deep breath. "I know I won't be able to. I want space. So please..."

"Kit. Please. I love you," I said.

She turned to look at me one last time, then she was gone.

Over the next few weeks, I tried everything. I called, texted, and emailed. I went to Creekstone. But when I got there, Aunt Rita looked worried and sad as she told me Kit had left Creekstone, and she'd left explicit instructions not to tell anyone where she was. I found Veronica and begged her to help me talk to Kit, but she regretfully told me that she couldn't.

"I'm so sorry, William," Veronica said. Her lips pushed into a frown. She stood on the front stoop of her Grant Park house. "She's not here, and she made me swear that I wouldn't tell anyone—especially you—where she was."

"Please, Veronica," I pleaded from the pathway leading up to the stoop. "I just want to explain to her what happened. I just want to tell her I'm sorry."

Veronica looked down at her feet and said, "I wish I could, William. I really do, but I promised Kit, and well, I don't want her to cut me off like she cut you off."

I nodded. I understood. Losing Kit was one of the worst things that had ever happened to me. I understood that Veronica didn't want the same thing to happen to her.

"Will you just tell her that I came by and want to see her?" I asked, defeated.

Veronica nodded. I turned and started down the concrete path toward my car, then Veronica called out to me. "William, wait."

I turned to see Veronica standing with her arms crossed, biting her lip with worry. Finally, she said, "I don't know how much time she'll need, but she just needs time. She loves you, William. Just give her space so that when you two do talk, it's on her terms. That way she can recognize that she's fully choosing what's happening."

I nodded and gave a little wave. "Thanks, Veronica. You're a good friend to Kit."

I left that day hoping Veronica was right. That small bit of hope was like a candle in a dark, dark place. It got me through the first two months without Kit. I still believed it could be temporary. Surely, Kit loved me the way I loved her, and she would feel the void I was feeling. Surely, she would eventually call. But as the summer dragged on—with no communication and only silence from her family and friends—reality was starting to set in. I had lost Kit, maybe for good.

CHAPTER 27: KIT

27

Kit

After my fight with William, I went straight back to Creek-stone. I told Aunt Rita what had happened. She encouraged me to wait before I did anything rash. She thought I should talk to William when I calmed down, but I just couldn't. I didn't trust myself not to get manipulated again. I kept replaying our conversations, and I kept coming to the same conclusion. William had played me to get what he needed for the promotion. Our relationship was just a byproduct of that manipulation. I believed that William did love me, but I also believed his initial effort to get to know me was just part of a long con to get me to sell my land. If he really loved me, he would have shown me enough respect to explain to me what he was really doing in Creekstone. I just couldn't trust any other narrative.

I moved to D.C. and lived in my dad's guest room for the summer. He traveled so much that he was barely there, but when he was there, he was careful not to push me on any topic around William or Creekstone. He was careful not to ask me what my plans were for the future or if I had talked to William. Instead, he just let me stay there in his Dupont Circle flat. I spent my days languishing. I read and did some writing. I visited the museums and played chess in the park. I reconnected with a few of my old graduate school fellowship friends.

By the end of the summer, I had decided that since I was already in D.C., I might as well stay and finish my fellowship. I arranged to start in August. My dad offered to let me stay in his apartment because he was going to be doing an assignment in southeast Asia, and he wouldn't be home much.

For the first few months, I was very stuck on feeling betrayed by William. He was texting and calling me occasionally, begging to talk. I knew he had been to see Veronica and Aunt Rita, but I told everyone I didn't want to hear anything about William, so there was no way for anyone to help me work through my anger. I stayed mad until about mid-July, when I decided I'd be staying in D.C. for my fellowship. I knew I wouldn't be back to Creekstone or Atlanta any time soon. After that, staying angry at William felt pointless. And once the anger was gone, a sadness slipped in—one unlike anything I had ever experienced. The grief I felt when I lost my mom was different. It was something that had been accumulating for years before she was actually gone. Even though we had time to prepare, it still felt like a cloud that stayed with me.

This felt like a different type of devastation. It was sudden, jarring. Mistakes were made, and trust was broken. I kept recalculating what could have been done differently or what I should do now, but I couldn't make sense of my thoughts.

Even though I tried to keep busy with friends from my graduate fellowship, I always found myself alone at the end of every night. That's when the deep sadness would resurface and a darkness would take over. Eventually, I realized that I needed to restart therapy, and I found someone who specialized in grief and loss.

The therapist's name was Kathy. She was a petite Asian American woman with a small office just a short walk from where I was doing my fellowship. Our sessions started slowly. I tried being upbeat and inadvertently downplaying what was bothering me. Kathy was patient.

Once I got comfortable and started to get into the real reasons I was in therapy, Kathy listened without judgement. She asked soft questions like, "How is this breakup different from your breakup with Matt?"

That was easy to answer. Matt had never manipulated me the way William had. Kathy let me lay out my entire indictment against William. I told her all the reasons his nondisclosure was a betrayal and how I was certain I could never trust him again. She never pushed back. She let me work myself back up into a defensive frenzy. Then one day, I said I figured William must feel the same way—he'd stopped calling and texting me, after all. Even though I had done nothing to encourage William to send those messages, part of me clung to them as a sign that he still loved me.

Kathy then said gently, "Do you regret creating a non-communication boundary with William?"

"No." I was defensive and explained that I just felt that it was a sign that he had lost interest, like I knew that he would. I didn't see it as William respecting my boundaries.

And Kathy, in the calmest voice I've ever heard from someone saying something so unpleasant said, "I think it's fair for William to assume you wanted him to move on. You stopped communicating with him two months ago. Is that not what you hoped he'd do?"

I had to sit with it for a while. Our next session it came up again. I admitted that I missed William and wished I could talk to him. I wished all the hurt feelings would go away and everything could go back to normal, but I just couldn't get over it. Kathy waited a full minute and then asked, "What is stopping that from happening?"

I knew the answer was me. That was easy to admit, but the next part wasn't. I was afraid I had ruined everything. I was afraid that the way I recoiled and put up my defensive wall made me a giant red flag. I was afraid William had realized he was better off without someone like me and that was why he had stopped calling me. I was afraid I'd walked away too soon and now we'd never have a chance to work it out.

In one session, Kathy asked me what was special about our relationship. She noted that it seemed to be such a short amount of time, overall, less than six months, that we were friends and lovers. I had been with Matt for nearly five years, and I didn't experience this level of sadness after the breakup. I knew why. I felt a connection to William that was unlike any connection I'd ever had before.

William was attractive. He was fun. We loved to spend time together. He was kind and thoughtful. It was easy to be happy with William. But the truth was, William was also easy to be with when things were hard. He didn't get defensive or shut me down during arguments. William didn't try to solve my problems when I was stressed. William didn't ask me to handle my grief within parameters that were more manageable for him. That feeling of safety and acceptance opened the door for me to be more vulnerable with William. So when I felt hurt, I recoiled all the way to the furthest, safest place I could go.

Kathy was great, but like all therapists, she didn't have any concrete answers for me. She didn't push me to make decisions or act. Instead, she helped me realize that I wasn't preventing myself from getting hurt by walking away from William. Without ever talking to William again, I was still hurting months later, and it was possible some of this hurt could be resolved by talking with him. Kathy wasn't trying to put the blame on me for what William had done, but she pointed out that I had to take responsibility for ending things. William had tried for two months to work things out with me, and I had shut him out completely.

I did that because I wanted to feel like I had control again, but I was left with a sense of emptiness and a lot of what-ifs. Maybe I could have forgiven William. Maybe I had missed the boat with William. Maybe it was true that it was over, but unless I was willing to put myself back out there, I would be alone. Kathy was helping me think about whether I might be willing to put myself back out there—with William, or, if not him, maybe someone new. I had gotten comfortable thinking about it in a theoretical way in therapy, but I wasn't ready to take the next step. I couldn't imagine how awful it would be to send William a text and for him to leave me on 'read,' or how it would feel if I called and he didn't pick up, and I realized I had done all of that to him.

Aunt Rita came to visit me a few times during the fall. She was traveling with a new boyfriend, and anytime she passed through Washington, D.C., she would make a point to schedule a layover long enough to see me. During one of her visits late in the fall, we met for coffee before she left town. She pressed me a little about coming home for the Christmas Tree Decorating Contest. I hesitated, but Aunt Rita was adamant. I told her that I wasn't ready. She said she was getting married over New Year's, and Christmas might be the only chance to meet her fiancé before he became her husband. I was shocked. I wanted more information about this fiancé, but she stood her ground. She said that if I wanted to know more about her engagement, I needed to come home.

"This isn't fair," I said. "You're being awfully coercive."

Aunt Rita's eyes grew wide, and she laughed in amazement. "Kit, what's not fair is that everyone has been walking on eggshells around you for six months. We're all afraid to tell you that our lives have progressed and grown because we can't talk to you about William or Creekstone without fear of you cutting us off. That's pretty damn coercive."

I sulked. "I'm sorry I made you feel that way."

Aunt Rita straightened up and took a sip of her coffee, keeping her eye on me. "Kit, I know you're hurting, but a lot of good things have happened in Creekstone since you left, and some of them have been because we sold that land. I hope you're going to be able to see that when you come home."

I sighed. "I'm sure I will." I was pouting a little.

"Can I tell you a story, Kit?" Aunt Rita asked softly.

"Sure," I said without looking up at her.

"Both of your parents avoided telling you the whole truth about their relationship. They wanted you to focus on the love they felt for you, not what was between them. But when your mom and dad dated, things were getting serious. Your mother was in love with your dad. Your dad was a war correspondent and traveled to some unsafe places. Your mom asked him to get reassigned. I guess you could say it was kind of an ultimatum. He kept saying he would, but he never did, and he went away for a two-month assignment. When he came home, your mom was gone. She had moved back to Creekstone."

"Oh," I said leaning forward. "I didn't realize."

"That's right," Aunt Rita said, leaning back in her chair. "Your dad finally figured out where your mom was and came to Creekstone—only to find her six months pregnant with you. He wanted to stay. He begged her to be with him. He promised to quit his job. He said, had he known she was expecting, if he'd had all the information, he would have done everything differently."

"Why didn't she tell him?" I'd heard some of this story before, but not like this.

"Your mom was stuck on the fact that he didn't ask for a reassignment. She felt betrayed and lied to. So, she told him she had moved on. Your mom later told me she had a certain vision for the kind of life you needed and how she wanted to parent you. It was in Creekstone. She said that even though she loved your dad, she didn't want him to quit his job entirely. She believed he was—and still is—a talented journalist, and she didn't think it was fair for him to give that up. So, she made the choice for him. For those first few years, your dad made overtures that he wanted to be with your mom again, but your mother always said no. It was brutal."

I was stunned. "I had no idea."

"Now, listen," Aunt Rita said sternly. "I didn't tell you this to change your opinion of your parents. They both loved you and wanted to be in your life. They both had full lives. And I believe they've both been happy since all that happened. I know we can't change the past, and I know your mom was just following her instinct to protect herself and to protect you. But I have always wondered—if your mom could have found it in her heart to forgive your dad—would things have turned out differently? I've always wondered if it's possible that your mom was too rigid about what was best for you and for her.

"And now it's like—" Aunt Rita's voice cracked. "I'm watching it all happen again."

I let my eyes fall back to the table.

"Kit, I'm not asking you to get back with William. I'm just asking you not to shut down and shut everyone out. You've got to be able to grow, even when you're hurt. You have to heal, dear."

I was quiet. Aunt Rita nudged me. "Kit?"

"This seems silly because it's still several weeks away, but I promise to come home for Christmas." I crossed my arms and muttered, "That was quite the speech."

Aunt Rita smiled. "I rehearsed it with the lady I was sitting next to on the plane." She laughed and stood up, giving me a hug. She had to head back to the airport. Aunt Rita had given me a lot to think about, but one thing was for sure, I had to go home for the holidays.

28

William

All I owned was a sofa, a coffee table, and a bed. I had a television, unplugged, leaning against a stack of boxes in the corner of the dining room of my new house. I ate most of my meals at the office or standing at the sink in the kitchen.

I decided to go ahead with the purchase of the house, but I didn't have the heart to unpack or buy new furniture. The thought of decorating without Kit was too painful and disappointing.

The only people who had been to the house were Meredith and Addison. When they came to bring me a houseplant as a housewarming present, Addison immediately said, "We got you this houseplant, but it may be too much to ask you to take care of another living thing right now." And she discreetly tucked it back into her oversized handbag and brought it home with her.

Meredith tried to goad me into putting a little more effort into decorating the house, but I just didn't have it in me. When my mom came back from the Philippines in the early fall, she wanted to visit me and see the new house. I bought a few painter's drop cloths and tarps and covered the boxes. I told her I was about to get the house painted and do some renovations before I moved the rest of my furniture in. Uncharacteristically, she didn't push the issue. Perhaps she let it go because I promised to take her where I had really been living for the last six months: Creekstone.

Before my mom arrived, all I did was work and lament about losing Kit, so the two-hour drive to Creekstone with her was a welcome change of pace. Mom had a backlog of stories and observations to share from her time away in the Philippines. She regaled me with stories of cousins, slimy expats, and tourists. Eventually, as we got closer to Creekstone, my mom got quieter. She looked out the car window and observed the quiet beauty of the north Georgia mountains.

Eventually, she said, "Once your dad brought me up here."

"Really?" I said, surprised. I thought I had heard every story my mom could tell me about my dad, but I had never heard that one. "When?"

She tilted her chin up thoughtfully and pushed her large glasses up as they slid down her nose. "We had been dating for a few months. He was on spring break, and Atlanta was known for a particularly rowdy spring break event. He felt like it might be too much for me, so he suggested we take a trip together. This is where he took me."

"Freaknik?" I asked. "Are you saying Dad didn't want you to experience Freaknik so he brought you to Creekstone?"

"And what do you know about Freaknik?" My mom looked at me over the top of her glasses. Her lips pushed down in a disapproving frown. "Anyway, I don't think it was Creekstone, just somewhere up here. I fell in love with your father in these mountains. In fact, somewhere up here is where we..."

"Okay, Mom," I said loudly. "I don't need to know all the details of your romance, but it's nice to hear this story about Dad. Did he like the mountains?"

"Oh, yes," she said, smiling reminiscently. "We both did. For me, it was so different than where I'm from, and for your dad, well he loved river fishing."

"Fly fishing?" I asked.

"I guess so." My mom said with a shrug.

Mom continued to tell me stories about Dad. Hearing any new detail about Dad always helped pull me out of a fog. Maybe my mom knew that, and it was part of why she was telling me.

When we arrived in Creekstone, I took my mom to the house first. I worried it might feel weird bringing my mom to Creekstone, where Kit and I had been together. But Aunt Rita was there in the foyer waiting for us.

"You must be William's mom, Bonifacia!" Aunt Rita declared.

"Yes, you can call me Bonnie. You must be Aunt Rita."

The two hit it off. Aunt Rita took my mom on a tour of the house. I trailed behind them. I'd been back to Creekstone a few times for work since the breakup at the beginning of summer, but if I could make it a day trip, I did. I decided not to give up my lease on the apartment, just in case I wanted to stay overnight. Part of me was struggling to let go.

When we reached our second-floor apartment, Aunt Rita turned to me and said, "The renters across the hall have left.

They were finally able to buy a home, thanks to some new affordable housing that was developed near town." Aunt Rita beamed. "So, I made up that room for your mom to stay in while she's here visiting."

"Oh, you didn't have to do that." I was surprised at the gesture. "You can add the cost of her stay to my monthly rent."

"William, don't be crazy. You're family." Aunt Rita shook her head insistently. Aunt Rita meant well, but it made me feel terrible. It reminded me of all that I had lost with Kit. Over the months, I'd gotten better at not sinking into such a noticeable bad mood. I'd learned how to mask it a little better so my friends and family would be less concerned, but I was still blown apart by losing Kit.

I thought about it all the time. Maybe we moved too fast. My promotion and need to move back to Atlanta may have put our relationship into a pressure cooker, and the first chance Kit got to hit the eject button, she did it.

My mom and Aunt Rita made dinner at the house together. The next day, Rita offered to take my mom around town while I worked, then we met for lunch at The Pub. I had two meetings at the newly opened entrepreneurship center. Braithway had started volunteering with me there, and when the meetings were over, I invited him to lunch.

I introduced Braithway to my mom and Aunt Rita. I noticed a smile and expression I'd never seen on Braithway's face before when Aunt Rita said, "I think we met at a volunteer coordination meeting at the hospital."

After lunch, Mom told me that she wanted to head back because jet lag was catching up to her. When we got into the car, Mom leaned over and said, "I think they like each other."

"Who?" I asked, buckling my seat belt.

Mom rolled her eyes and said, "Puh-leease. William. Are you blind? Rita and your boss."

I couldn't help but laugh, and I said, "I guess I hadn't noticed," even though I had.

Mom shook her head. "You'd have to be blind not to see that chemistry." Then she said, "Just because they're retired doesn't mean they don't want to have someone to be with. Most people are very sexually active in their senior years."

"Mom," I said. "I just...could we not talk about this?"

Mom giggled. "William, you've got to lighten up."

"I guess I haven't been able to think much about dating since..." My voice caught in my throat. I hated even saying it. "...since Kit left."

Mom nodded and looked out the window. "Rita thinks she'll come back to you."

I whipped around to look at my mom. "What did she say?"

"William," Mom said seriously. "Before I tell you, I think it's important that you decide what you want. Kit left you with no chance to even explain yourself. She listened to three gossips in a bar and threw your entire relationship out the window. Does she deserve a second chance?"

"What did she say?" I insisted, ignoring my mom's questions.

"Rita said she knows Kit. She and Kit's father have spoken, and they both think Kit has made a mistake. They think Kit is still in love with you and will come back to you when she sees you again."

"Oh." I swallowed the lump of disappointment that had formed in my throat. "But Kit didn't actually say anything to Aunt Rita or anyone. That's just how Aunt Rita feels?"

"Yes," Mom said, "But Rita knows."

I shook my head. "All Kit's family and friends thought she should get back with her college boyfriend, Matt, but Kit never wanted that. So, this is probably the same thing." The last thing I wanted was to be another ex-boyfriend pining away for Kit long after she had moved on.

My mom squeezed my arm. "Just be patient, Anak."

I looked back at my mom. "Thanks, Mom. I know you're all trying to help, but I need to be realistic or I'm never going to get over this."

29

Kit

December rolled around, and it was time to make good on my promise to Aunt Rita and go home to Creekstone for the holidays. I flew into Atlanta, and Veronica picked me up from the airport. She let me borrow one of their cars to go up to Creekstone for a few days. Veronica stressed that I could come back to her house at any time if I felt overwhelmed. I knew it was a possibility that I would see William because he had kept his rented room at the house. Aunt Rita had casually mentioned that the front room was still rented to the same person, but they worked out of town and spent most of their time traveling. The rest of her rooms were rented, which was great news as far as covering the cost of running the house.

When I arrived, it was early evening. Whatever anxiety I had about being in Creekstone instantly melted away because of how beautiful the town looked. Streetlamps were wrapped in garland and lights. Wreaths hung on every storefront. Holly and poinsettias lined the windows on Main Street. Several of the buildings had been given impressive facelifts, new paint, new windows, new shutters, and new sidewalks.

I went straight to the library. I wanted to see the Christmas trees before the library closed for the night. When I walked through the doors, I felt like I was home. The warm blast of air accompanied by the scent of library books was so familiar and comforting that I smiled.

"Kit!" Trent screamed from the circulation desk. He jumped over the desk and bounded toward me like a huge, tattooed puppy dog. "I have missed you so much." He wrapped me up in a huge hug.

I let out a surprised laugh and said, "Buddy, I've missed you, too."

"Sasha, Melissa, and Nick are going to be so fucking jazzed you're home," Trent said, holding me by my arms. "We should all meet at The Pub!"

"Yes!" I agreed, actually feeling excited by the thought. "But not tonight. I promised Aunt Rita I'd come home for dinner tonight. Tomorrow?"

"Yes, tomorrow for sure!" Trent said. "Hey, I gotta do my closing rounds and check all the stacks. We got about fifteen more minutes. I can't wait to hear about D.C. tomorrow night! Enjoy the trees. Some of them are pretty good!"

"Okay, I should be out of here before closing," I smiled.

Trent gave me the rock and roll signal with his hand and said, "Rock on, Boss Lady!"

I started wandering around the library looking at the trees. There were more trees than last year, and they all looked great. Some of the groups had recycled their themes from previous years, but a few had new themes. The scouts decided to make ornaments that looked like holiday themed merit badges. That was adorable. The high school STEM team did a Star Wars Christmas theme that I found oddly enjoyable.

The last tree was from the Creekstone Chamber of Commerce. They'd made ceramic ornaments that looked like little replicas of buildings in Creekstone. They had one of the courthouse, library, The Pub, The Bean, and most of the businesses. In addition to the ornaments shaped like buildings, there were little ornaments that looked like street signs, simple lights, and tinsel on the tree. The perfecting touch was an old-fashioned star on top of the tree. It had a sign across it that said, 'Welcome to Creekstone.' Although simply done, the tree was perfect.

As I stood admiring the tree, a man walked up and stood next to me. I turned to see Mr. Braithway. It took me a second to realize it was him because he wasn't wearing a suit and his hair was a bit longer with a full beard.

"Oh, hi," I said, surprised to see him there.

"I think we've met before," Mr. Braithway said, extending his hand for a handshake. I took it. Mr. Braithway's hand was smooth and warm, but his handshake was firm.

I nodded. "We have met. I'm Kit Campbell."

"Well, Kit. Do you like the Chamber's tree?" Mr. Braithway asked.

"I do," I admitted. "I love the Creekstone-themed ornaments. I was just admiring all the detail that went into making them."

"William insisted," Mr. Braithway said. "I wanted to hire a designer to decorate a tree like we used to do at the office in Atlanta, but William told me that was too impersonal and Christmas decorations were a visual expression of joy and hope. So according to William, a lot of thought had to go into them."

I turned and looked at the tree. The mention of William's name made my cheeks feel hot. Finally, I said, "Well, they're very well done, and I can feel the love for Creekstone in this tree."

"Good," Mr. Braithway said gruffly. "The custom, hand-painted ceramic ornaments cost me an arm and leg."

I chuckled. I turned to Mr. Braithway and said, "If you don't mind me asking, what are you doing in Creekstone?"

"Well, I am building a retirement cabin just up the road, so I'm staying here in town for the holidays. Getting to know the town a bit," Mr. Braithway said, smoothing his beard with one hand.

I licked my lips and nodded. "It's the best place to be at Christmas, so you're in luck."

Mr. Braithway stood next to me for another minute, and I turned to him and said, "How's semi-retirement?"

"Crazy," Braithway said. He surprised me by disclosing something personal. "I decided to try dating since I was retired, and I met a woman I'm madly in love with."

"That's wonderful," I said.

"I'll tell you what it is. It's scary," Mr. Braithway said, almost annoyed, his mustache twitching as he looked back at the tree. "After I lost my wife, I never thought I'd date again, but my daughters insisted I try. It's been almost twenty years, and I met someone who makes me feel absolutely alive."

I nodded and laughed. "I think that's what they say."

Braithway looked at me and said, "William is the one who encouraged me to stick with it. He said if I found a love that made me feel this alive, I should do whatever I could to keep it."

"That's good advice," I hadn't heard from William in four months. I wondered if he'd moved on. I swallowed hard and asked, "Is William in Atlanta for the holidays?"

Braithway shook his head. "He's spending the holidays with his mother this year. They were overdue to have a holiday together."

Mr. Braithway shifted his weight as if he were about to leave. I realized this was my one chance to find out something that had been tormenting me for months.

I took a deep breath and said, "Mr. Braithway, I have to ask you something." He looked at me curiously, then I blurted out, "Was William's promotion contingent on my family selling our land to Braithway & Randall?"

Mr. Braithway tilted his head to the side and crossed his arms over his chest. He smoothed his beard with one hand. "Not necessarily. William was given the assignment to come to Creekstone and earn the trust of the people he was working with. He was told to strike a balance between what was good for the company and what would truly help Creekstone avoid total ruin." Braithway paused. "I needed to know the next CEO was going to be someone who wanted to help communities. Not someone who was driven by the bottom line like Meredith, and not someone who just wanted influence and power like Charles. Both are amazing at their jobs, but we need a balance in the CEO position. I needed to know William could come to a place like Creekstone and do his job in a way that would benefit the community."

I turned back toward the tree. "Do you think he did that?"

"Absolutely. The work he's done here has been phenomenal. It's on a very small scale, but William has helped the new mayor usher in some economic changes that will totally revitalize Creekstone for generations to come. He prioritized acquiring land that would help the community if it were developed, rather than land that would only serve narrow investment interests. Creekstone was a dying town, and now there will be growth. Young families will want to live here again. William showed great instinct and demonstrated his ability to foster community engagement, but the sale of your land wasn't left up to William. He came to me in the spring and told me he had a conflict of interest and couldn't represent the company in the land deal. All my employees sign an NDA and non-compete, so I wasn't worried that he'd double-cross the company. He would never risk that, but that's why I sent Charles to negotiate that deal."

"He did?" I asked almost in a whisper and as I tried to fight back tears. "I didn't know that."

Braithway's eyebrows twitched as he examined me. "Did that have something to do with your breakup?"

I didn't answer.

Braithway sighed. "This all makes sense now. William tried to back out of the CEO position in July. He claimed to be too broken-hearted." Braithway didn't look at me. He kept his eyes on the tree. "No one knows that except for me. He came to me in July. He said he had a shift in his priorities, and he resigned. Wanted to give the job to Meredith."

"Wha..What did you say? What happened?" I couldn't hide my shock. I felt my heart beating faster, my face flush.

"I refused his resignation," Braithway said as if this should be obvious. "I've been preparing William for this job for five years. I've invested quite a lot in him. We've created entire management structures that play to his strengths and personality. He's going to have to tough it out."

Tears finally broke free and streamed down my cheeks. Braithway looked a little flustered. "Was it something I said?"

"No," I shook my head. "I just realized I jumped to conclusions because I was hurt and feeling defensive. I should have stayed and tried to work it out. I've really ruined everything."

"Look, I've had my heart broken before. When I lost my wife, I was destroyed. It's not quite the same, but one thing that doesn't change is how impossible it is to think straight when you're broken-hearted. When William asked to resign, I told him to wait a year. If he still felt the same after some time had passed, then he could submit his resignation to the board. Until then, I wanted him to give it more time. A lot can happen in a year."

He said more gently, "I have four daughters, and I'll tell you what I'd tell them, when people are hurting, they can do things that make sense in the moment, to stop the pain. But it doesn't usually lead to actual healing. Everyone deserves a little grace when they're hurting."

I blew a puff of air out of my mouth and turned back toward the tree. "Well, William really wanted that job. I'm glad he didn't quit." I wiped a tear from my cheek.

"I should be going," Mr. Braithway said quietly. "Merry Christmas, Kit."

"Thanks, Mr. Braithway. Merry Christmas to you, too."

I headed back to the house. I waited in my car for a minute before going in. I sighed and looked at the house. Aunt Rita had decorated with garland across the banisters and a beautiful new wreath on the front door. Every window in the house had a candle in it. I looked to see if the light was on in William's room, but it wasn't. I couldn't help but feel some disappointment.

Did William really recuse himself from participating in the purchase of the land? Had he been telling the truth all along? Had William really tried to quit his job? Why didn't he tell me? But I realized the answer as soon as I thought of the question. I wouldn't have listened. I wouldn't even take his phone calls. How could he have told me?

I went inside was immediately hit with the sounds and smells of home during the holidays. The crackle of the fireplace and the smell of fresh baked cookies. No one was in the front room, so I hurried into the kitchen. The kitchen island was covered in a sight I never expected to see. There were delicious serving platters of food. Usually, I cooked for Aunt Rita, so I was slightly skeptical when she insisted on making dinner at home, but maybe she had learned how to cook while I was in D.C.

Aunt Rita was standing by the back island, beaming. I walked over and gave her a huge hug. "Where did all this food come from? Did you cook this?" I was amazed.

"Well, we wanted to do something special since you were going to be home tonight," Aunt Rita said.

"This is awesome," I said, "But did you cook all this? Did your fiancé cook all of this?"

"Actually," Aunt Rita said slowly, "Bonifacia cooked it."

"Bonifacia?" I asked.

Aunt Rita said slowly, "Bonifacia is a new renter. She's rented the room across from William's."

"Oh, that's great," I said. I was still unable to fully process what was happening. "The food smells delicious. Is she joining us for dinner?"

Mr. Braithway walked in. He was holding two bottles of wine and a bottle of whiskey. "Happy Holidays!"

"Mr. Braithway," I said as my eyes darted from Aunt Rita to Mr. Braithway.

As if to make things clearer, Mr. Braithway set the bottles on the counter and walked over to Aunt Rita. He slid his arm around her waist and gave her a quick peck on the lips. Aunt Rita smiled up at him, then said, "Kit, I know you've met Mr. Braithway before. We've been dating."

Aunt Rita put her hand out and I blinked, wide-eyed at the biggest diamond engagement ring I'd ever seen. "Wow! Congratulations! But this is a lot to take in."

"I know it's a lot," Aunt Rita said softly. She looked up at Mr. Braithway, who still had his arm around her waist, and smiled. "But we are incredibly happy, Kit. I hope you'll be happy for us too."

I took a deep breath and held it in for a second before I said, "I am. I really am. It's a surprise, but I am happy for you two. But how did you two even meet?"

Aunt Rita looked up at Braithway and said adoringly, "George has been volunteering with the chamber and the hospital. I'd seen him around at the hospital."

Braithway let a little smile slip, and he said, "From the moment I first saw her, I just knew."

"The rest is history." Aunt Rita blushed. I had never seen her so happy before, and I didn't want to rain on this parade, but this was a lot to take in.

Aunt Rita said, "Dinner will be ready in about ten minutes."

I was grateful for the distraction. "I think I'm just going to go upstairs to clean up," I said. I turned and hurried down the hallway and to the foyer. My head was spinning. George Braithway and Aunt Rita had just given me so much to process. I darted for the front door, tempted to run back to my car and drive straight back to Veronica's house in Atlanta.

My hand was on the knob of the front door when I saw someone standing by the Christmas tree, putting logs onto the fireplace. He had his back turned toward me, but I recognized his broad shoulders.

In that moment, a thousand scenarios raced through my mind. All of which felt too scary to face. I wanted to run. I reached out for the doorknob, but William's muttering stopped me.

"Why won't this fire light?" I heard him say under his breath.

"William," I said softly." Merry Christmas. Need help with that fire?"

William turned and his dark eyes showed their surprise and then something like relief washed across his face. His full lips parted and he said softly, "Kit, I am so happy to see you."

William took a step toward me but then stopped himself. He shoved a hand in his pocket and bit his lip. I felt emotional hearing William say he was happy to see me. It was a relief, but I still felt anxiety in the pit of my stomach.

"I'm happy to see you, too," I said quietly. "I didn't expect to see you in Creekstone. Mr. Braithway told me you were spending the holiday with your mom, so I just assumed you were with her in the Philippines."

"Oh, yeah." William ran his hand through his hair and then shoved his free hand in his pocket. "My mom is renting a room here now. I brought her to Creekstone in the fall, and she just loved it, so I helped her rent a room."

I stepped into the front room, unsure of what to say next.

We were silent for a moment until I pointed toward the kitchen. "Sorry if I seem out of it. I just saw Aunt Rita and Braithway kiss, and I have so many questions, but I am not sure I'll ever be ready for the answers."

William chuckled.

I swallowed. "I saw your Christmas tree. The one in the competition. It's perfect." My voice caught a little in my throat.

William closed the distance between us. He stood close enough to touch me, but he didn't. After all this time, I couldn't believe how I longed for him. He asked in a low voice, "Can we talk upstairs?"

I nodded and I followed William to his studio apartment. I'd played out so many scenarios in which William and I would see each other for the first time. For the last month, I'd imagined the conversation over and over again. I'd practiced what I would say with anyone who would listen: my therapist, my best friend, the lady who cut my hair in D.C., and the plants in my dad's apartment. I thought I was ready for this, but standing there, all I could think about was what Mr. Braithway had told me in the library.

When reached William's room, it was exactly as it was when I left, only now a small Christmas tree stood by the fireplace. I walked over to the tree and admired it.

"Is it okay if I shut the door?" William asked.

"Yes, of course," I said. William walked over and stood a few feet away from me by the mantel.

"I just don't want to make you uncomfortable." William looked sheepish. "Plus, Aunt Rita, Braithway, and my mom are a gossipy bunch, so as soon as they figure out, we're up here..."

I laughed. "I can't imagine."

William looked relieved to see me laugh.

"It's nice that your mom stayed in the states for the holidays," I said.

William shrugged. "I've been having a hard time..." William's voice trailed off for a moment before he added, "She thought it might be nice to spend the holiday here with my friends."

My head jerked back a little when he said, 'his friends.' He stood with his hands in his pockets, looking at the floor.

"Kit, I am so sorry. I should have told you everything. I thought it was better to keep work separate from our relationship," William said, "but I see how that was wrong—and that you feel like you can't trust me. I hope that you can forgive me, and that we can at least be friends," William said. His jaw flexed and his eyes searched my face for a reaction.

We stood in silence. I took a deep breath, and I said, "We can't be friends."

William sighed and his shoulders slumped, almost as if resigned to it. "I'm sorry, Kit. I understand. Thanks for hearing me out, at least."

"I don't think you do," I said gaining confidence. "I can't be casual friends with you because I can't be anything casual with you."

William looked up at me. I smiled. "I'm in love with you, William. I have spent every minute of the last six months trying to make sense of why I couldn't move on, but it is clear to me now. You said it best the night of my birthday party. There is no turning back from this."

William was against me so quickly. His hand cupping my face and then his lips against mine. The kiss was soft at first. I wrapped my arms around his neck.

William spoke against my mouth. "I love you, Kit." Almost like no time had passed, William's hands were around my waist pulling me against him.

I looked up at him and said, "I know we need to talk. I know we have a lot to work out, but I want to try."

"Me too. I'm so sorry, Kit. I'm so sorry I hurt you." William pressed his forehead against mine. "Please forgive me."

"I'm sorry, too. I shouldn't have left like that. I should have tried to communicate what I was feeling instead of just running away. You didn't deserve to be treated like that," I said. "I hope that I didn't ruin everything by leaving."

William paused and said, "It really hurt me that you left without even trying to work things out, but I understand how hurt you were, and I'm sorry. But Kit, you have to know, I would have waited for the rest of my life for you to come home."

William held me in a tight embrace, almost as if he were afraid to let go. I pressed my face against his broad, muscular chest. I closed my eyes and breathed in his wonderful scent. I could feel him doing the same in my hair.

Then after a few moments, William said softly, "Kit, can I ask you something?"

"Yes," I whispered, my eyes still closed.

"Where have you been? I looked everywhere for you."

I laughed. "In D.C. staying with my dad and finishing my fellowship."

William pulled back, and I looked up to see his handsome, crooked smile. "I can't wait to hear about it, but we have to go downstairs and act very cool in front of some very nosy family members now."

I chuckled. "This might be the best Christmas yet."

William looked amused and said, "Better than last year?"

I let my fingers lace into his as we started to walk toward the door. "Our impromptu holiday movie marathon is going to be hard to beat, but I suppose we have time to try and top it."

"Yeah?" William asked, his crooked smile spreading across his lips.

"I think we're due for a lifetime of perfect holidays."

Epilogue

Four months later

Okay, just one last toast before dessert," I announced, standing up as I lifted my glass. I glanced over at Kit, who looked a little nervous despite her smile. I cleared my throat as everyone seated at our poolside patio table quieted down to hear me.

Six months ago, I thought I had lost the most important person in my life. So having Kit, my friends, and my family all together in one place meant the world to me. I looked out at the table and saw the people I cared about most gathered together in our new house in Atlanta. Of course, Kit, Aunt Rita, Kit's dad, and my mom were there. Veronica and Gus were sitting across from Meredith and Addison at the far end of the table. Mr. Braithway, his four daughters, and his three grandchildren were all there. Over the last three months, they'd become like family to me.

"Okay, I'm going to try not to be too sentimental..." I started, looking over at Kit. "I just wanted to say thank you to Braithway and Rita for letting me commandeer his Saturday night family dinner for an impromptu birthday celebration for Kit. I thank each of you for being such a wonderful, supportive family. It wouldn't be a celebration without each of you here, and I wanted to tell Kit, thank you for being so incredibly easy to celebrate. You do so much for everyone around you. We all love and appreciate you. Happy Birthday, babe."

Kit blushed, and I said, "Okay, this isn't a birthday party without singing and cake." I pointed to the glass patio door where Aunt Rita and my mom emerged, each carrying two large white cakes. They started singing as they walked toward the table and everyone joined in. I watched Kit's face light up as the cake with the candle made its way in front of her. As soon as the song was done, she closed her eyes and made a wish.

Veronica and Addison immediately began clamoring from their end of the table, "Speech! Speech. Birthday Girl, give a speech!"

I gave Kit a little nod, winked, and pulled her to her feet. She rolled her eyes and laughed but let me pull her up beside me. Kit put her hand in her pocket nervously. I slipped my arm around her waist.

"Okay, okay. Quiet down you over there in the peanut gallery!" Kit joked. "Like William, I just want to thank you all. I feel so lucky to have such a wonderful group of friends and family, and I'm especially glad you're here so you can help us make a big decision."

Kit paused and looked up at me nervously. I gave her a reassuring nod.

She told them, "We have four different kinds of cake tonight because I was hoping you could try them all and help us decide which flavor to serve at our wedding in December."

There was a clatter at the end of the table. Veronica had dropped her fork as she jumped up. "Are you engaged?" she shrieked. A huge smile spread across Kit's face as she nodded and looked up at me. Veronica cried, "Show us the ring!"

Kit pulled her hand out of her pocket and showed off her ring. "Holy shit, congratulations!" Veronica practically leaped across the table to give Kit a hug. There was the bustle of people standing up to give congratulatory hugs and handshakes.

Meredith and Addison both came up and gave me a hug. "William, I'm so happy for you," Addison said. "The two of you are perfectly matched."

"At the very least, Kit got you to buy real furniture, so she's already improved the quality of your life dramatically," Meredith quipped.

"And she's brought sharkcuterie to my parties, so that's another improvement," I added.

I turned to see Braithway talking to his second daughter, Aracely. "Well, Cely, have you given any thought to what your sisters have been telling you? Take a page out of William's book. Might be time to start looking for someone more serious."

"Dad," Aracely said, looking annoyed.

"You're older than William and Kit," Braithway pushed, as he typically did "And I'm worried about you being alone."

Aracely's face looked hurt, and she quickly said, "I'm dating someone. Just trying not to rush things."

I stepped in. "Braithway, Aracely is destroying her competition globally by building a video game empire." Aracely was, in fact, building one of the most successful video game companies in the world. "She can't be bothered with dating. When it happens, it'll happen, and she'll have no choice. Trust me." My eyes flick over to Kit who was laughing at something Veronica was saying about the size of her ring. Seeing Kit that happy was everything to me.

Braithway started to interject, but I took a page out of his book and pushed. "After all, look at how it happened with you and Aunt Rita. The two of you met, fell in love, and were married in less than a year. Who's to say that won't happen to Aracely?"

Braithway gave a little chuckle and walked over to Kit to give her his congratulations. Aracely looked over at me, grateful, and I gave her a knowing nod.

Two of Cely's sisters, Terra and Iggy, joined us. Terra, the oldest, asked, "Where will the wedding be?"

"Definitely Creekstone," I said with a laugh. "Kit wouldn't have it any other way!"

Acknowledgement

I want to start out by acknowledging my sisters, who first encouraged me and then gently chastised me into completing this project. Without your support, I just don't know where I'd be.

Thank you to RT for all you have done to help complete this project. You are the most patient person I know.

Thanks to Lauren and Jimmy for listening to all my story ideas over the years. It really takes a special kind of friend to read all those long text messages. Thank you to my friends and first readers, Erin and Deb. Without you two, I am not sure I would have shared this project with anyone else. Thank you, Bryn Donovan and Rebecca Eller-Molitas, for your excellent editing. Thanks to my cousin, Stacy, for all the advice and encouragement.

So many friends and family members encouraged me along the way, too many to name, but a special thanks to the LDP crew for being rad. Thanks to my kids for giving me a reason to be good and decent. And, last but not least, thanks to my parents, who continue to support me. You two are the best.